W9-BJK-611

We hit the deck too hard, too fast, and plowed in first with a wrenching crash that I thought would buckle the whole shuttle frame. I could feel her groan with the impact. If there really are insane gods who watch over shuttle pilots and fools, they were with us that day.

The port panel skids sent up a shower of sparks and the tearing scream of metal against stressed metal. I jockeyed to keep us from going over, but the endpanel wall was coming up on us too fast, and when I hit the landing baffles nothing happened. The warning light over the baffle switch wasn't on; it must have burned out when the control did. There was nothing else to stop us from smearing ourselves up against the wall like so much rockdust.

Look for all these Tor Books by Melisa C. Michaels

SKIRMISH
FIRST BATTLE
LAST WAR

MELISA C. MICHAELS

LAST WAR

A TOM DOHERTY ASSOCIATES BOOK

To my parents,
Carol and Bill Evans,
with love and gratitude

This is a work of fiction. All the characters and events portrayed in this book are fictional, and any resemblance to real people or incidents is purely coincidental.

LAST WAR

Copyright © 1986 by Melisa C. Michaels

All rights reserved, including the right to reproduce this book or portions thereof in any form.

First printing, March 1986

A TOR Book

Published by Tom Doherty Associates
49 West 24 Street
New York, N.Y. 10010

Cover art by Bruce Jensen

ISBN: 0-812-54570-2
CAN. ED.: 0-812-54571-0

Printed in the United States

0 9 8 7 6 5 4 3 2 1

PROLOGUE

There are ghosts among the asteroids. Ghosts of warriors and workers, ghosts of pilots and passengers, and ghosts of the Gypsies who originally settled the Belt. The Gypsies speak in ancient Romani, and ask nothing of anyone but that they be left to their dreams.

I never heard them before the accident. I never had nightmares before, either. Nor a metal plate in my head to hold my brains in. At first I wondered whether that had anything to do with it, with the ghosts and the nightmares. But when I asked the med-techs, they muttered polysyllabically about survivor guilt, said I should feel grateful my pretty face wasn't marred, and suggested I might be due for a vacation.

I took one. I learned to live with myself, and with my responsibility for the accident that killed Django, who had been my love. He had been one of the last few Gypsies in the Belt, but I didn't lose the Gypsies' songs; I can still hear them. And he was one of the few real heroes I ever met. I tried not to lose that, either. In a way, I suppose I tried to take his place.

I tried to become a Gypsy hero. Risk taker, law breaker, outlaw queen . . . Skyrider. That's me. I can't ever be a Gypsy, so I don't try; and I can't be the kind of hero

Django was. But I followed his ways as well as I could, and I did it so long that they have become my ways.

Naturally, some of me showed through even at first, and the ratio kept increasing. Django would never have bartered with the Company before agreeing to go on a rescue mission to save one of their passenger liners, but I did. He wouldn't have held the passengers hostage to extort additional payment from the Company for the pilot who helped with the mission, but I did. He wouldn't have insisted on one of Earth's newest shuttles in payment for rescuing a different group of hostages from terrorists, but I did.

And when the long-foreseen war between Earth and the Colonies seemed imminent, his first move wouldn't have been to make one last smuggling run to Earth. I did that, too. It wasn't just the money, you understand. I had a reputation to maintain.

CHAPTER ONE

I damn near killed him, just because he was there. Nobody was supposed to be at the landing site. Anyway, nobody friendly. And I was jumpy to begin with; making a covert landing on Earth isn't an everyday activity, even for me.

Putting my Falcon down on a landing strip instead of a flight deck wasn't difficult, even on the down-sun or dark side of the planet; the strip was clearly marked. Because of Earth's mass and consequent gravity, the really crucial part of the landing had been choosing a trajectory while I was well outside atmosphere. My computer assisted with that, and with reflecting and/or dodging Earth's defensive sensors on the way down. But then I was down. Planetside. Expected to climb out of my cockpit without so much as a breathing unit between me and the starred night sky.

I'm not a native Belter, but I'd lived out there for twenty years. Caution is a way of life in the asteroid belt. One does not survive carelessness there, not for long. I'd spent the first ten years of my life on Earth, but the twenty years since then of living in enclosed environments had produced in me a strong conviction that to open my cockpit under a domeless sky would be suicidal.

That's why I decided not to kill the stranger I found waiting for me by the landing strip. Which sounds contradictory, since it's also why I was nervous enough to consider it. But it took only a moment to realize I hadn't yet done anything illegal, and that his presence there wasn't just a rude intrusion into my personal smuggling plans. He provided an example with which I could bolster my courage. If he could stand out there in his shirtsleeves, no space suit and no breathing unit, so could I. And he was standing there, under an open sky where frayed wisps of clouds rode a high wind between me and the stars. I popped the hatch.

I didn't realize I was holding my breath till I was halfway out of the shuttle. That was silly, and would have been useless in a vacuum. But I'm often silly. And it wasn't a vacuum. And those are only two of the reasons I'm still alive.

He moved forward to greet me when he saw the hatch open. I didn't draw my handgun; he was unarmed, as far as I could tell, and I'm a fast draw when I have to be. More important, I didn't know why he was there and maybe he didn't know why I was there. If he was a friend, I wouldn't need my weapon. If he wasn't, I might need to look innocent. It's difficult to look innocent with one's weapon drawn. I climbed on down, swung the hatch shut, locked it, and turned to face him, ready for anything and hoping I didn't look it.

"Skyrider?" He peered uncertainly through the darkness between us. At least he wasn't wearing the familiar red-and-black of the Patrol.

"Who wants to know?" I meant that to sound casual; but standing in the open like that, with air moving past us so briskly my instincts said the chamber had sprung a leak and I should dive for a space suit, made my voice harsh. The air smelled damp and moldy, like neglected hydroponics, and I wasn't convinced there was adequate oxygen in it.

"I'm sorry, I know you weren't expecting anyone to be here." The stranger offered me an unconvincing smile. The lights on my Falcon were all off, but he'd got near enough to one of the muted landing lights that I could see his face. It was narrow, pale, and dominated by large startled eyes like the eyes of a child. He wasn't much more than a child. I was glad I'd decided not to kill him.

"Look, kid, I have things to do. Tell me what you're here for, if anything, and then get lost, okay?"

"Well, I have a message, but listen, I don't want to get lost, I want, um, that is, afterward . . ."

"Afterward what?" My eyes were adjusting to the dark. I could see a low building off to my right, behind him. There were no lights, but the squatting shape of it was visible against the lighter sky, and it was a shape I'd been told to look for.

"Well, I guess the message, um." He gestured toward the building. "The people in there, I know them, they're Earthers. They couldn't be trusted with a message from the Belt, so I brought it, because I need . . ." He looked at me, looked away, took a deep breath, and looked at me again. "I'd have brought you the message anyway."

I was losing what little patience I had. "Pull yourself together, kid. *What* message?"

He hesitated. "You *are* the Skyrider?"

"It's been said. D'you have a name?"

"Oh, sorry. Igawa. My name's Igawa."

"That's nice, Igawa. Now, if you have a message for me, why don't you deliver it now, so I can get on with my business?"

"It's about the homesteaders." He glanced around anxiously, as if suddenly fearful of an audience in the windy dark around us. "About their new right to claim their rocks, you know. Or their land, on Mars. The Redistribution." A fleeting look of anger crossed his face, briefly changing the angular shadows there. "Earth's generous concession to the Colonies."

"I'm familiar with the Redistribution." It would have been extraordinary if I weren't; the Redistribution Act was the primary topic of conversation these days in the Colonies, and I'd have been surprised if it hadn't received almost as much attention on Earth. It was a controversial measure, to say the least.

An investigation, led by my old friend Board Advisor Brown, had forced Earth to reassess her treatment of colonists: one of the resultant benefits was that a lot of land on Mars which had for years been in the possession of rich Earther families who neither used it nor allowed its sale to colonists who could use it was suddenly made available for purchase; and residents of the asteroid belt, including freefall mutants, were granted the right to own real estate in the Belt where, since the last war, *all* the rocks had belonged to Earthers one way or another. Even those rocks homesteaded or mined by freelancers, some of whom had been out there for generations, had become Company property after the last war. I made my living smuggling supplies to the colonists who refused to leave them.

"Well, anyway, I guess it's working on Mars," said Igawa.

I became conscious of a strange, chirruping sound in the dark all around us. A loud, creaky, mechanical noise. "What's that?"

Igawa looked at me, his eyes glittering in the dark. "What's what?"

"That sound."

He listened, tilting his head to one side in concentration. "I don't hear anything."

I moved nervously, and the nearer sources of the sound fell silent. "An indigenous life form?" I peered through the darkness. "I don't see anything. But I certainly hear it."

He cocked his head again for a moment, then looked at me, startled. "You mean the *crickets?*"

"What's a cricket?"

"An indigenous life form," he said drily. "An insect."

"You can't mean that raucous clamor is coming from an insect. How big is a cricket, anyway?"

He held up one hand, the thumb and index finger about a centimeter apart. "About so. Not very big. But if you mean that squeaky kind of singing, that's crickets."

"Jeez." I looked at him. He was trying not to laugh at me. I resisted the impulse to kill him by reminding myself that he was a child. "Look, kid, I'd like to get my business transacted and get off this rock. I am not accustomed to indigenous life forms only a centimeter across that make more noise than a shuttle in flight. What is this message you have for me?"

"Well, it's about the Redistribution. The Company has found a way to use it against colonists. Not on Mars: as far as anybody knows, it's working all right on Mars. But not in the Belt."

"What d'you mean? Aren't the homesteaders being granted their rocks?"

"It doesn't look that way. It looks like just a new and better way to get them *off* their rocks. Which is something the Company couldn't manage before, even in the last war."

"What are they doing, exactly?"

"When the colonists come in to register their claims, they're told their rocks already belong to somebody else." He looked surprisingly fierce. "The 'somebody else' is always a member of one of the Earth-based Company families that have always controlled the Belt."

"Not quite always," I said absently. "How are they taking it? The colonists, I mean."

"How would you expect? They're being told they can't return to their rocks. They can't even go home to get their belongings; the Earthers say that would be trespassing. The truth is they know they'd never pry the poor bastards off again. They've got 'em off and they want to keep 'em off." He hesitated. "Some try to go home anyway. Most of them, at first. The Patrol got them."

" 'Got' them?"

"Killed them."

"Damn. I *knew* I shouldn't leave the Belt."

"I understand they're building an army, out on Mars Station."

"You shouldn't listen to spaceport gossip." In light of the Redistribution, our efforts had been regarded in some circles as singularly pessimistic. I had, in fact, hoped our detractors were right. With even freefall mutants suddenly granted the right to own real estate, I'd hoped our pessimism was downright silly. I have a lot of foolish hopes like that.

"One thing I learned in the last war," said Igawa, "was *which* spaceport gossip to listen to."

"Earther." I meant only to sound impatient, but it came out nearly a curse. "What most of us learned in the last war was that we didn't want another. Besides, you were too young then."

"For what? To learn anything? I was never that young. I'm not as young as I look, and I'm a damn good pilot. And a Colonial sympathizer. I want to go to Mars Station."

"So do a lot of Earthers. Go away; I have work to do."

He looked stunned. "But I brought you the message."

"And I forgot to say thanks. Thanks. By the way, who sent it?"

"Rat Johnson. He went in to stake his claim."

"Rat did? Oh, space. Won't they let him go home?"

"He wants you to take him. They confiscated his shuttle."

"But . . ."

"It's getting light."

The sky to my right did seem to be paling. The squat shape of the building in which I was collecting my contraband seemed darker against a hint of blue. "Wait here," I said. "Let me think about this. I've got to make my pickup."

"Remember," he said, "the people inside really are Earthers. They'll sell to you because smugglers pay more than legitimate buyers. But they aren't sympathizers. Don't trust them, okay?"

"I don't trust anybody. If there weren't any risk in this business, it wouldn't pay nearly as well. If you won't leave, at least don't touch the *Defiance*. She doesn't like strangers."

"The *Defiance*? Oh, your shuttle. No, I won't touch her." He stood still in the frail light of first dawn, watching me walk toward the warehouse.

Even without his warning I'd hardly have trusted the

people inside the warehouse any further than I could throw
them; and since they were all rather large men, and I'm a
rather small woman, that wasn't far. They were all, as
Igawa said, Earthers. One can't always tell on sight whether
someone is *not* an Earther, but one can almost always tell
if someone *is*. It's something in their attitude, I think, that
shows itself in their movements and expressions, particularly when they are confronted with a colonist; and even
more particularly when the colonist is, as I was, known to
be more sympathetic than not toward Colonial Insurrectionists.

They were polite enough. They welcomed me somewhat
clandestinely into the warehouse and led me to the goods
I'd contracted for. We didn't say much beyond what was
essential to the transaction: which goods I was to take, and
to whom I was to pay what amounts in exchange. Nobody
offered to help me carry the crates to my shuttle, but that
wasn't their job and it was only a short distance. I did
think that, owing to the speed at which their planet was
rotating us toward the up-sun side, it might have been
wiser of them to assist me just to get it done before full
light, but I didn't say so.

I had it done in three loads. It wasn't much in quantity,
but it was worth enough to justify the trip. Igawa watched
the process, standing near my shuttle, apparently not very
much inclined to be seen by the men in the warehouse
since, as we moved up-sun, he moved not quite furtively
into the shadow of the *Defiance*. But he didn't, as I'd more
than half hoped he would do, go.

Between the strained friendliness of the Earthers, the
horror of moving air around me every time I stepped out of
the warehouse or my shuttle, and the lurking and inadequately explained presence of Igawa watching everything I
did, I was in a foul mood by the time I'd loaded the last
crate into the *Defiance*.

When I started to close the cockpit hatch behind me
after the last load, Igawa was there in a flash. "So can I
go with you?" he demanded.

"Can you *what?*"

"Can I go with you." He sounded impatient; and when I physically blocked him from entering the *Defiance*, he frowned at me. "I thought you understood. I'm a pilot."

"So are half the other people in the Solar System. What's that got to do with me?"

"I'm also an experienced piloting instructor."

"So am I. So what?"

"So the Colonials need more pilots, don't they? And more instructors? And there's no legal transport to Mars Station." He was nearly dancing in his anxiety to get on board the *Defiance*. "I need a ride. Listen, what are you, scared, or what?" The last was said with a certain tentative mockery.

"I certainly am," I said. "But not of you." I glanced around at the awful landscape behind him. Rolling green hills that went on forever, dotted with clusters of trees, groups of houses, sudden high-rise multi-family dwellings, and occasionally an anachronistic little farm nestled in a shadowy valley. What rocks I could see were small, worn by wind and weather I didn't even want to imagine. And although the crickets had fallen silent, now there were birds singing. More birds than I could believe in. Even on a rock the size of Earth, surely there couldn't be *that* many birds.

"What, then?" asked Igawa.

I looked at him. "Are you still here?"

"Of course I'm still here. I want a ride."

"Do I look like free public transport to you?"

He tilted his head and looked at me through ridiculously long eyelashes. "What are you afraid of?"

I glanced behind him again. "Birds, I guess."

"Birds?"

"Have you ever been to the Belt?" Stupid question; I could see that he had. Even a kid's eyes get a look about them, a haunted darkness, when they've looked too far toward stars.

"I was born there. I just came to Earth for school. A

course I wanted to take, and one they wanted me to teach. Now I can't legally go home.''

"I suppose you taught piloting. What was the course you wanted to take?''

"Geology. Listen, shouldn't we be leaving? It'll be full light soon. The Patrol will spot us for sure.''

"My *Defiance* can outrun anything they've got.''

"Even a Sunfinch?''

"Shut up,'' I explained.

"Oh.'' He delved suddenly into a pocket of his tunic and emerged with a handful of malite markers. "I can pay my way, you know.''

I reached for the chips, and he gave me them without hesitation. "Where'd you get all this?''

He shrugged. "Earthers don't play Planets very well. I do.'' He grinned disarmingly.

I put the markers in my own pocket and looked past him at Earth. "It's not enough: the price of an illegal run from here to Mars Station is high.''

His grin didn't falter. "It's all I've got.''

I thought about it a moment, shrugged, and turned away. "Get on board if you're coming.''

He didn't wait for an engraved invitation. In fact, he nearly bowled me over in his haste to get on board before I could change my mind. "Thanks, Skyrider.'' He laughed out loud. "I knew I'd got you when you put the markers in your pocket.''

I reached past him to lock the hatch. "How old are you, kid?'' I asked.

"Old enough.'' He settled comfortably into the auxilliary seat and had the grace to look embarrassed when I took the pilot's seat and waited, watching him. "I'm sixteen, if it matters so damn much.''

"If true, you're old enough, all right. Old enough to know better.'' I switched on the *Defiance* and listened with real affection to the smooth rumble of her powerful engines.

"Know better than whom?''

I saw no reason to dignify that with an answer. "Fasten your shock webbing and hang on. You're right, the Patrol may just spot us. In which case we'll be in for one hell of a ride.''

"Great! Let's go."

We went. The Patrol spotted us. And it was one hell of a ride.

CHAPTER TWO

The crates were stowed well enough in the concealed hold made when I had increased my Falcon's fuel capacity; and without finding those, the Patrol couldn't have done much to me just for being in Earth's atmosphere—if Igawa hadn't been along. With him along, I didn't know what they could do if they caught me. Not knowing, I decided my best choice was simply not to get caught. But then, it would have been, anyway.

The *Defiance* dodged and bounced sensors on the way out as efficiently as she had done on the way in; but the Patrol was out on maneuvers and caught sight of us anyway. "Patrol boat to starboard," said Igawa, watching the sensor screens with alarm.

"I see it." There was one to port as well. And a whole squadron aft. I couldn't tell whether any of them had spotted us yet. When in doubt, run like hell, I always say. I ran.

At least none of them had Sunfinches. I had, on occasion, outrun Sunfinches when I had to, but their new conversion drive engines made it a considerable job. These were only Starbirds, which are as fast as the average Falcon but haven't its fuel capacity for distance. And mine wasn't the average Falcon.

"They're coming up behind, too," said Igawa.

"They're Earthers. They think flat." I swung away from the plane of their attack formation and hit the thrusters for all they were worth. It took the Patrol a moment to figure that out; but one of them was a better gunner than he was a pilot. He was the last to follow me, but before he made the turn he snapped off a shot that caught deadcenter in my starboard shield. The laser glared blood red as it hit, and the shield sparked yellow, then flared into a sheet of sickening green as it burned out.

The light of it was almost blinding in the cockpit. Circuitry fizzed and popped and the starboard sensor screen went out. I swung away to port till I could catch most of the Patrol squadron in my other screens. They were straggling along after me, their exhaust chutes trailing wasted malite in the form of glowing gases.

"You can't outrun Starbirds, can you?" asked Igawa.

"Watch me." I flipped the *Defiance* over, threw a laser burst at the cluster of Patrol boats behind me, and cut in the thrusters again to stop our backward ride away from them. Before we'd overcome inertia and started moving forward again, all the Patrol boats had passed us, and not one of them got in a shot worth firing.

They took up formation on a plane again, and I dodged right out of it again. We repeated that a few times, with none of us getting in any more effective shots and the Patrol never figuring out that in space a battle just won't stay neatly on one plane: with each maneuver, I got a little farther ahead of them, till at last I was right out of range. After that it was just a matter of ꞏꞏꞏꞏꞏꞏ ꞏꞏꞏ I ꞏꞏꞏ ꞏꞏꞏꞏ ꞏꞏꞏꞏꞏ ꞏꞏ ꞏꞏꞏ ꞏꞏꞏꞏꞏꞏ to Mars Station. Starbirds are great for infighting, but they just can't run; no stamina.

"I wouldn't have believed that if I hadn't seen it," said Igawa.

"I thought you said you're a pilot."

"I am a pilot. Hell of good, too, if you want to know." He grinned almost sheepishly. "But I never said I was the Skyrider."

"Maybe it's time you told me who the hell you are."

"I told you. I'm Igawa."

"That doesn't mean a whole hell of a lot where I come from. What's an Igawa?"

"Oh, sorry. There's no reason you'd have heard of me. Um, I said I know Rat Johnson, didn't I?"

"A lot of people know Rat Johnson, I expect."

"I'm his grandson."

"You're what!" I stared at him. "One of Rat's progeny? Don't be silly. Rat's a Gypsy. And an antique. He'd hardly have any slant-eyed grandkids your age."

"He may be an antique, but he's not a fossil."

"Point well taken. He's still a Gypsy. Are you telling me he married a slant? Or is it supposed to be one of his offspring who did that?"

He looked prim. "Usually what people do, what polite people do, when for some reason if they want to talk about those so-called racial characteristics such as what you call slant eyes, usually what they say is they say 'Oriental.' "

I grinned at him. "You may not be a Gypsy, but you've hung out with some. Only a Gypsy can mangle Company English in quite that way. Rat usually doesn't, but he can. Did you learn that from him?"

He looked smug. "Sure. I can talk Rock, too."

"Spare me. So okay, you claim you're Rat's progeny, and you want to join the Colonial Fleet. What for? Blood and thunder?"

He looked sheepish again. "Some of that, I suppose."

At least he was honest. "And?"

"And . . . damn it, I'm a Belter. An Insurrectionist, then, okay? I couldn't just sit on Earth while they make their fancy promises and take away my people's homes. I couldn't just watch at a distance, could I?"

"It's been done." I sounded grim, even to myself.

"Yes." He avoided my eyes. "I know. But you must have had, I mean, I always supposed you had . . . well, reasons."

"Sure, I had reasons." Hotshot Skyrider. Risk taker. Law breaker. Hell on wings to hear some people tell it.

And all I did, last war, was sit safely in the asteroid belt making Company runs and telling myself the war wasn't my problem. "Well, it's not up to me, kid. You know that. They'll decide at Mars Station whether they can use you or not. And hell save you, if you're not on the level with them. We don't think well of spies in the Colonies."

"Nobody thinks well of spies except other spies." He sounded almost as grim as I had, but when I looked at him there were no unexpected shadows in those dark, boyish eyes. "How long will it take to get out there?"

"Depends. You're in for a wait, in any event."

"And I'm delaying your run, aren't I? I mean, you would've delivered your contraband before you returned to the Station?"

"Maybe." I looked at the screens. They were clear of Patrol, so I looked instead out the viewport at the unguarded stars. "You know I might have killed you back there. I nearly did. On the landing strip, when I first saw you."

"I know."

"I wasn't expecting anyone."

"I know."

"It seems rather a chance to take. There must be other ways out to Mars Station."

"None that included bringing you Rat's message."

"Rat's message. Yes. How did he get it to you?"

"Comm phone."

"Clear?"

"Well, we did have a sort of a code we use. But it wasn't meant to handle a message like this, not really."

"So some or most of it got said over the phone, in clear, right?"

"Well, um."

"Rat's no fool, and he must've thought it would be okay or he wouldn't have done it. But I still don't like it."

He grinned at me. "Rat said you'd say that."

"*Did* he?"

"He also said you'd bring me anyway."

I picked up another Patrol boat in the scanners on my up-sun side, but he was too far away to worry about. "That's if I didn't kill you on sight. Did he mention that?"

"He emphasized it. He thought maybe I should try to reach you by Comm Link."

"You're not serious. That would've got the Patrol on me in a flash."

"That's what he said, when I asked why he didn't do it himself. I guess he knew I'd want a ride badly enough to take the risk of being there in person, and he wanted to make sure I knew the risk was there."

"If he'd emphasized it adequately, you wouldn't be here."

"You didn't kill me."

"There's that."

"He said you were his best chance of getting home. I couldn't tell you that over the Comm Link. Not, anyway, without getting you caught and losing his chance. And mine. I had to come."

"Such a hero."

"He also said your only quality stronger than temper was curiosity, which might decrease the risk."

"That sounds like Rat." I checked our course, made a minor correction, punched it into the computer, and stood up. "Okay. You're here. All speed no stops to Mars Station. Want a cup of coffee while you tell me everything you know about the Redistribution?"

If he wasn't a pilot, he was at least an experienced passenger. He didn't give the control board a glance as he unfastened his shock webbing and stood up to join me. I've had passengers go all hysterical when I walked away from the controls. "*Real* coffee?" he asked.

"Sure, real coffee. You think I only collect contraband for other people?"

"Well, coffee isn't exactly contraband, even in the Belt, is it?"

"Strictly speaking, no." I led him into the galley and

punched up an order for dark French roast. "That is, there's legal coffee in the Belt, brought out by Company ships on Company runs. That isn't how I get mine, but who's to know?"

He looked startled. "You can afford the legal variety? Of *real* coffee?"

"I wouldn't have it as a gift." I handed him a steaming mug of the genuine article. "You take it black? I warn you, this isn't a thin commercial brew."

"Black, please." He smelled it appreciatively.

"But to answer your question, yes, I can afford the legal variety. I can afford just about anything I like, short of a Sunfinch, and I'm not quite sure I couldn't have that if I asked nicely."

"If you're so rich, what are you doing making smuggling runs like this?"

"Nobody can have too much money."

He looked thoughtful. "Then you don't do it because otherwise the colonists couldn't have the supplies you bring?"

"Do I look like the Red Cross?"

He didn't answer that; he'd tasted his coffee. "Whew! I doubt if this would be legal, even on Earth!"

"I assure you it is. You were going to tell me what you know about the Redistribution. I can't believe they got Rat off his rock by trickery. You're serious about that?"

"I'm serious."

I shook my head. "Jeez, if it's a trick, we all fell for it."

"It was very convincing. In fact, I think maybe the Earthers—the Corporation—expected it to work. Maybe they even meant it to work. Certainly it seems to be going okay on Mars. I think it's only the Belt branch of the Corporation—the Company—that's turned it into a trick."

"I *know* that some who went in got their rocks, same like the Company said they would."

"Sure. And who were they? Who went in first?"

"I don't know. What d'you mean?"

"That's what got Rat in, you know. The fact that the

first ones in actually got their rocks, as promised. It was
only after he'd been denied his rock that he started looking
into the backgrounds of those who got theirs. For instance,
did you ever make a run for the Robinsons?''

"I don't even know them. But I'm by no means the
only smuggler in the Belt.''

"I know, and you can't know everybody. How about
the Beothys? Ever make a run for them? Or the Shellabar-
gers? How about old lady Ngaio, out in Delta sector?''

"I've heard of some of them, but I've never made a run
for any of them. So what? Somebody else ran for them,
that's all.''

"Nobody ran for them. Or rather, no smugglers. They
didn't need their supplies smuggled. They're homesteaders
and miners, for sure, and they had no more legal right to
be on their rocks since the war than Rat had to be on his,
but they weren't supplied by smugglers. Guess what? The
Patrol supplied them.''

"The Patrol?''

"The Patrol. They're all at least distantly related to the
old Earther families. They all had the Company's approval; not legally, but in practice, to stay on their rocks.
When the Redistribution Act went through, they were the
first to make their claims legal. And they were granted all
they asked. I'm not sure it was planned in advance as a way
to convince the old Belter families that the Redistribution
worked, but that's what happened. People who couldn't be
pried loose from their rocks by all the violence of the last
war—''

"Which never got as far as the Belt," I said.

He nodded. "Which never got as far as the Belt, okay,
not as far as open battles were concerned, but you can't
deny the violence was there.''

I thought of the freefall mutants I knew, and the homesteaders trying to stay alive where the Company didn't
want them, and I nodded. "Okay. Sure. The Company
wanted to get them off their rocks. That's obvious.''

"So these people, all of whom the Company has been
trying to displace for years, have come in to Home Base to

register, expecting to be granted what is, in effect, their birthright—most of them were *born* on those rocks, rocks that have been in their families for generations, that were claimed in the early days of settlement before the Company even existed—and they're told their rocks belong to somebody else.''

"To whom?"

"Different people. With one thing in common: they're all old Company families, same like those who went in first." He sipped his coffee, watching me. "Sometimes you have to go pretty far back to find the link, but it's always there if you look far enough."

"There'd be a link somewhere back for a lot of us; we *are* all Terran."

"But most of us wouldn't willingly act as agents for the Company in this. Most of us wouldn't let people be dispossessed in our names, just because there was some multi-distant relative we had in common with some Company muckymuck."

"Of course not."

He was still watching me, his expression unreadable. "Will you help Rat get home?"

"Hell. I don't know."

"The war's started at last, isn't it?"

I thought of Jamin, who was a freefall mutant, and of his adoptive son Collis who not only wasn't a mutant but who got dangerously ill in freefall. For his sake, the two of them still lived on Home Base, the Company's headquarters. They had meant to get away somehow before the war started. Now maybe it would be too late. "I'm afraid it's starting. *Damn* it."

Igawa was clearly trying to control a boyish excitement. "In the last war—"

"The last war wasn't the Last War. Obviously."

He stared. "What?"

"Maybe there'll never be a Last War."

"Oh." He frowned into his coffee mug. "We can beat them this time, for sure."

"Beat Earth? Are you joking?"

"You don't think we can?"

"We may win the war. This war. It's conceivable, though it isn't probable, I'm afraid. But even if we win this time, do you really think that'll be an end to it?"

He looked uncomfortable. "But . . ."

"War isn't a game, Igawa. Whatever they've taught you on Earth, or you've imagined from reading adventure chips and watching holos, war isn't a grand experience fraught with heroic excitement and wonderfulness. It's a nasty, shoddy, awful business in which people, real people that you know and love, are going to *die*. You and I may die. And whether we do or we don't, we won't have proved a damn thing by being there."

"But I—"

"Nobody'll prove anything. War doesn't prove anything. We'll just fight till we're tired of dying and then we'll quit, same like last time. The issues will still be unresolved. Just a lot more people will be dead. That's all war ever does. It just kills."

Oddly, he sounded very much more mature in response to that. "I hope you're wrong."

I sighed. "So do I. But we've been through the last war, and now look."

"I have looked. And we can't keep on this way."

"D'you really think killing people will improve anything?"

"I don't know. It sounds absurd when you put it like that. Do you think we'd be better off not wanting what's ours? Not insisting on basic human rights for everyone?"

"Of course not. But I wanted to find another way."

"Most of us did. It seems there isn't one. We have to face that."

I smiled. "Did you think I wasn't facing it?"

"You sounded . . ." he said, and paused, frowned at me, and looked away.

"D'you know what that contraband is I've just collected from Earth?"

"No, of course not."

"Medication for freefall mutants to survive in gravity.

A prescription will be required when there's a war on; it helps the Earthers keep track of all the nasty mutant Insurrectionists. No proColonial firm manufactures it, and I knew we'd be needing it. I just hoped we wouldn't need it so soon.''

CHAPTER THREE

I dropped Igawa at Mars Station and went straight on to Home Base. It was one of the larger asteroids, tunneled and hollowed to provide quarters for Company offices and employees. I had made my home there for twenty years, as long as I'd worked for the Company. Jamin and Collis had been there less long, and Rat shouldn't properly have been there at all.

If the war wasn't begun, it was hell of close. Home Base was surrounded by armed Patrol boats, diligently examining and challenging all comers. I identified myself and answered a number of stupid, officious questions before I was granted Comm Link access to Granger, the Flight Controller on duty.

"Cleared for Panel Three," he said formally.

"I understand Rat Johnson's on Base," I said.

"I repeat, you have clearance," said Granger.

"Is it that bad down there already?"

"Just bring her down, Skyrider."

"Sure thing, Granger." I did as I was told. With the *Defiance* linked through her synch system to the ground-based computer, there wasn't really a lot for me to do but sit back and watch the landing, delicately controlling here and there more because I wanted to than because there was any real need.

The flight deck was unexpectedly crowded. At least, there were a lot of shuttles on board. There were very few people visible. Most of those I could see were Ground Patrol. I put *Defiance* where Granger told me to and climbed down out of her warily. Ground Patrol converged on me, their weapons drawn.

"What's this?" I hoped I sounded only mildly perturbed.

"We'll have your weapon, sir."

"You'll what!" I started to put my hand on it, thought better of that, and just stared at them. Even in normal times one small woman would be a fool to try to take on six hulking male Ground Patrolmen, and these weren't normal times. But colonists had been granted the legal right to bear non-lethal personal arms at the end of the last war. If there hadn't been a new war openly declared, they had no right to confiscate mine. Unless they knew what I carried in the hidden hold on the *Defiance*.

"Just till you leave Home Base, sir," said the lead Patrolman. "It's a new ruling; on account of civil disturbances."

At least they were being polite. I unstrapped my weapon, reluctantly, and stood there holding it, looking at them.

The lead Patrolman was one I'd met before, in better times. He looked embarrassed. "We'll tag it, sir, and give you the stub, so you can reclaim it when you space out again."

"Civil disturbances," I said.

He actually shuffled his feet. "Yes, sir." He hesitated. "Some of the freelancers had trouble with their claims. Owing to the Redistribution. I know this seems highly irregular, but it's a temporary local ordinance." He thrust an electronic scroll at me. "You can read it, sir. Section ten, sub-paragraph B."

I took it from him, read it through while they waited, and handed it back with a grimace. "The Company starting its own little war, maybe?"

"Please, sir."

"Oh, space." I handed him my weapon. "I want that stub."

He carefully tagged my handgun and its holster, handed me the stub, gave me a miserable little smile, and led his troops away. Someone behind me said, "It's beginning." She sounded unutterably weary. "S'pose we shouldn't be surprised."

Still thinking about the implications of confiscated hand-guns, I turned to look at her. "Jake! What're you doing on Home Base? I thought you were down at Mars Station."

"Shhh!" She glanced around us, her long brown face drawn tight with fatigue and worry. "This is enemy ground."

"It always was." Which may seem an odd thing to say about one's home, but it was true. I looked at Jake's stained white Damage Control suit. "Is that what you're doing for a living?"

She made a wry face. "Let's say so and let it go."

"Anything I can do?" I didn't mean about Damage Control.

She shook her head so slightly that the tight dark curls around her face didn't even bounce. "Not just now, I don't think. Looks like you ran into some trouble?" She was looking at the carbon scars on the side of the *Defiance*, where the Patrol boat back at Earth had got in its lucky shot.

"Starboard shield and screen burned out," I said. "No time to deal with it. Have you seen Rat? Or Jamin?"

"Rat Johnson? They've given him temporary quarters down on Level Two." She studied my face for a moment. "I'll see what I can do about the *Defiance* if you think you'll be here on Base a few minutes."

"Why? Because I asked about Rat?"

"You'll try to help him, I s'pose?" She was eyeing my Falcon, thinking about the proposed repairs.

"If he makes it worth my while."

She looked at me. "Sure. Always the Skyrider."

"Who else would I be?"

She grinned reluctantly. "Nobody. Jamin and Collis are probably in their quarters: Jamin just got in from a run."

"Good. I wanted to see them before I leave."

The flight deck at Home Base looked like an open tunnel into space. At the open end one could look out at the stars; an invisible screen held in the atmosphere, responding to alloys in a shuttle's hull to let the ships through while keeping the vacuum out. Jake looked through it now, at a bright little short-runner synching up for landing. ''You'll be going back out to the Station?'' She asked it absently, without apparent interest, but her gaze when she turned back to me was penetrating.

''After the other run we mentioned, yes.''

She nodded, looked at me a moment longer, then turned and walked away without another word.

I went down to Level Two in search of Rat. That whole level was crowded with the newly dispossessed of the Belt: freelancers, miners, and homesteaders, many of whom had never been to Home Base before and weren't glad to be there now. Presumably they had all been assigned quarters down there, but they tended to cluster in the corridors instead of in their chambers.

Some of them must have expected to make a brief holiday out of their visit; they were dressed in bright party clothes and surrounded by luggage. Others wore their work clothes and had no visible luggage; they must have expected to make a quick run in and out again, and left everything at home on the rocks to which the Company now said they could never return. The whole crowd looked odd to me, and it took a moment to figure out why: none wore handguns. Ordinarily we all wore them, always. It was a small thing to have had them confiscated, but it was demeaning and, in a peculiar way, dehumanizing. I was too aware of the lack of weight at my own hip. I felt as though I couldn't walk quite normally without it.

There was a brief silence as I entered the corridor from the lift to the flight deck level. Nearly everyone turned to look at me. Their eyes were hollow, haunted. Nobody smiled. Nobody spoke. Nobody missed noticing the empty place at my hip where my holster should have been. After a moment they all turned back to their little clusters of conversation or areas of silence. All except Rat Johnson, who had been standing alone near a wall, watching the entrance to the lift. He stepped toward me, his face a wrinkled brown mask of indifference in which his beady little black Gypsy eyes glittered with all the emotions his face didn't express. "You saw Igawa?"

I nodded. "I brought him out to Mars Station."

He glanced anxiously around and drew me aside, into a tiny chamber just large enough for a bed and a chair. "Will you do it?" He closed the door behind him and stood leaning against it, watching me, his eyes bright and hard.

"You know I will." With Rat there wasn't any need for the ritual bargaining. He knew me too well.

He seemed to relax all at once, though I hadn't been aware till then how tense he was. After a moment he awarded me a battered smile and gestured toward the chamber's only chair. "Sit?"

"Thanks." I sat and watched him move from the door to the bed. He didn't sit on it, but stood staring absently at the PA speaker on the wall. I said, "Rat . . ."

"I know." His gaze moved to my face and those eyes startled me with their awful intensity. "I'm not asking miracles. Just . . . I want to try."

"You're a foolish old man."

"Tell me something I don't know."

"Not here." I glanced at the PA speaker. It had never been established whether the Company listened to private conversations over that, but it was widely suspected and perfectly possible; most communications systems could be made to work both ways.

He grinned suddenly. "You are a paranoid young woman."

"I hope so. Is Igawa really your grandson?"

"He said that?" He winked. "I should be so young. The boy is my great-grandson. The youngest of his generation."

"He didn't like it when I asked had you married a slant."

"He doesn't know you." Suddenly jolly, he sat on the

edge of the bed and began to gossip about his family, absent-mindedly dropping into the odd Belter argot that Company-English speakers called pidgin but which we more often called Rock talk. He spoke fondly of his wife, now dead for fifty years; and of his eight sons, three of whom had died in the last war and three of whom had made their homes on Mars or on Earth. The other two were still in the Belt somewhere, but it wasn't clear exactly where or what they were doing. When he started on his grandchildren I soon lost track; there seemed to be dozens of them. Some were in the Belt, some were on Mars, some had died in the war, a few had emigrated to Earth, and a few had joined the ambitious expeditions beyond the Solar System, whose fate would probably not be known in my lifetime, much less in Rat's. He seemed most proud of those, and not without reason.

"They get one start new out there, 'ass why," he said. "Stay too muchi guru, w'at you t'ink? Maybe they go stay come one future mo' bettah no Eart'ers!"

The grammar and pronunciation of Rock talk is even odder than I portray it; it is comprised of a great many languages from the pioneer days of the Belt, not all of which are still in use anywhere else by now, and each of which has affected the grammar and pronunciation of the others. We all spoke Rock to some degree, and there were Belters who had no other language. It was easy to fall into it for casual conversation.

"W'at you t'ink," I said. "Eart'ers make war already?"

"Da kine wen take all our rocks, hey, rien, maybe? All Belters down Home Base come, t'row one pahty, so des' ka? Maybe say who knees rock, yeah? Who knees? I one rock need, 'ass who. All my fambly knees one rock already. Da kine wen take, you bet one war!"

"Igawa t'ink war muchi guru. Wen stop Mars Station fo' teach, fight."

Rat shrugged. "He go grow up yet." He looked at me with sudden curiosity. "That boy you like?"

Startled, I said, "Rat, that boy fo' *days* young!"

He grinned. "Not. He groween. You like? One woman knees one man, yeah?"

"Not this woman need one man."

"So des' ka? Skyrider fly solo, hey?"

I shrugged. " 'Ass why."

He studied me. "You that one Gypsy wen like but."

"Django?" I shook my head. "Django's dead." He died of a clogged air filter that blew its top and damn near killed me with him. I should have checked the filter before the flight. It took me a long time to understand that didn't make me guilty. It took even longer for me to stop *feeling* guilty. I still felt responsible, and I didn't want to talk about it.

"So," said Rat. "Bumbai you one new fellow like."

"Bumbai. Peut-être."

He shook his head lugubriously. "Bear no' wait fo' days, getteen old."

I laughed. "You talk already!"

After a startled second he laughed with me. "Voice of experience, yeah?"

" 'Ass why."

He stood up, still grinning, and dropped the Rock talk as readily as he had taken it up. "You ready to go, or what?"

"What," I said. "I have to see somebody first. Meet you on the flight deck in half an hour?"

He nodded, watching me seriously. "No fights till we're off this rock, Skyrider. No matter how the Earthers act. Okay?"

Most people who knew me at all wouldn't have even tried to get away with a line like that; I'd have killed them. I guess Rat knew me well enough to know he was safe. I said, "Yessir," saluted, grinned at him, and walked away, conscious of his level gaze on my back. I hoped Jamin and Collis, when I found them, would be doing as well in the circumstances as Rat was. Of course, they hadn't had a rock stolen from under them. But Jamin was a freefall mutant. In the best of times Earth never treated freefall mutants well.

According to the *Encyclopedia Terra*, the freefall mutation first developed on Station Challenger way back when
the pioneers first began to colonize space. The mutants
were absolutely human in every way, except that they
could not tolerate gravity. Some of the early ones died of
gravity shock before the problem was fully understood.
After that they just stayed in freefall if they had any sense.

By now the human race was divided into three categories: Fallers, or freefall mutants, to whom gravity was a
health hazard; Grounders, who were like the original
strain in that they could live happily in gravity and could,
with adequate exercise and nutritional supplements, survive quite long periods in freefall; and Floaters, like me,
who had one gene for gravity and one for freefall and
could "float" at will between the two environments or live
in either.

Most Earthers were Grounders. They controlled the Solar System, and they regarded Fallers as something less
than human. An Earther med-tech had once actually referred to Fallers, in my presence, as "monsters." The
colonists on Mars and in the asteroid belt were a fairly
even mix of all three genetic varieties, politically divided
into at least three more confusing categories: those who
openly sided with Earth, usually called "Earthers" regardless of where they lived; those who couldn't make up their
minds or didn't want to rock the boat or didn't give a
damn; and those of us who openly opposed the continued
government of the Colonies by Earth. Members of the last
category were called Colonial Insurrectionists, as a group,
and traitors, as individuals. Either label might have been
applicable, I don't know. I think the line between "pa-
triot" and "traitor" is often very finely drawn.

Earthers tended to regard all Fallers as Insurrectionists
(or traitors); which, while it wasn't strictly accurate, was a
logical error. Fallers were "monsters" physically unsuited
to life on Earth; why would they want to be governed from
Earth? (Some of them did, but never mind.) Earthers
therefore singled out Fallers for the strictest regimentation
when hostilities threatened. I was worried about Jamin.

I'd been worried about Jamin for some time. The impending war wasn't exactly unexpected. We'd been warding it off with decreasing success for years now, almost since the last war ended. I'd tried to talk Jamin into moving off Company ground. He wouldn't go. His son Collis needed gravity to live, but there were plenty of stations and rocks with gravity sections. Collis would have been confined to those sections, and would have had to go through freefall to get to them, but that could have been managed easily enough. Jamin just didn't want to put Collis through that inconvenience and discomfort if it wasn't absolutely necessary.

As a result, they might both be put through quite a lot worse. Already it might be too late to get them safely off Home Base. I couldn't do it myself till I'd made the run for Rat's rock, but I did want to have another go at convincing Jamin to make the move, if he could.

CHAPTER FOUR

Collis, at least, was glad to see me. He nearly bowled me over with one of his whirlwind hugs when I arrived at their door. A person who is almost seven years old may be pretty reserved in most situations—almost seven is, in the Belt, damn close to grown up—but even a grownup might respond with visible delight on seeing an old friend after a separation of weeks, particularly in difficult times like these. And Collis was never going to be the cold, aloof, undemonstrative type like his father.

Two people could hardly have been more dissimilar, either in appearance or in temperament. Jamin was tall, dark, and handsome, as the saying goes. He was also astonishingly thin, his face a region of planes and shadows, his blue eyes the color of deep ice. Collis was small and blond, as cute and cuddly as a teddy bear: a Buddha-faced boy still plump with baby fat whose eyes, though they were exactly the color of his father's, reminded one not of ice but of the clear summer skies of Earth.

When I first met them, I had disliked Jamin on sight and Collis had enchanted me with one blinding smile. Since then I had grown fond of both of them, and learned to recognize Jamin's arrogance for what it was: an embarrassed effort to conceal his discomfort in a gravity environment. Understanding didn't make his behavior any easier to endure, but I couldn't slug him in gravity where I had such an unfair advantage, and he didn't behave half so badly in freefall where we could have had a proper fight.

Jamin looked up when I came in, and didn't smile. "Back from the wars and the Patrol didn't stop you?"

"Wars?" Collis brightened visibly. "Wars?"

"Figure of speech, bumpkin," I said. "The war isn't properly started yet." I looked at Jamin. "But it's not long off, and the two of you ought to clear out of here while you still can. *If* you still can."

Jamin frowned and shook his head in a curt negative, with a glance at Collis to emphasize his point. "Have you seen Rat Johnson? I heard he was looking for you."

"I've seen him. They took his rock, you know. He's pretty upset about it: he recited the history of all his progeny to me again."

"I suppose you agreed to take him—"

"I agreed." I said it quickly, before he could announce my plans aloud.

He glanced at his phone unit and grinned. "Paranoid, aren't we?" he asked maliciously.

"It seems prudent. Yes, thanks, I will sit down." He hadn't asked, but I felt silly standing in the middle of the chamber like an unwelcome guest. Better to sit in the middle of the chamber like an unwelcome guest. I reached automatically to adjust my holster as I sat, but of course it wasn't there. I withdrew my hand from my hip with a feeling of irritation that must have showed, because Jamin grinned sardonically.

"You don't seem comfortable with the new ruling."

Collis climbed confidently into my lap and I glanced at Jamin, but he didn't seem to be paying attention, so I let Collis settle with his head against my shoulder. "What new ruling?" he asked, twisting his neck to look up into my face.

I looked at Jamin. "What have you told him?"

"Told who?" asked Collis.

"Nothing," said Jamin.

"That's typical. You think if you ignore it, it'll go away?"

"Not exactly," said Jamin.

"What'll go away?" asked Collis.

"Never mind," I told him. "Your father and I don't always agree on policy."

"What's policy?"

"Oh come on, you know what policy is."

"Yeah, but I don't know what you mean, 'ass why."

I grinned at Jamin. "I keep telling you, you're raising a Belter kid."

"What's that got to do with anything?"

"Quite a lot, actually. For instance, how old were you when you flew your first shuttle?"

"Ten, I guess," he said suspiciously.

"That'd be solo. I meant flew, at all."

"I don't know."

"You know, all right. D'you remember how you felt? D'you remember how old you were, inside? Age is only numbers. You can't keep treating Collis like a kid."

Collis looked triumphantly at his father. " 'Ass why."

"Don't start showing off, Toad. You'll ruin my presentation."

"Oh." He settled down again, his head against my shoulder.

"It's not a matter of treating him like a kid or not treating him like a kid," said Jamin. "It's a matter of—"

"What, then? Your own cowardice?" I felt Collis move in my arms, but I had spoken cheerfully and he had unreasonable trust in me. He only looked up at me silently.

Jamin lifted one dark eyebrow. "Watch your mouth, hotshot."

"If you'd just act right," I said. "Jamin, for space sake, what are you thinking of? You *know* they'll deny you departure clearance if you wait too long."

He sighed. "I have a Company run to make that I contracted for some time ago. After that, maybe we'll reconsider. *If* I can find somewhere safe for both of us—"

"You'll have to lower your standards. Collis could—"

"I'll decide what Collis could."

"Damn you." I said it with more impatience than conviction.

He smiled distantly. "You're too late. God did that already."

"She had nothing to do with it. It's your own stubborn arrogance. There are a million Fallers in the Belt—"

"Only a million?"

"All right, millions. I don't know. There are a *lot* of Fallers in the Belt. And of them all, you are undoubtedly the stubbornest, most arrogant—"

"You said that already."

"Preposterously dim-witted—"

"Careful there."

"Unreasonable damn *jockey* of the lot!"

"You may be right." He winked at Collis.

"You could go to Mars Station. They have gravity quarters there, I'm sure. Or you could send Collis to Mars, to my cousin Michael's family, for the duration."

"For the duration. Fine phrase, that," he said. "Only it just might mean the rest of our lives."

"You won't live that long if you don't do *some*thing."

"Opinion noted."

"You are insufferable."

"I know it." He grinned suddenly, and it transformed his face from dark mockery to cheerful friendliness. "It's no use, Skyrider. You can't pick a fight with me here, and you aren't going to change my mind anyway. You may as well give up."

"You mean you won't stop acting like a fool."

"You may be right. Think of it this way. At least *I'm* not making a run for a confiscated rock." His eyes were flat blue mirrors.

"You call that logic?"

"Call it what you like." His face was a mask of polite indifference, but his voice betrayed his weariness. "I wish you hadn't taken that on, Skyrider."

"And I wish . . . Oh, bother. I suppose we're even, then."

"In a sense." He closed his eyes briefly, then opened them again to stare at me without expression.

"Well . . . get off, then, Toad. I have a run to make."

Collis climbed obediently out of my lap and stood by my
chair, looking from me to his father and back again.

"You guys mad at each other?" he asked.

I stood up. "I don't know."

"No news from Earth?" asked Jamin.

"I didn't stop long enough to ask any questions. Picked
up a new pilot instructor for Mars Station. One of Rat's
progeny." I glanced at the phone as I said it; but if anyone
were listening, he'd heard enough by now to incriminate
us both. "Something else. Have they got your medication
on the controlled list yet?"

"I don't need a prescription, but I can't stockpile it,
either. Prescriptions will be the next step, I guess."

"Well, if it becomes a problem, let me know, okay?"

He lifted a single eyebrow at me again. "Is that why
you went down to Earth?"

"Somebody has to plan ahead."

He grinned at me. "Your logic is impeccable."

"Usually that's my line." I returned his grin without
quite meaning to. "You really are a hopeless damn jockey,
you know."

"You may be right." He looked at me seriously for a
moment, as though he intended to say something more; but
if so, he decided against it.

"Well, good luck, damn it," I said.

He didn't answer. I found it unexpectedly difficult to
leave them. With the whole Solar System gearing up for
war, there was no way of knowing when or whether I
would see them again. Collis hugged me in the open doorway, right there in front of God and random passers-by,
and I hugged him back without even thinking till afterward
how it would look if any of my fellow pilots saw me
hugging a six-year-old. When I did think of it, I didn't
care. Even an outlaw queen can have friends. And they
don't all have to be grownups. Anyway, I think I half
hoped someone would see us, and try to make something
of it. I could have done with a good fistfight just then,
regardless of Rat's stern warning.

Nobody even looked twice at us. Most of the passers-by

were strangers; the pilots I knew were almost all at Mars Station, trying to turn farmers and freelancers into fighter pilots. I said goodbye to Jamin and Collis and went on down the corridor to my own quarters: or to what had been my quarters for the nearly twenty years since I got my pilot's license. The chambers were small and musty and oddly unfamiliar, as though they belonged to a stranger; which, in a way, they did. The woman who had grown up there was a scrapper, but she wasn't a warrior. Like an eternal adolescent, she took the universe too personally and herself too seriously: flaws I couldn't remedy by recognizing them, but it was a first step.

I moved through my quarters slowly, touching the relics of my past with nerveless fingers. The holograms I'd brought back from my holiday on Earth nearly a year ago winked their bright colors at me, speaking in images of green hills, cloud-strewn skies, wind-bent forests, wide emerald seas. An ancient wooden box caught my eye: smaller than my hand, it held pebbles from rocks Django had visited, including Earth. It was the only thing of his I had kept. I opened it, and the little shards of rock shifted inside with a tiny rustling sound. I put a finger in to stir them absently. They were cold and silent under my touch. They were only pebbles. They held nothing of his smile, or his laughter, or his love. I closed the box and moved on.

The phone unit was dented on one side where I hit it once in a fury over something Jamin had done. I couldn't hit him, so I broke my hand on a mindless machine. It hadn't changed anything. It hadn't even made me feel better. It just dented my phone and broke my hand.

The table was scarred from years of rough usage; burned places and knife scars from my brief attempt, years ago, to learn to cook; tool marks from various small mechanical problems I had brought home with me; a few rounded dents from hammering and deep burns from soldering, made when I decided to teach myself carpentry. . . . The dispenser in the middle of the table was programmed with all my favorite recipes. Whoever had my quarters next would probably wipe them without a second thought.

I touched the rock wall beside the table and looked at the familiar blast scars left from the original tunneling of Home Base. If an Earther got my quarters, he or she would cover the rock with fabric or furs in the Earther fashion. Probably cover the furniture, too, or have it replaced. Earthers couldn't seem to tolerate the existence of bare rock and metal in the living quarters. In pilot territory, all the quarters were naked rock furnished with simple metal and plastics, perhaps not only because we liked it that way but also because we were rough on our furnishings, and metal and plastic could take it. During the coming war Earthers would live here. How would they cope?

It wasn't my problem. I didn't care. I checked the locker to be sure I hadn't left anything irreplaceable, and found only standard tunics and slippers, undergarments, an old newsfax sheet of no particular interest, and my one dressy jumpsuit. I wouldn't be needing that.

In the bathroom there were only standard toiletries, all of which were duplicated on my shuttle and, in any event, easily replaced. Django had bought me a sturdy plasteel mirror when I broke the old glass one the Company had supplied with my quarters. The Earther who lived there next might appreciate that. I'd almost never remembered to look in it, though Django had always said I should, "to remind yourself how pretty you are." But "pretty," like "outlaw," is only a word.

There was one thing in my quarters that I did want to keep, and that I hadn't yet transferred to the *Defiance*. I'd brought it back after the Station Newhome incident, and concealed it in a pocket of rock behind the bed. I hadn't known, then, exactly why I kept it; it wasn't something for which I hoped to find a use. But now it might be a very good thing to have.

I had to leave the holster behind, but the laser itself fit nicely into the inside pocket of my flight jacket under my arm. It was a very small unit that would carry only a short charge, but it was deadly and, thanks to the Patrol, it was the only weapon I had. Besides all its other qualities, it was illegal as all hell, which actually added to my pleasure in carrying it. I suppose I was feeling defiant about the confiscation of my legal weapon.

Thus comfortably armed again, I left my quarters without further delay. Twenty years is a long time; but my chambers were only hollowed rock in a warren of hollowed rock. I felt more at home on the *Defiance*; I'd spent most of my life in shuttles, and she was the best.

I was stopped twice on my way to the flight deck: once by a cluster of Patrolmen who demanded to know my business but backed off when they heard my name; and once by a single Patrolman who must not only have been new at her job but also straight out from Earth on the most recent Company transport. She spoke Company English with an Earther twang and affected total ignorance of both my name and my nickname. She studied my ID and frowned at me while I said yessir and nosir obediently to her every query, as perfectly and patiently as a cadet. Rat would have been proud of me. She didn't openly insult me, but I probably would have let her get away with that, too; much as I'd wanted a fight when I first left Jamin and Collis, I'd had ample time since then to calm down. Now I just wanted off that rock and safely back out into space where I belonged.

Rat was waiting for me beside the *Defiance*. He looked relieved when I showed up. "Skyrider," he said in surprise.

"That's my name."

"Not," he said accurately, because my name is really Melacha Vandy Rendell. "But I'm glad to see you; I wasn't sure you'd manage not to mix it with the Patrol."

"I managed. Climb aboard." I unlocked the *Defiance* and looked around for Jake. "I'm going, you can stay or come."

"You bet." He went inside and I closed the hatch behind him. There were Ground Patrolmen all around, but none of them seemed troubled to see Rat climbing aboard my shuttle. I wanted to find my handgun before I left Home Base. With any luck, maybe they really would give it back. But first I wanted to find Jake.

She was working on a battered Starbird not far from the *Defiance*. When I approached she looked up and offered me a frayed smile and a weary sigh. "*Defiance* should be okay now," she said. "Lead panel was charred. Replaced it."

"Thanks." I hesitated, not sure how to phrase my request and not really sure I should make it.

She straightened from her work to study me. "Something else you want?"

"Jamin won't leave."

She looked at me steadily. "Want me to keep an eye on 'em for you?"

"Could you?"

"Don't know it'll do much good."

"I know." I shifted uncomfortably. "I'd feel better if you would, anyway."

"Okay." She glanced past me at an approaching Patrolman. "Here's your handgun."

Startled, I turned to see the same Patrolman who had taken my handgun approaching with my tagged holster in his hands. He looked embarrassed, but determined. "I saw you put a passenger aboard," he said. "You're going off-station?"

"As soon as I have my weapon back."

"Here it is. Do you have the stub I gave you?"

I had it. "I don't believe this. I thought . . ."

"You thought you'd have to fight for it if you got it at all, right? Space, Skyrider, I think the new rule's rockdust, same like you, but it's my job. What am I going to do?"

I studied his face while I strapped my holster on. He looked young, worried, and vaguely puzzled. "There are alternatives," I said.

"Alternatives to obeying the law?"

I didn't answer directly. "You're a Belter, aren't you? I mean, you were born out here?" The handgun was a comfortable weight against my hip. I straightened and settled the holster into its familiar position.

"Sure, but space, I'm a Patrolman."

"So you are." I didn't smile. "No matter what?"

"I don't know what you mean." His eyes were the

color of pale amber. They looked even younger than his face.

"I think you do. If a government breaks faith with its people, should the people just sit back and take it?" A shuttle popped the screen behind me, engines whining, and slid down onto a landing panel, trailing hot gases and the stench of burning malite.

"There's always legal recourse," said the Patrolman.

"Space legal recourse. We've had legal recourse. What d'you think this latest fuss is about?"

"You don't have to break the law," he said stubbornly. "You can fight within the system—"

"Okay." I shook my head. "You should be right. I wish you were. Hell, I hope you are."

He still looked worried. "But you don't think so?"

I couldn't remember his name. "I don't know." Suddenly the conversation didn't seem very important. "I don't know. It's your life. Nobody can live it for you."

He hesitated, ready to take offense, but uncertain whether any was meant. "Meaning?"

"Meaning, I guess, that if the world is going to be saved, it'll have to be done by somebody too young to know it can't be done."

"I'm fifteen standard years old." He sounded defiant, thinking I'd just accused him of youth. Which, of course, I had.

"Good for you." I glanced at the shuttle that had just come in. It was the Company transport, off-loading a new batch of hopeful colonists who had, by coming in, lost the very thing they had come to claim.

The Patrolman shifted uneasily. "Skyrider . . ."

"Thanks for the handgun." I couldn't offer him the standard wish for a long life; soon I might be the enemy warrior who would end it. I walked away.

CHAPTER FIVE

We lifted off Home Base without any interference from the Patrol. I checked the starboard screen, and it was working. The computer reported optimum strength in the starboard shield. I hoped it was right; I was going to need all my shields on this run.

We made it all the way to New England without incident. There were plenty of Patrol boats in evidence along the way, but none challenged us or made any effort to intercept us. I had filed a flight plan to one of the Company's "relocation centers" (read internment rocks) out that way, which kept us legal till we turned off for Rat's rock. That I contrived to do right in the middle of a heavy flurry of wild rocks, which are frequent in the New England area, and which I hoped would confuse the Patrol's sensors long enough to give us a head start.

They must have been expecting me to do exactly that. Going in, I could have sworn there wasn't a Patrol boat anywhere near us. In the flurry I was too busy dodging rocks to notice. When we came out, there were six boats waiting for us in battle formation, their weapons armed and their shields up.

"Attention, *Defiance*," said the Comm Link. "You are in violation of your recorded flight plan. Please respond. You are entering an off-limits area. Do you copy?"

We were moving at a good clip, and it's a truism that you don't make sudden turns or stops in space, at least not in a Falcon. I'd been told the Sunfinch's new malite conversion drive supplied enough power to overcome inertia in so little space it seemed able to turn square corners and stop on a pebble, but I had never flown one long enough to find out. Anyway the *Defiance* couldn't turn a square corner or stop on a pebble, so I did the next best thing: the unexpected. I flipped her end-for-end and let inertia carry us backward, still on course, right through the Patrol's careful formation.

It meant I didn't have them on my laser screens till we were past them, which worried me; but it worked. If I'd gone through frontward, they'd have fired on us. Riding backward, there was a chance we were trying to stop. I hoped they wouldn't fire if we seemed to be complying with their demand, and they didn't. As soon as we were through their formation I had them on my laser screens again, but they didn't all have us on theirs; some of them were slow to flip over.

I punched several Comm Link controls, deliberately breaking up my signal. "Wild rock knocked out scanners and controls, will attempt to comply, do you copy?"

"Say again?" The Patrol boats had all flipped by now, to get us back on their screens. "Your signal is garbled, *Defiance*. Say again?"

I jockeyed sideways, let the *Defiance* yaw unsteadily, and said in a tight voice, "Damage to controls, wild rocks, I cannot, do you read?" If they scanned the heat loss from my jockey thrusters they would recognize the ruse at once, but I had to edge away from them to get a good run for Rat's rock. Still allowing the apparently uncontrolled yaw, I jockeyed again and started a pitch that would bring me end-over-end aimed, if my calculations were correct, in the direction we wanted to go. "Please assist, please assist," I said, watching my screens. "Shuttle *Defiance* out of control, I say again, please assist. . . ." We were headed the right way, and they hadn't fired yet. I hit the thrusters for all they were worth and watched my aft screens. The Patrol boats scrambled after us, but we were in luck; they still didn't fire. They might not fully believe me, but they weren't yet ready to commit to disbelief.

Through all this, Rat had sat stolidly in the auxilliary control seat, watching the scanners without a word. He looked startled when I kicked out the thrusters and let the *Defiance* fall into what I hoped would seem an awkward and unintentional tumble. We came up facing the boats again, riding away from them tailfirst at an angle that kept us on course and them all in my laser screens. The Comm Link was spitting static and I flipped it off.

"This can't last, you know," said Rat.

"Sure it can."

"The two Falcons are lining up to fire," he said.

"So they are." The other four boats were all Starbirds, better for infighting than my Falcon but unable to outrun us in the long haul. The Falcons were what worried me, and it was disheartening to see that their pilots were the first to decide this was to be a firefight, after all. But Rat was right; I couldn't reasonably have hoped they'd hold off forever.

I jockeyed off their screens, threw a blind shot their way, and gave up the pretense of being disabled: flipping over one last time, I aimed straight for Rat's rock and kicked in the thrusters all the way. They would eat fuel like a cargo hog, but I had plenty of fuel; the Patrol Falcons hadn't. Nobody had redesigned their innards to accommodate twice the original fuel capacity. I hoped.

Their first shots missed us by a healthy margin. The Starbirds scrambled after us, then fell behind one by one as their fuel gauges signaled the risk. The Falcons lumbered sturdily after us, still firing. We were squarely in their laser screens now, and for all my dodging we hadn't really a hope of getting off their screens again except by outrunning them, which would take time. Meanwhile I poured what spare power we had into my aft screens and thought about praying. We were closing on Rat's rock.

With those Falcons after us, we would have to swing on past and ambush them from the other side . . . if they didn't knock us out of space before we had the chance.

That was when the second squadron of Patrol boats floated up out of the scanner shadow of Rat's rock. All six of them were Falcons. I just had time to redistribute shield power before they fired.

The next few minutes are not altogether clear in my memory. Rat says I yelled something, but if so, I've no idea what it was. I remember the blinding red of the lasers and the shield sparks like new stars: bright green and yellow shards of light against the black of space on our down-sun side, blanking the real stars; and sun-washed yellow sheets on our up-sun side, less beautiful but not less deadly.

Inside the cockpit there was a sudden stink and spit of burning circuits; the reek of sealant as Rat grabbed up a cylinder and inverted it to seal a minute, whistling hole in the bulkhead just aft of his seat; the flash of warning lights that burned out almost as quickly as they came on; and the unholy *blaat!* of warning klaxons as my systems burned out.

We had one tiny chance in hell of escaping, and I took it. We'd been moving at top speed when we were hit. The lasers hadn't slowed us; it takes more than that to overcome the inertia of a racing Falcon. I cut the thrusters and hit every scanner-visible control on the board, including life support, and we rode on past Rat's rock in dark, dead silence.

If the Patrol didn't buy it, if they didn't believe they'd killed us with those first blasts, if they fired even one last shot to make sure of us, we were dead. There was nothing between us and their lasers but vulnerable bulkheads: no shields. It had to be that way. If I'd left so much as an air filter running they'd have taken that last shot for sure. This way we had a chance. Nothing exactly to crow about, but a chance.

Oddly, I couldn't even hear the Gypsies singing. They had sung me through every tight spot I'd been in since

Django died; but this time, they were silent. The whole world was silent. The thickening air in the cockpit stank of burnt wiring. Now and then a fading spark hissed from a dying panel, but there was no other sound. The winds of space are silent winds, and the stars with all their tales to tell never say a word.

The scanner screens were out, but I could watch the starred black of space through the viewport. There was nothing else to watch. The reflected light inside the cockpit was inadequate to see by. Tears burned my eyes and the sharp tang of sealant choked me and the deathly silence frightened me and I stared at the distant stars.

Without scanners, I couldn't tell what the Patrol boats were doing. Without any readouts I couldn't tell how fast we were traveling, or whether we were being followed, or even whether in that last desperate maneuver we had developed some hideous error in course. We might be headed straight for a field of wild rocks; they were common in that area.

I couldn't even tell exactly how foul the atmosphere inside the *Defiance* was getting. I knew it was bad, but I had to judge entirely by feel when "bad" turned into "dangerous." If I misjudged that, and passed out without reactivating life support, there'd be nothing to save us.

I could feel Rat watching me. But he was an older hand at this sort of thing than I: he wouldn't panic. He would wait, stolidly, calmly, and without comment, for me to make the decision. This was my ship, my command, my responsibility.

The stars glittered against the black of space, cold and bright and beautiful. I was absurdly grateful that we were facing down-sun, so I could watch their jeweled display. The air seemed to be clearing; my eyes weren't blinded by tears, and though my throat felt raw and I could hear Rat audibly gasping for breath, at least I could see the cruel beauty of the universe while I waited for the Patrol boats to drop behind; for the Gypsies to start their song; for time to heal, or stop, or change the rhythm of its ceaseless, meaningless parade. . . .

I was never aware of reaching for the controls. I must have manipulated them entirely by feel, since in that aching, dizzied darkness I could see nothing but the fire and ice of stars. The artificial lights inside the cockpit came up slowly, and the atmosphere control whirred busily into action with a quiet hum that matched the hum of blood in my ears. I was only distantly aware of the renewed gentle thrum of engines as gravity returned and the control board blinked back into battered operational mode.

Rat was clinging to his shock webbing with silent resignation. His eyes barely wavered from their intent gaze out the viewport at the stars. He didn't even check the scanners; if we hadn't lost the Patrol, there was nothing he could do about it, anyway.

I checked them, though I wasn't sure there was anything I could do, either. As it happened, I didn't have to; we'd lost the Patrol. I could just make them out, up-sun so far they couldn't possibly scan us for life signs now. "They bought it." My voice cracked, and I cleared my throat. "They stayed behind."

Rat looked into the scanner screens and found the one that showed his rock tumbling silently away behind us in the feeble light of the sun. "A whole squadron." His voice was as harsh and as weary as mine. "A whole damn squadron for my rock."

"Both squadrons were for your rock; why else would that first group have been there? There's nothing else around here for them to protect."

"Protect!" He closed his eyes. "Gods damn them all."

"If there are any gods, they will." I had asked the computer for a damage report. Reading it, I almost wished I hadn't asked. "And if the gods don't do it then by space I will!"

He looked at me, his eyes bright with bitterness and fatigue. "We're not out of this yet."

"Oh, hell, Rat. I've been in tighter spots. We can make

Mars Station, easy. Why sound so fatal? You haven't even looked at the damage report.''

''I don't have to. I can feel it. Don't try to fool me, child. I've lived a long life, most of it on shuttles and rocks, and I know how they should feel. This shuttle, believe me, doesn't feel right.''

''We can make it to Mars Station.''

He shrugged ineffably. ''Believe what you need to believe.'' That should have been offensive, but it wasn't.

''You'll see.'' I gentled the *Defiance* into a broad turn that put her nose toward Mars. She moved awkwardly, but she moved, and she went where I told her. It took more time and more care than it should have, but now that we'd left the Patrol behind and got the life support systems back on, we had plenty of time; and for the *Defiance* I had plenty of patience.

In the condition she was in, she couldn't have docked with Rat's rock even if the Patrol had suddenly deserted it for our convenience. I don't know that I wouldn't have tried it anyway. Fortunately I didn't have to make that decision; the Patrol wasn't leaving.

We couldn't return to Home Base all battle-scarred and broken. If the Patrol we'd tangled with hadn't reported us, the others would guess anyway if they saw us. And if they didn't knock us out of space on general principles, the inquisition we would have to face from Ground Patrol when we landed would be insufferable and would almost certainly end with both of us headed for an internment rock.

That left Mars Station—if the Patrol didn't find us on the way and decide to eliminate us just for having the temerity not to be dead already. Once I had us pointed in the right direction I read the damage reports again, checked a couple of failing instruments, held my breath, and kicked in the thrusters. That was a calculated risk; if they malfunctioned, they could throw us into a terminal dive for the sun; and if the dying navigational computer had miscalculated the desired trajectory then even if the thrusters functioned correctly we might end in a deep-space dive that we wouldn't have either the power or the functioning instruments to correct in time.

If I'd been satisfied with less thrust, we could have made the journey a lot more safely, and it would have taken only a little over twice as long. I guess I was reacting to Rat's calm assertion that we couldn't make it at all. The first time Jamin had ever called me "hotshot" I had promptly risked my life to show him what a real hotshot could do. Now Rat said we couldn't make Mars Station and I promptly risked both our lives to show him just how easily we could make Mars Station if I said we could. Once a hotshot, always a hotshot.

The thrusters didn't malfunction. The Patrol didn't intercept us. The trajectory calculations were correct to the last decimal. And we even had fuel enough left when we got to Mars Station to retrofire into a safe orbit and ask politely for landing clearance.

The majority of our instruments were useless and the greatest part of the control panel was dead by then, but all we really needed were life support, the Comm Link, and the jockey thrusters, all of which had survived so far. It would have been pleasant to have the synch system as well, but one can't have everything. I'd landed often enough before without a synch system. I could do it one more time.

My cousin Michael was on Flight Control. He cursed when he scanned our damage, and suggested with terrible patience that a pilot with any damn sense would abandon ship and let a salvage crew bring shuttle and passengers in separately. He knew as well as I did how rarely I've been accused of having any damn sense. I said, "Negative. We'll come in on our own."

"Melacha, don't be a fool. Even you can't land that wreck, and you know it."

"This *wreck* is my Falcon, Michael, and I'm damned if I'll abandon her to the scavengers. I went through worse than this to get her, and it will take worse than this to get her away from me."

"Special dispensation," he said. "I'll lead the salvage crew. No claim. We'll just bring her in for you."

"Now who's the fool? You couldn't get a team to go after her on those terms, and you know it."

"I can and I will. Abandon ship, for gods' sake."

Maybe he could have done it, I don't know. I wasn't about to take the chance. "Negative. Do I have landing clearance, or shall I try to make it down to Mars?"

"Oh, hell." My Comm screen was out, but I could imagine his predatory expression as he leaned over his scanners, his big hands dancing across the controls, his pale eyes anxiously studying the results. "Oh, hell, Melacha. Honest to gods, nobody could land that thing."

To my surprise, Rat spoke up for the first time. Without a glance at me he said in his sharp old-man voice, "The Skyrider can."

Michael sighed audibly. "If you could see her from here . . . Oh, hell. Give me time to clear the panels and call out Damage and Fire Control crews." He did that, and came back on Link to swear at me. "If you kill yourself in this damnfool landing, I swear I'll knock your face in."

"If I kill myself, you're welcome to do anything you like with my face afterward."

"Yeah, okay, I get the message, hotshot. You're cleared for landing. Come on in if you can."

I looked at Rat. "You're sure? You could jump ship you know. The scavengers bring in passengers for free."

He shook his head. "You got us this far. Bring us on in."

I broke orbit, jockeyed into position at the opening of the tunnel that was Mars Station's flight deck, carefully calculated the axial rotation and orbital velocity of the Station, and did my best to match them with my failing controls. That's what a synch system is supposed to do; if the landing ship isn't traveling at very nearly the same velocity as the flight deck is in its orbit around the sun or planet that holds it, and at the same time rotating on its axis at exactly the same rate as the flight deck, the landing will be a disaster. With a shipboard synch system linked to the flight deck's computers, everything is safely synchronized by electronic minds and there's very little chance of misfortune. Without a synch system the whole procedure is a chance at misfortune: and with limited and malfunctioning controls, most people would consider it a rather complicated method of suicide.

I don't approve of suicide, but I have different ideas from most people about what constitutes acceptable risk.

CHAPTER SIX

I've made better landings. If there really are insane gods who watch over shuttle pilots and fools, they were with us that day. My calculations were off by a very small margin. That's all it takes. We hit the deck too hard, too fast, and port side first, with a wrenching crash that I thought would buckle the whole shuttle frame. I could feel her groan with the impact.

The port panel skids sent up a shower of sparks and the tearing scream of metal against stressed metal. I jockeyed to keep us from going over, but the endpanel wall was coming up on us too fast, and when I hit the landing baffles nothing happened. They should have snagged into the panel slowscreen, to keep us from crashing head-on against that wall. The warning light over the baffle switch wasn't on; it must have burned out when the control did. There was nothing else to stop us from smearing ourselves up against the wall like so much rockdust.

One doesn't retrofire on-station. There are engines for liftoff and landing, and there are engines for flight, and the two types are distinct and different. The mechanics of the difference are too complex to go into here: it should be adequate to say that the interaction of flight engines and landing deck niceties like the slowscreen is not always a happy affair. The danger, however, is primarily to the shuttle involved and to any groundcrew members standing too near the landing site. Michael had cleared the deck to accommodate us, and a new danger to the *Defiance* could hardly be worse than the one we already faced. If I didn't do something, they'd be scraping us off the endpanel wall for a week. I took a chance on retrofire.

We didn't immediately burst into a ball of flame and a shower of hot shrapnel. That was promising. We did swing hard around till we were skidding down the panel with our starboard side forward before I could cut the retrofire. One of the retro engines must have failed, to spin us around like that. The construction of a landing panel is such that there wasn't any danger of skidding off ours onto another unless we rolled, and so far the landing wasn't quite that bad. But we were still approaching the end wall at an alarming rate, starboard first now, and further retrofire would only swing us on around and then speed our progress toward the wall, tail-first.

All this took place in seconds. I was making decisions faster than I can retell them; and after the first bone-jarring impact with the panel that proved my initial calculations wrong, I never for a moment thought we were going to survive. I was just trying to make the end a little less spectacular. It if had to be said that the Skyrider died of a flubbed landing, let it at least be said that she came closer to saving it than an ordinary pilot could have done.

I reached for the retrofire button again, and Rat had time to give me one startled glance of resigned amusement before I hit it. One second of fire and off again, and we were ass-backward on the panel, still rushing for the endpanel wall, but at least not trailing a fiery tail of sparks from the panel skids. Retrofire off: liftoff engines on: if I'd timed it right, the retrofire should have straightened us exactly enough for the liftoff engines to try to take us straight back out into space. They couldn't do it, of course; there was too much inertia still to overcome, and the engines were not in the best condition to begin with. But, again if I had timed it right, they might stop us before we splattered up against the wall.

I counted under my breath without even looking at the screens. One second, two seconds, three seconds, cut the engines. . . .

In the sudden silence afterward I looked up, almost reluctantly, at the screens. We were at a full stop with five meters left between us and the end wall. I'd done the impossible. We were alive.

"Very showy." Michael's voice over the Comm Link sounded dry and unexpectedly loud.

I released a breath I hadn't known I held. "Thanks, if that's a compliment."

"I'm not sure it is."

"Then watch your damn mouth, Martian, or I'll put my fist in it."

He laughed. It was a rustling-paper sound occasioned more, I think, by relief than by amusement. "You're not in the Belt now, hotshot. Try anything like that and I'll have you up on charges so fast it'll make your head spin."

I said unsteadily, "My head's already spinning."

"I mean it, Skyrider." There was still a hint of laughter in his voice, but there was a much stronger note of warning. "I know you Belters like a good fistfight after a bad run the way a normal person likes a nice hot container of caffeine and room to hang loose. But on this station you're going to have to find some alternative means of letting off steam. We're here to fight a common enemy. We *don't* fight each other."

"Yessir, Flight Controller, sir."

"Melacha , , ,"

Rat interrupted him. "She'll be okay. You just get your people to put her shuttle back together, 'ey? This is Rat Johnson speaking. Where do new pilot instructors sign on for duty?"

Michael told him, and I shut off the Comm Link. We unfastened our shock webbing in the musty silence of the half-dark cockpit, unaccountably avoiding each other's eyes. "Rat, I'm sorry about your rock."

He shrugged ineffably. "I'm sorry about your shuttle."

"My shuttle can be mended."

"My rock can be reclaimed."

We looked at each other then, and grinned like idiots. "You *bet* one war," we said simultaneously, and laughed as if we'd said something funny.

Mars Station was a freefall station, and now that we were down and had our webbing unfastened, the effects of that became obvious. The *Defiance* wouldn't float off-panel till the holding magnets were disengaged, but there was nothing to hold down anything we'd left loose inside her. During the period in space when we'd had the life support systems turned off, it had been too dark inside to see how many bits and pieces of her had come loose in the cockpit as a result of the battle; and when we turned the life support back on, the gravity came with it, so everything loose at the time had floated back down roughly where it belonged, or out of sight.

Now it all floated up again; wiring, loose panels, switches, bits of air filter material, tools from a locker that had sprung open, and us. We kicked free of our seats and dodged the debris on the way to the hatch, which functioned perfectly in spite of all we had been through.

The Damage and Fire Control crews that had been waiting behind crash barriers to see how many pieces they would have to pick up were out in full force and already beginning their investigatory scramble over the outside of my *Defiance* when we floated through the hatch. I left it open for them; they couldn't do it all from the outside.

Rat thanked me for the flight and went to report in to our flight training school. It would have been polite to accompany him, but I wasn't feeling polite. And I wasn't ready to report in for routine flight training duty. I greeted a few of the Damage Control people, most of whom were old friends from the pre-Redistribution days, and accepted their dubious praise for a bad landing well saved. Then I went off to look for the container of caffeine Michael had mentioned, and the place to hang loose after a bad run.

The ready room was almost deserted. I changed from

flight suit to Belter tunic, tights, and slippers, strapped my stun gun back to my hip with a feeling of having achieved very little by reclaiming it, and put the little illegal laser in my locker with my flight suit. If it turned out to be useful at all, it wouldn't be on Mars Station.

One of the nearby gaming tables produced a container of caffeine when I punched the request into its dispenser keyboard. I hooked one foot over the back of a chair for balance and floated next to it, sipping iced caffeine from a condensation-beaded plastic tube. At the neighboring table, a group of Martians I didn't know were having a game of Planets with magnetic pieces and a miniature grav tray to hold the pot. They had looked up and nodded at me when I entered, then returned to their game. Aside from them, the room was deserted; there wasn't much time for play on Mars Station these days.

Nor for relaxation of any sort: I knew I shouldn't really be there. I should have reported, as Rat did, to the flight training crews for instructor duty. The thought didn't thrill me. I wondered absently whether, if I could promote a shuttle in which to do it, and I went back to Home Base, I could get Jamin and Collis away from the Company before they got rounded up for internment. Jamin had relatives in high places in the Company, but that didn't guarantee him freedom forever. Relatives or not, he was a Faller.

Which reminded me of my undelivered cargo aboard the *Defiance*. Neither my battle with the Patrol nor my subsequent ungraceful landing on Mars Station should have done it any damage, but it might be as well to offload it now before anything further went wrong. The question was how to get the best value out of it. If I were an altruistic sort, I might just have handed it over to the Colonials with my compliments, but I'd never been particularly altruistic. I'd gone a long way through a lot of risk and trouble to get that load of drugs. I wanted something in exchange to make it worth my while.

Maybe the gods just sit around and wait for us to get uppity so they can take our expectations down a peg or two: I was deciding on an opening bid to ask of the three potential purchasers of my cargo (the Colonials themselves, in the person of what might loosely be called our governing body; a very wealthy Colonial Faller I knew who'd taken refuge with his family on Mars Station but would have liked to be able to make occasional visits to various gravity stations and rocks where Floater friends and relations of hers were living; and the leader of a commando group with whom I'd had some dealings in the past, whose members included several Fallers and who would have been delighted at the opportunity my medication would afford them to perform sabotage forays against Earthers in gravity locations), when my cousin Michael floated into the ready room.

"Off duty already?" I said in surprise.

"What do you mean, already?" He hooked an ankle under the table next to me and looked without interest at the dispenser keyboard. "I've been on duty for the last eighteen hours."

"Still short of personnel?"

He coded the dispenser for caffeine and frowned at the resultant container. "We're short of everything."

"If it's something I can smuggle, tell me, and I'll go get it."

He gave me an odd look. "In what?"

"In the *Defiance*, once your crews get her mended. Or isn't Rat's credit good with you?"

"It's good, but the *Defiance* isn't. She won't be mended."

"She what?"

"It just isn't worth it, Melacha. She's all torn up inside. Once we got a real look at her, none of us could see how the hell you brought her down without killing yourself. The frame's okay, and the body's only a little dented— nothing to bother fixing unless you plan to make a run into atmosphere—but the engines, the controls, the wiring, essentially everything that makes her fly, is shot to hell. She's a useless hunk of metal and plastic, and that's it."

"You won't fix her?"

"Skyrider, I'm not sure we *could* fix her, even if we had the time and parts and were willing to waste them on a piece of junk that should by rights be taken apart and *used* for parts."

"You won't fix her."

He sighed wearily. "I think that's what I just said."

I studied him uneasily. "How much?"

"How much what?" He was genuinely puzzled.

"How much would it take to get her fixed?"

"I've just told you, I don't even know whether we could. Certainly we won't try. We have a lot of shuttles out there that need fixing, and the ones in the condition the *Defiance* is in get taken apart and used to mend others. That's how we do it, Melacha. There's nothing I can do about it. She's just too wrecked."

"Damn it, tell me how much?"

"I'm not bargaining, don't you understand? I'm not trying to run up the price. I'm telling you there isn't a price. We can't do it."

"You *could*."

He made an unwary gesture that broke his tenuous attachment to the table and sent him floating gently off at an angle away from me, looking impatient. "Okay, okay, we could do it. Of course we could do it. Any group of mechanics and electronics experts and computer people could do it, if they had unlimited time, materials, and money. A manufacturing plant would be ideal for your needs. We don't have one. We don't have the time, materials, or money, and if we had, we couldn't waste them on your shuttle. We're getting ready for a war here, has that escaped your attention? The shuttles we fix are going to fly in it. We can't waste time on one that won't."

"What makes you think she won't? I'm as proColonial as the next guy, or I wouldn't be here, surely?"

He produced a wolfish warrior's smile. "Are you telling me you're going to fly in the Colonial Fleet? You? The Skyrider? Obeying orders like a rookie?"

"I can fly formation with the best of them. Hell, I taught a lot of pilots myself. I'm damn good, and you know it."

"You're damn good, yes, as a pilot. As a warrior even. But not as a member of a team."

"I can—"

"And even if you flew in the Fleet," he continued inexorably, "you'd fly in one of our shuttles. You don't have one of your own anymore. You have a pile of scrap on which the Colonial Fleet is willing to make you an offer."

"I have a little something more than that."

"Yeah? What? Because if you think you can offer me enough money—"

"Not money."

He frowned at me, his pale eyes shadowed with weariness and maybe worry. "What could you possibly offer?" It was a rhetorical question; he didn't leave room for me to answer it. "I'm trying to explain to you, it's a simple exercise in logic or economics or something, damn it; look, the *Defiance* just isn't worth fixing. Maybe if you've got enough money you could buy another shuttle from us, I don't know, but I don't see how you could buy the fixing of that junk heap."

"If you've got other Falcons, you could use them to rebuild the *Defiance*, couldn't you?"

"It'd make more sense the other way around. We'd be essentially taking apart a whole, functioning Falcon to mend a broken hulk. That doesn't make sense."

"It makes sense to me. She's mine."

"Well, it can't be done. We can't afford it."

"Could you afford it in exchange for six full crates of gravity medication?"

"Six *what*?"

"Full crates of gravity medication. No, I take that back. Five full, one almost full. I need some for Jamin."

"Where would you get something like that?"

"I've got it already. On that broken hulk you've been insulting."

He shook his head. "No, you haven't. My people have been all over that shuttle, inside and out. If you had six crates of anything that interesting, they'd have told me."

"They won't have seen it."

"How could they not see it? I just told you, they've been all over her. They had to be, to determine the full extent of the damage. There's nothing like that aboard."

"There is." I grinned at him. "And now maybe you see why I want *that* Falcon, not some standard model whose innards nobody has improved. There are several things about her your people won't have noticed. And believe me, altering another Falcon to suit me would be a lot more costly in time and materials than it would be for you to just mend the *Defiance* with spare parts from whatever you've got lying around. Even if it takes a whole functioning Falcon to do it."

He hesitated, studying me. "You'd have to show me the drugs."

"Of course."

"And I can't make the final decision. I'd have to consult—"

"Consult all you like. Just don't take forever; I still have a run or two to make sometime soon."

"Jamin still at Home Base?"

"I don't quite see how that follows, but yes, he is."

He nodded. "Show me the drugs."

He came with me back to the flight deck, but I made him wait outside the *Defiance* while I got the crates out of her concealed hold. I put them in the standard hold and went back outside to get him. "You can come aboard now," I said.

He came aboard, looking dubious. The sight of six crates where he knew perfectly well no crates had been only minutes before shook him, but he recovered well. "Open one."

I did it, and removed a box of medication. "I'll keep this aside for Jamin. You can look over the rest. When you're satisfied, you can go consult with whoever. But the crates don't get offloaded till I have a firm commitment for repairs."

He didn't bother to open the other crates, though he did

peer suspiciously into one of the boxes in the open one. Then, looking properly impressed, he put it back in the crate, hooked the lid shut, and pressed the crate securely against the retaining panel I'd hooked them to. "I'll see what I can do," he said.

"You do that."

CHAPTER SEVEN

While they were repairing the *Defiance*, I put through a Comm call to Home Base to see if Jamin and Collis were all right. They were, and Jamin still wouldn't leave the Company's employ, so I hung up on him and went back to teaching Colonial Fleet recruits how to fly.

The group to which I was assigned was bright enough, as recruits go, which isn't saying much. However, we worked with what we had. I had three Martians and three Belters. Two of the Martians were past retirement age, and all three of the Belters were kids very probably younger than proper recruitment age, which left me with one woman about the right age to fly in the Fleet; and she'd have been better trained when she was younger. She knew how to pilot a Martian atmosphere skimmer and was convinced that gave her a head start in shuttle pilot training, which meant that what it would do instead was slow her considerably.

I gave them the standard introductory lecture and handed out the standard charts and schematics for study. The old folks were a married couple named Lem and Linda who seemed to think as a unit. They looked alike, finished each other's sentences, held hands constantly, and wondered whether they really needed two copies of everything; surely they could share?

"You won't be sharing a shuttle," I said.

They looked startled, their deep brown eyes peering
wetly first at each other and then at me. I wondered
whether they met the vision requirements and, if not,
whether Mars Station had the facilities to improve their
eyesight. "Oh, of course we won't," said Lem.

"We hadn't thought of that, but it's," said Linda.

"Perfectly logical," said Lem. He accepted his set of
charts and schematics with no further objections.

The three Belter kids were all Fallers raised in the Outer
Rocks. Unlike Lem and Linda, who spoke only Company
English, the kids spoke none; and their pidgin was so
heavily accented that I seldom understood what they said
on the first try. The youngest of them didn't speak at all
till I pointed out that the ability to do so was an absolute
requirement for Fleet membership. Then she piped up in a
tiny, musical voice that her name was Fred (a fact that
hadn't been wormed out of her before she came to me; her
ID had given only a Company number), that she was well
versed in astrophysics but hadn't ever piloted anything
larger than a lifeboat, and that she was sixteen years old. It
took three repetitions before I was sure I understood all
that, and I thought the last fact was probably embroidered
by at least five years, but I let it go. She was big enough to
reach the controls in a Starbird; I'd just have to see she
wasn't given a Ford by mistake.

The other two kids were boys: Bay and Ichi, fifteen and
fourteen respectively (and I believed them), one blond and
stringy, the other dark and plump. Each had flown Fords
and Chevys before, though neither had flown solo. "We
smaht quick but," said Ichi.

"I'm sure you will," I said. "But do bear in mind that
you may be assigned something other than a Ford or a
Chevy."

They consulted together, translated what I had said into
their brand of Rock talk for better understanding, nodded
over it with nervous giggles, and turned back to me.
"Whatkine anyway you t'eenk?" asked Bay.

"I don't have any idea. You'll get what's available. I
just wanted to remind you that it may not be anything with

which you're familiar.'' I was deliberately avoiding a tendency to fall into Rock talk in response to theirs; they were going to have to learn Company English to get along on the Comm Link with their wingmates and squadron leaders, not all of whom were Belters.

My final pupil, the woman who knew how to fly skimmers, was about twenty years old and rather spectacularly unattractive. She looked as though she worked at it; her clothes and her person were dirty and unkempt, her hair a stringy mat that shadowed her small staring eyes, and her posture oddly curled and twisted from the "neutral" position in which most of us floated in freefall. Her name was Bunz, which she repeated several times in an unsuccessful effort to get me to pronounce it correctly, and her occupation before signing on with the Fleet had been itinerant farmwork.

The worst thing was that it wasn't an atypical group. The Colonial Fleet would be comprised of people like these: children and social misfits and senior citizens who should have been resting on their laurels, or at least resting. While these six wouldn't necessarily form a squadron together—there was no guarantee they would even all survive the training or, if they survived, achieve the required expertise for Fleet pilot status—they were representative of squadrons recently formed. The thought of sending such a crew into battle was chilling.

"I want you all to study these materials very closely," I said. "We'll be doing a lot of studying before we ever step inside a shuttle."

"Already comprending astrophysics but," said Fred.

"Astrophysics isn't all you'll need," I said, "and it's not what's in these printouts."

"Not?" She held her printouts upside down, studying them intently.

"Fred, do you know how to read?"

She looked at me, her dark eyes huge. "Why, boddah you?"

"It's not a question of . . ." I paused. "But how did you learn astrophysics if you don't know how to read?

You must at least know how to read numbers." But if she did, surely she'd know which side up to hold the printouts.

"Get one good memory." She said it with a mixture of pride and defiance that was pitiable.

"So then you *don't* know how to read."

" 'Ey," said Ichi.

"What is it?"

He was looking at me with surprise and something like fear. "Fo' bean one pilot, knees *read*?"

"I take it you don't know how, either?"

He looked at Bay and they dropped briefly into conference in such fast and heavy pidgin that I missed most of it. Then he turned back to me and smiled broadly. "Fo' sure, you bet, readeen *easy*kine stuffs."

The meaning of that was ambiguous; he might have meant he could read simple things, or that reading itself was simple for him. Either way, I didn't believe it. "Bay? What about you?"

He looked startled. "Whatchu wan', yeah?"

"D'you know how to read?"

"Fo' sure you bet, facilité, no probs—"

I turned to the three Martians. "Do any of *you* know how to read?" All three nodded, but Bunz looked dubious about it. Out of six students, I had two who probably could read and four who probably couldn't. And there simply wasn't time to teach them all to read before I taught them to be pilots. If I *could* teach them to be pilots. "Okay." I sighed and turned to face my little class again. "To answer your question, Ichi, no. It's not necessary to know how to read in order to become a pilot. It would make it a hell a lot of easier if you knew how; but since you don't, I'll just have to do your reading for you. You *will* have to learn to read schematics and to interact with your computers on screens, and you'll have to be able to identify your shuttle controls by their names, but I don't give a damn whether you're able to read the labels or you just memorize the board, as long as you *know* the controls, where they are, and what they do. Understand?"

Ichi puzzled over that for a moment and confided in Bay

again before he turned back to me and nodded. "Comprend you bet," he said.

"Good. Okay. That means we're going to be here a little longer today than I'd intended. Instead of going to your quarters to study the materials I've given you, you'll stay here and we'll study them together."

Ichi and Bay whispered quickly and nodded together.

"How long have you two been in from the Outer Rocks?" I asked.

They consulted. Ichi said uncertainly. "T'ree day maybe one week, yeah?"

I had been thinking of separating them, but if they'd been in only a little over a week they might actually need each other's help to understand the proceedings. "Okay. Thank you. Let's get started." We went over the charts and schematics together. I had trouble getting Fred to hold hers the right way up, but everybody seemed to understand the principles fairly well if given time to absorb what they were told. Since they couldn't refer to the printouts after the meeting, they would have to work extra hard to memorize what was said during class, but they seemed willing and capable. By the time we ended the session I had decided that my initial assessment of them as a group had been hasty. Initial assessments often are.

When I finally dismissed them for the day, I returned to the flight deck to see how the mechanics were doing with the *Defiance*. My presence there was discouraged, which wasn't altogether unreasonable. The flight deck was crowded and busy; the whole of Mars Station was busy these days , , , and these "nights," only of course we didn't divide our time that way anymore. In deep space, day and night are artificial innovations brought by Humankind, and we hadn't time for them when we were gearing up for war.

Back when Jamin and Michael and I were involved in the Station Newhome affair that eventually resulted in my showy interruption of an assassination attempt on the President of the World, Incorporated, the Colonials had managed to cobble together a makeshift Fleet with which to face down the Earth Fighters who tried to interfere. Our

Fleet had been a clumsy and untrained force, half the shuttles without firepower and the other half flown by people who had never fired a lethal weapon before (I do exaggerate, but not by a hell of a lot).

It had looked well, it had moved well as a fleet, it had done what had to be done. And afterward it had straggled home to Mars and the Belt as best it could, in anxious little clusters. As many ships had been lost to faulty equipment and inexperienced piloting as might have been lost in battle by a well-trained, properly equipped force. They were still bringing in the pieces. Still salvaging the sad, battered hulks that had been left behind with engines failed, or with rusty bulkheads burst, or run into wild rocks by inexperienced pilots, or even into each other in their nervous exhaustion and the aftermath of fear.

Colonists from Mars Station went out in the best ships they had left, snagged the debris, and toted it on-station to see what the mechanics could do with it. The bodies of the poor lost pilots who hadn't had time or training to save themselves were cast into solar dives when feasible or left to float forever in the dark of space when nothing better could be done for them. They had company enough out there. *There are ghosts among the asteroids. . . .*

After several increasingly firm suggestions that if I really wanted my shuttle repaired I should get the hell off the flight deck and out of the overworked mechanics' way, I decided maybe I should get off the flight deck and out of the overworked mechanics' way. But waiting has never been one of my better tricks. I hadn't yet committed myself to real work on this station, and I was as out of place everywhere else as I was on the flight deck.

I bounced off the walls in the quarters I'd been assigned, doing my best to settle down and be patient, for a whole ten minutes or so before I finally gave it up as a bad job and went to the rec room to see if anyone else was off duty who had energy (and credit) for a game of Planets.

My work shift had been short because I'd been assigned, so far, only the one group of students. Everybody

else had at least two groups and usually three; and
the people who weren't currently involved with pilot
training were mostly all up on the flight deck, mending
wrecks. The rec room was completely deserted when I
floated in.

I almost floated right out again; but I hadn't anywhere
better to go, so I ordered up a container of caffeine and
looked through the entertainment computer for something
to read. Nothing appealed. It was a dumb idea; nothing
would appeal till I knew my *Defiance* was operational
again.

In a fit of impatience I punched off the entertainer and
tried the newsfax instead, but it was on its "World News"
cycle, which meant mostly news about Earth, which was
of negligible interest to me. Drought in the United Soviet
Socialist Republic of China. A hurricane off the coast of
the Florida Chain. Workers rioting in England. Workers
rioting in Old New England. Factories put on twenty-four-
hour schedules to produce "defensive" armaments and
spacecraft. There were parades for peace in the Capitol,
and antiColonial parades in the Capitol. Mothers Against
Mutant Accession was being sued by a woman who claimed
MAMA had kidnapped and murdered her only son, a
Faller.

"Can't you find anything better to do than to watch that
rubbish?"

Startled, I banged against the console in my effort to
turn quickly. "Oh, Rat. I didn't hear you come in. Look,
did you see this bit? MAMA has killed a kid, and their
defense—which seems to be working, since the trial is
taking place on Earth—is that it can't be called murder
because the kid wasn't, properly speaking, human."

"What was he then?" Rat asked with interest.

"A Faller."

He was looking at the newsfax screen. "Look at this."

I turned to see what had caught his attention. The
headline said, "LAND REDISTRIBUTION ACT WORK-
ING WELL IN COLONIES." There were holos of happy
Martian families holding up the scrolls that proved their

land belonged to them. There were also holos of happy Belter families holding up similar scrolls about rocks, which didn't make any sense. As far as I knew, no such happy Belter families existed.

We watched the whole article through before either of us spoke. "Damn," said Rat.

"D'you suppose Earth really doesn't know?"

"It would seem not," he said.

"That's ridiculous. I don't believe it. Somebody had to hire the actors to portray the contented Belters."

"The Company could have hired them and made the report without the Corporation's knowledge or approval."

"The newsfax people would believe a story sent in by the Company, wouldn't they?"

"Damn betcha," said Rat. "What's more, so will the public that sees the article."

"So will the whole Corporation. Somebody should tell them the truth," I said.

"How do you propose to do that?"

"Could we send in the real story to the newsfax people? How do they usually get their reports?"

"Roving reporters, probably. Why would they believe a story from a couple of Belter Insurrectionists? They'd think we made it up."

"Same like the Company did."

"Same like."

"There must be something we can do."

"Teach your little groups of future warriors how to fly."

"I only have one group. And you wouldn't believe them. How the hell are we going to make any kind of army out of the material we're getting?"

"With difficulty," he said drily. "I doubt your group's any worse than either of mine. I'm getting a new group tomorrow, and I don't expect any better. They're all kids or misfits or senior citizens who should be home tending their pensions." From Rat, that particular comment was quite a condemnation. "Half of them can't read, and the other half can't speak any language I know. What the hell can you do? I'll teach them to fly, 'ass why.'' The newsfax caught his eye again. He turned me to face it and waited while I read it.

The Company had begun to round up freefall mutants.

CHAPTER EIGHT

The newsfax didn't put it so baldly, of course. What it said was that a number of Colonial Insurrectionists had been arrested for various crimes against the Company. But it listed their names, and more than half of them were people I knew, few of whom had ever had any active Insurrectionist tendencies, and all of whom were Fallers.

Jamin wouldn't be collected in the early batches. He had relatives (Floaters and Grounders all) among the Company's high muckymucks, and that would keep him safe for a while. But Jake should have called me, anyway. Jamin and Collis must have been confined to quarters or at least to Home Base by now. I could get them off Home Base, but I wouldn't be able to get them off an internment rock once they were sent there.

"Now he'll have to listen to reason," I said.

"Who?" asked Rat.

"Jamin. A friend of mine on Home Base."

He looked sympathetic. "A Faller?"

"And one of the stubbornest men in the Belt."

"You'll be going after him?"

"For what good it will do. I don't know whether he'll come away, even now."

"He's not a Company man, is he?"

"Not in the way you mean. He works for the Company,

71

but he's not an Earther.'' By which I meant he didn't sympathize with Earth; obviously a Faller couldn't be the sort of Earther who *lived* on Earth. "But he's a damn fool."

"Why hasn't he come out here?"

"Sheer rockheadedness," I said uncharitably. "He has a Grounder Kid who gets sick in freefall."

"There are gravity quarters here, aren't there? Or the kid could go down to Mars." He paused, looking at me oddly. "A Faller can't have a Grounder kid."

Genetically, of course, he was right. Each parent contributed one of his two genes for the gravity/freefall trait, and both a Faller's genes for that are for freefall, so even if the other parent were a Grounder (with both genes for gravity), the kid would as a result get one gene for gravity and one for freefall, making him heterozygous: a Floater, like Rat and me. "The kid's adopted," I said. "His mother died in the war. I don't know who his biological father was."

Rat nodded. "Well, you'd better get them off Home Base if you can. You want me to take on your students?"

"That would help. . . . Oh, bother!"

"Now what?"

"The *Defiance*. They probably haven't fixed her yet."

"There's a way to find out."

I was already on my way to the flight deck to see. Rat followed me somewhat diffidently, saying as we went, "If she's not ready, maybe I can help you promote another shuttle."

"Another one won't do. At least, it would be a lot harder. Unless there's another as well outfitted for smuggling as mine."

"That I doubt. But we'll find something that'll do, don't you worry."

"I'm already worried."

"Well, wait till we see, anyway." Which was sensible advice not easily taken.

Fortunately, the trip from the rec room to the flight deck wasn't a long one, so I hadn't long to worry about what

I'd find when I got there. Unfortunately, what I found was exactly what I should have known I'd find. The *Defiance* was still in pieces. Of course she was. The idea that she could have been mended in the time since I left her was laughable. They were working on her, but the Patrol had done her a lot of damage that my ungraceful landing had compounded. She wouldn't be ready to fly for hours yet; possibly days.

"Space and bother," I said, and kicked off toward the head mechanic. Rat caught my arm with one hand and a freefall handhold with the other. His grip was powerful and unexpected, and the strength of it combined with the force with which I had started away from him swung me right around in a circle and nearly banged my head against the wall. "What's this in aid of?" I untangled myself from him and from the wall but not from his firm grip on my arm.

"There's no reason to attack the mechanics," he said mildly. "They're all working double shifts and they're probably tireder and crosser than you are at this point. I know you'd like a good fight about now, but is it really the most useful thing you can think of to do?"

I stared. Rat was the last person from whom I would have expected philosophical suggestions about social behavior. "Why, boddah you?"

His eyes glittered in the light. "Once a Belter, always a Belter. No, don't waste your energy on me, either; I won't fight you, you know. You want to get your friend off Home Base. Will picking a fight at Mars Station help you do that?"

"Of course not." I must have relaxed as I said it, because he promptly released his hold on my arm. "It's just that . . ."

"It's just that the customary Belter reaction to any frustration, mild or severe, is to pick a fight with somebody, right?"

"Well, hell." In fact, the customary Belter reaction to most *any* adverse circumstance was to pick a fight with somebody, but he was right: that wouldn't help Jamin and

Collis. "What d'you suggest? And don't say another damn shuttle, because there ain't another damn shuttle that can do the job."

"You're not the only smuggler in the Colonies, are you?"

"I'm the only one with a Falcon outfitted for the job."

"I happen to know somebody with a Sunfinch that's outfitted pretty well. You think maybe you could make do with that?"

"Damn you, this isn't a time to make jokes."

"I'm not joking."

I frowned at him. "You can't know somebody with a Sunfinch that's outfitted for smuggling. There's only one Sunfinch in the Colonies: the one I stole from the Earthers out at Station Newhome. And that one's been taken apart so the experts could study her new conversion drive and go into production on a Colonial version."

"You're behind the times, Skyrider. I'm surprised at you. They took that Sunfinch apart, all right: then they put her back together again, and since then they've built two prototype Colonial versions of the same thing. Strictly speaking, you're right, they're not Sunfinches. They don't even look like Sunfinches. But that could be to your advantage if you're going to try for a peaceable landing at Home Base. And I happen to know that the first model, which looks a lot like a Falcon if you don't look past the outer shell, has a nice little concealed cargo hold that ought to be big enough for your friends if they squeeze a little."

I had known that Colonials were working every waking minute to get the Colonies ready for whatever Earth might throw at us; I hadn't known how much they'd managed to accomplish in the time since I brought out that stolen Earther Sunfinch with its remarkable new malite conversion drive. I looked around the flight deck, half expecting to see an unusual Falcon with the Sunfinch drive resting against a nearby retaining wall. "You've been isolated on your rock till recently; how would you know about anything like that?" I asked suspiciously.

He grinned. "I been out on my rock. I was never isolated. I had Comm Link, same like anybody else, and I got a few friends in the Colonies, as you ought to know."

"Where is it, then? Whose is it? Who's been flying it? Why haven't I heard of it?"

"It's here, belongs to the Colonial government, Jake's been flying it, and why would you have heard of it? Who's heard how the *Defiance* is put together?" He made an impatient gesture. "Okay, everybody, *now*. But before you brought her in in pieces? The Patrol hasn't ever caught up with Jake, and she hasn't crashed, so who'd know what she's got inside the Falcon shell? Only the people who put it there, right? And her pilot."

"Okay, what makes you think Jake's shuttle is here? She's on Home Base."

He looked patient. "I know Jake's on Home Base. And I know her shuttle's here. She only flies it, she isn't physically attached to it. It doesn't even belong to her; it belongs to the government, like I said."

"The Colonial government."

"That's right."

"So why are they going to let me fly her?"

"Are you kidding? The Skyrider? On a rescue mission?"

"Listen, we're nice folks and all that, but I don't see the government, such as it is, risking one of their first two Sunfinch conversion drive shuttles to rescue one more freefall mutant. They'll be sympathetic as all hell, but they're not idiots. At least, I hope not; I'm counting on them to govern wisely. And Jamin's rescue from Home Base isn't exactly crucial to the war effort."

He grinned triumphantly. "No, but you may be."

I shook my head. "You know that, I know that, but who told the government about the wonderfulness of myself?"

"Nobody told them, yet." He had floated away from me, and had to catch my arm to propel himself back into reach of a handhold.

"Oh, and you're going to, I suppose?" Unbalanced by

his tug on my arm, I floated gently away till the ankle I'd hooked to a handhold stopped me.

"We are." He had a grip on a handhold now. I was floating through an arc around the axis of my ankle. He reached out his free hand to help me stop it.

"They'll believe us, I suppose, just like that, because we say so."

That triumphant grin again. "Well, I did sort of have a plan."

I probably looked suspicious. "You want to tell me it?"

"I haven't worked it all out yet."

"Which means you've only just thought of it?"

"You could say that."

I sighed. "Which means it probably won't work. What is it?" A white-suited mechanic floated past us and paused at the nearest shuttle to pry at a blackened panel.

"You know the President, right?" said Rat.

"Of the Colonies? We don't have one that I know of."

"Of the World, Incorporated."

"Oh. Well, yeah, I've met her."

His look said what he thought of modesty. "And she filled your credit account because you saved her life, right?"

"What are you getting at?" The mechanic had got the panel off and was fussing with wires inside, tangling herself in the panel cover's tether while she was at it. I watched her absently, wondering if we were getting to the point now where our mechanics were as inept as our prospective pilots.

Rat didn't even glance at her. "I don't think Earth knows what's going on out here. Somebody's got to tell them. That's what I'm getting at."

"Oh, space, Rat. I thought you had an *idea*." I pulled my ankle out of the handhold and kicked off from the wall, back toward the rec room. "Forget it. I'll find Jake's shuttle myself, and steal her if I have to." The mechanic glanced up as I passed her.

Rat followed me hastily. "We could supply you with data to bring the President," he began.

A warship caught my eye and I hooked one leg over an old Nissan's tail fin to stop myself while I looked her over. "Better yet, I'll steal that mother." She was a big old-fashioned dreadnought bristling with ancient guns and massive with primitive armor. The average modern passenger liner could probably outfly her, and those thick clumsy plasteel defenses wouldn't hold off lasers worth a damn. If she hadn't any modern shielding, a photar could cut her in half. But she did have a lot of guns. And she was big enough to face down Home Base itself, if I worked it right.

Rat caught hold of the same Nissan I was anchored to and looked from the warship to me and back again. "You're joking. That thing couldn't outfly a rock."

"With me in the pilot seat she could."

"Space," he said, looking from her to me again. "If you're going to steal anything, steal Jake's shuttle."

"That's more like it." I grinned at him. "Where is she?"

He led me to her. She looked, as he'd said, like a Falcon. They'd used a Falcon body, but I could tell there was something funny about her engines, maybe only because I knew it before I saw her. It seemed to me that the engine nacelles were just slightly the wrong size and shape. Aside from that, she could have passed for the *Defiance*. She wasn't even painted with the blazon of the Colonial Fleet, as I'd expected. It would be the work of minutes to paint over her registration numbers with those of the *Defiance*, and then Home Base would have no way of knowing there was anything funny about my coming in on her.

"You could paint your own registration numbers over hers," said Rat.

"Great minds," I said. "But I won't have time, if I'm stealing her."

"You won't let me talk to them about a trade? They let you borrow the *Steadfast* and in return you talk to the President?"

"Jake named her the *Steadfast*?"

"Don't try to sidetrack me, Skyrider."

"No, I don't want to try to make a trade. Suppose they

turned me down? Then what chance would I have to steal the *Steadfast*? They'd be alerted. Besides, what makes you think I want to run back down to Earth to ask for an interview with the President? You don't really think she'd remember me, and grant it, just like that?"

"Yes, I do."

"Rockdust. A Colonial ship coming in clear at a time like this? They might just blast me out of the sky, and *then* where would you be?"

"I'd still be on Mars Station."

"And I'd be dead."

"Yes."

"And the Colonies wouldn't have gained a damn thing."

"But I don't think it would happen that way. You underestimate your legend, Skyrider."

"What I don't underestimate is the value of my life. I like living, I really do. I don't see any damn reason to throw myself at the mercy of the Earthers just because you think they'll be gentle with me."

"I didn't say they'd be gentle."

"Okay, rough, but impressed with my damn legend."

"Damn it, Skyrider—"

"Will you help me steal this bird, or not?"

He studied me a moment before he answered. I looked past him and noticed the same white-suited mechanic who'd been working on the shuttle next to us when Rat first suggested my going to Earth: now she was inspecting the shield nozzles on the *Steadfast*. I glared at her, which for some reason made her blush and move hastily away.

Rat sighed. "Go put on your flight suit," he said. "I'll paint the damn numbers. Beyond that, you're on your own."

"That's all I need." I grinned at him, flipped over to see if the path was clear, and kicked away toward the ready room before he could change his mind.

The flight deck was busy and crowded, but everyone was too involved with his own work to notice what anyone else was doing if it didn't interfere. The mechanics working on the *Defiance* saw me board her on my way to the ready room, but they didn't see what I retrieved from her cockpit locker. Probably nobody even saw a wrinkled old space-browned Gypsy in miner's trousers and a battered tunic carefully overpainting the registration numbers on an ordinary, flight-worn Falcon named the *Steadfast*. Certainly nobody stopped him. By the time I got back, the job was done, as promised.

He didn't even say anything. He just looked at me and moved away as I boarded her. At least I didn't have to burn my way in; she was unlocked. I settled into the pilot's seat, turned on the gravity, and fired up the engines with a feeling of perfect familiarity. The control board was very like that of the *Defiance*, with a few minor differences that might have put me off if I'd never flown a Sunfinch before, but I had, so it wasn't a problem.

Somebody in Flight Control sounded very startled when I fired up her engines. "Shuttle, ah shuttle F53146 . . . what in space is going on? That's the *Defiance*'s reg number. Will the shuttle that has just fired its engines please identify, I say again, identify, you are *not* cleared for liftoff, please identify."

I flipped on the Comm transmitter. "You better clear me, Flight Control, because I'm going."

"Who is that? Identify, identify. You are not cleared, I say again, you are not cleared, please identify."

I turned on the visual so I could glare at him. "This is the Skyrider, rookie, and I'll blast my way off this tin rock if I have to, so you'd better clear me, do you read?"

"I read you, ah, Skyrider, ah . . ." He looked bewildered, glanced to one side, shrugged, and a new voice came on Link. "Melacha, what in space do you think you're pulling now?"

"Oh, hi, Michael. I thought you were on school duty."

"I am." He moved on-screen so I could admire his pretty blue eyes. "Flight Controllers have to be trained, too, you know."

"Well, train that one to give the Skyrider clearance." I had the engine pressure where I wanted it, and the lasers were hooked directly into the converter, which meant they were ready, too. I probably wouldn't really have blasted my way off-station, but I didn't want to have to make the choice. "I'm on a rescue mission. Let me go."

My cousin Michael was never a slow thinker. "That's Jake's shuttle. You think the Patrol will mistake it for yours?"

"That's what I'm hoping. Do I have clearance?"

"Jamin?"

"I said it's a rescue mission. Now are you going to let me go or do I have to fight my way out?"

"Clearance granted." He hesitated. "Good luck, Sky-rider."

"Thanks, Michael. I just may need it."

"Bring her back in one piece, will you?"

"Sure, what about me? You don't mind how many pieces I'm in, as long as your precious shuttle is okay?"

"Just go." He turned away. "Some people never grow up." I don't know whether he meant me to hear that. The Link clicked off on the end of the last word; maybe he'd thought his trainee turned it off sooner.

It didn't matter. I had clearance, that was what counted. I lifted off-panel gently and turned the *Steadfast's* nose toward space, glad I wouldn't have to ram my way past Colonial shuttles to get free. A landing Starbird swooped in out of my way and I jockeyed out through the protective force screen into the down-sun dark outside.

CHAPTER NINE

The trip back to Home Base took less time than it would have in the real *Defiance* even though I didn't push the *Steadfast* since if I happened to cross paths with the Patrol I didn't want them to notice anything odd about my shuttle. The *Defiance* was a good ship, but she didn't have that new conversion drive. With it, the *Steadfast*'s moderate cruising speed ate space like it wasn't there. It was fun to think what she could do if we got in a hurry.

I did cross paths with the Patrol, and they didn't notice anything odd about my shuttle. I thought they might hold it against me that when last seen in the *Defiance* I was trying to break a Patrol cordon around Rat's rock, but either the ones I met didn't know about that or all was forgiven. I didn't appear to be doing anything illegal now, and nobody challenged me to prove it.

They did challenge my right to land at Home Base, but only in the way they had done when I came in from Earth in the *Defiance*; checking to make sure they knew me and that I wasn't bristling with Colonial weaponry and hostile thoughts. My weaponry didn't bristle and my thoughts were even better concealed, so I was granted landing clearance without undue fuss. The first real trouble I ran into was the owner of my borrowed shuttle. She was on the flight deck, and she didn't mistake the *Steadfast* for the

Defiance any more than I would have done if it were the other way around.

She was waiting for me when I popped the hatch and climbed down onto the panel. "Oh, hi, Jake," I said with what I hoped would sound like cheerful innocence.

She was looking at the *Steadfast*. "I suppose you have a good excuse?"

"It's not one I want to advertise here." I glanced around at the Ground Patrol converging to perform their weapons confiscation routine. "But I think you'd approve."

She nodded, looking grim. After a long moment she turned her gaze from her shuttle to my face, and her look didn't get any less grim. "Break her and you're dead." She said it quietly, but with evident sincerity.

I tried out a devil-may-care grin. "Probably."

"I mean it, Skyrider. If this is one of your damn profiteering, self-serving adventures—" She paused and waited while Ground Patrol took my stungun, tagged it, and handed me the stub. Luckily they didn't look for anything more than the holstered weapon I wore openly.

When they were gone I asked Jake, "Have you seen Jamin around?"

She studied me impassively. "Okay. If that's it, okay. But just remember, you may have half the Belters you've ever met convinced you're some kind of god in outlaw's garb—"

"But the other half want to kill me. I know."

She couldn't help grinning at that. "He's probably in his quarters. You know he's been confined to Base?"

"I was afraid he'd have been confined to quarters."

"Not yet. Would have called you in that case. To the he still has his cousin Board Member Willem to back him. But even Willem can't halt progress forever."

I turned away from the ersatz *Defiance*. "I wanted to ask you about the spare hold on your *Steadfast*."

"Hatch control in the pilot's locker. Get out of here before somebody wonders what we've got to chat about."

"Thanks." I walked away, wondering only absently why I felt like hitting her. It didn't really matter since I hadn't acted on the impulse. I couldn't afford the adverse attention it might have drawn from Ground Patrol.

Home Base was no longer familiar territory. Already it had changed somehow, in atmosphere if not in fact. The corridors looked physically the same, but the people walking through them were different. The doors led to the same chambers they always had, but inside the chambers the activities taking place were subtly altered. Business was probably being carried on as usual, but with new directions, new purposes, and the inevitable urgency that occurs when the threat of war is finally becoming a reality.

Most of my friends were gone already to Mars Station, where they were training Colonial pilots and amassing Colonial weapons of war with the same purposeful intensity that I could detect in the Earther activities here at Base. The people I encountered were not all strangers; in the years I'd worked out of Home Base I'd come to know and even like a number of Earthers, most of whom were still at work here now; and there were Colonial stragglers like Jake who had business of one sort or another to accomplish here before they felt free to join the Colonials at Mars.

There were also a great many freelancers and miners who had been tricked off their rocks and hadn't yet found transport safely off Home Base, nor been summarily shunted onto internment rocks by the Company. Some of them had gone, willingly or otherwise, since I'd been here to pick up Rat, but more had arrived and many still remained. Ground Patrol was out in force to keep them in order.

Not that they looked like they needed much keeping in order. They looked like refugees always look: pitiable and not particularly brave, but oddly relentless in that silent, unconquerable way a conquered people have.

Belters are necessarily a hardy breed, but simple hardiness won't solve the problems of a people from whom everything they really care about except life itself has been systematically taken by means for which there is no obvious recourse. Now even their lives were in danger, and they knew it. If there had been an enemy they could confront they would have torn him to shreds. But their common enemy was the Company; the Belt branch of the World, Incorporated; the government. That was too big for them. They weren't an army. They were only a homeless rabble.

They had nowhere to go and nothing to do, so they went nowhere and they did almost nothing: they stood or sat or reclined on their bits of luggage in the corridors, apparently having overflowed from Level Two where the Company had been trying to keep them when Rat was there; and they watched the Earthers with the flat sullen stare of the displaced and the homeless; and they made Ground Patrol nervous. You could tell they did, because the normally unflappable Patrolmen were all on edge, walking around with their hands on their weapons, now and then trying to start some minor altercation with somebody who happened to catch their attention, just to relieve the strain. The objects of their efforts moved silently aside, humble and obedient and imperturbably *there*.

A few of them watched me from their hooded eyelids as I went by. Those who didn't know me watched with such veiled hostility I could almost feel it as a tangible wall of hatred, slowing my progress. If the Ground Patrol was getting that treatment, no wonder they were on edge. The refugees who did know me tended to look away quickly when they recognized me. I thought at first it was embarrassment or a milder manifestation of hostility; it was only afterward that I realized they were protecting me. They knew me. They guessed I had business on Home Base, or I wouldn't have been there; and they knew that at the smallest provocation I would interrupt my own business to pick a fight with Ground Patrol on their behalf.

Due in large part to their consideration, I made it to pilot territory without incident. The refugees and attendant Ground Patrol hadn't got that far, and the corridors seemed deserted by comparison. In fact they were as crowded as ever, perhaps more than before I left. Most of the people I met were strangers to me: new pilots brought out from Earth to fill the gaps in the ranks left by the departure of

Colonials to Mars Station. New cannon fodder: untried
warriors as fierce in their innocence as any of those we
were training for the Colonial Fleet.

They eyed me with cautious disapproval. I wasn't wearing a blue Earth Fighter uniform, or the red-and-black of
Patrol; and I was obviously familiar with Home Base. I
hadn't been arrested or drafted, and I didn't act like a
refugee. They couldn't tell where I fit. It wasn't safe to
express overt hostility, in case I turned out to be a superior
officer; but neither was it necessary to show any particular
friendliness, since I probably wasn't any kind of officer at
all. Fortunately for their continued individual well-being,
none of them interfered with me, even when I stopped at
the door to the quarters of a mutant.

"Mutant" has always struck me as a rather odd or
unsatisfactory word. I really believe Earthers might have
accepted Fallers more readily if the genetic change that
created them had never been referred to as a mutation. Of
course it was a mutation, scientifically speaking, but we
aren't all scientists, and a long history of strange literature
had turned the word "mutant" into the stuff of horror
stories long before freefall mutants ever came on the scene.
The man whose quarters I was entering was certainly a
mutant, but he was by no means a monster.

At least, he looked perfectly normal. The freefall mutation didn't affect his physical appearance in the least, and
as a human he was even a reasonably attractive model.
Thin, arrogant, and maybe too handsome for everyone's
taste, with a look of sardonic amusement more or less
permanently set in his expression that wasn't my favorite
at all; but there was nothing monstrous about how he
looked.

His mental attitude was another matter. I sometimes
wondered how he had managed to live so long. I had come
to rescue him: he greeted me not with glad cries or with
any sign of relief, not even with ordinary friendliness.
but with a murderous scowl and a demand to know what in
space I was doing on Home Base.

"I've come to rescue you."

He didn't quite laugh at me. "From whom or what, if it isn't too presumptuous of me to ask?"

"Oh, space, Jamin, what's got into you? You're confined to Base now. How long do you think it'll be till you're herded off to an internment rock somewhere that I can't get you off?"

He turned away from me abruptly, but not before I saw the shadow of some terrible pain in his eyes. "Don't be silly. I'm fine. I don't need you. Go away."

I stared. "You said you only had another run to make, and then—"

"Go *away*." He didn't shout. He didn't have to. He could make his tone so coldly reproving one felt shouted at when he hadn't even raised his voice.

But I've never been a very obedient sort. I sat in the nearest chair and studied him dispassionately. "What a rockhead you've become in your old age. Are you scared, or what?"

I thought that might anger him into saying what was really wrong. It certainly angered him. He swung around and I really think he almost hit me. But at the last second he remembered who and what and where he was—and possibly how often I'd broken his jaw before. He didn't hit; he didn't even look at me. He hesitated a moment, then leaned wearily against the back of a chair, turning his face away, and said in a casually indifferent tone, "I guess I'd forgotten."

"Forgotten what?"

"Your incredible arrogance."

I grinned at him. "I'm not surprised. I'd certainly forgotten yours."

His face was shadowed. I thought his expression changed, but I couldn't read it. "Did anybody ever mention to you, even in passing, that the great Skyrider isn't always welcome to interfere? Has anybody even mentioned that it *is* interference when you trample into somebody's life and start ordering him around?" He faced me, then, and there was nothing in his eyes but the same dull, frustrated anger I'd seen in the eyes of the refugees outside. "You think you're God's own gift to Humankind, but you're not, you know. You're a nosey, interfering, self-important law-breaker with a penchant for getting in the way of decent people trying to do their jobs.''

''Yeah, I'm pretty fond of you, too, rock jockey.'' I'd figured out by then what was wrong, or I was afraid I had. ''Where's Collis?''

I'd got it right on the first try. He didn't exactly collapse into a quivering heap of helpless fatherhood, but he had the kind of face that for all its innate arrogance did crumple under stress. It was painful and oddly shocking to watch. He lost all his defenses. One moment he was a coldy superior bastard who would as soon step on some-body's face as talk to him: the next, he looked capable of tears. Mind you, he wasn't going to cry any. But he looked like he knew how. ''They've got him.'' Even his voice had lost its deadly mockery.

''Where?'' My own voice sounded harsh and unfamiliar.

''I don't know.''

''Then figure it out. How the hell are we going to get him free if we don't know where he is?''

He looked at me. I couldn't interpret the expression in those shadowed eyes. He had recovered some of his de-fenses: his face was a region of planes and hollows, dark and narrow and secret. There were blue smudges like bruises under his eyes. ''How the hell are we going to get him free even if we do know where he is? Don't you understand? They took him to keep me here. They know I'm a Colonial sympathizer. And they know I won't leave Collis. As long as they have him, I'll do exactly as they tell me, pausing only to ask how they want their colonists killed, and they know it. The one way they could buy me, they bought. You don't think they'll have put him in an indefensible playroom or anything? He's the price of my cooperation, and that's damn well worth something to them. He'll be where we can't get at him, you can be sure of that. He'll be where nobody can get at him.''

''The Skyrider can.'' That was a calculated risk; we'd both heard that line a few times too many, and he'd already said what he thought of the great Skyrider's abilities. But it was a line that other people had used before when we'd proposed to do the impossible and somebody had dared to suggest nobody could. If it didn't amuse him, maybe it would anger him enough to break through the helpless self-pity to the ruthless warrior underneath. I needed that warrior, if I was going to get him and Collis free of Home Base, which I was determined to do come hell or breached chambers.

It almost worked too well. I thought for a moment he was going to try to kill me. He hadn't a chance of succeeding on a gravity station, but I didn't want to hurt him. Fortunately reason asserted itself in time and after a brief hesitation he even achieved a frayed smile. "Sure. The Skyrider can do anything. Right. D'you have a plan, or are you just going to start walking and watch the Earthers fall away before your superior self-image?"

"How could I have a plan? I didn't even know they'd taken him. I still don't know where he is."

He sat down, carefully. In gravity all his movements tended to be careful, and a lot of the aloof unpleasantness of his manner was simply an effort to conceal pain. But not all of it. He could be fairly unpleasant in freefall, too, when the whim struck. "So you come barging in here demanding to know where my son is, and planning some wild rescue scheme that for all I know might get us all killed or at least imprisoned—"

"You're already imprisoned. And I just said I didn't have a plan."

"—and you're not even going to ask if I'm interested, you're just going to throw us all on the mercy of Ground Patrol, because—"

"Don't be silly. Ground Patrol has no mercy; they're Earthers."

"—you want to prove that the Skyrider can do any damn thing she pleases, laws or no laws, war or no war, and never mind who gets in her way."

"Do you *want* the Earthers to hold your son hostage?"

"Of course not."

"Well, then."

"Well then, *what*?"

"Well, then, I think we should rescue him."

"Just like that."

"Well, I had thought we might formulate a plan."

"That's great. That's just great."

"How do you know? We haven't formulated it yet."

"Damn you, Skyrider." He said it without any force or conviction.

"I think that may be seen to," I said. "Are you ready to think about a plan?"

"How can I be ready to—"

"For instance, you must have *some* idea where they're keeping him."

He sighed heavily. "Of course I have. I'm not as dumb as you look."

"Thanks awfully."

"I know exactly where they're keeping him. They've set up a créche for the children of Insurrectionists and other suspicious characters." He closed his eyes. Without the fire and ice of their anger showing, his face looked unutterably weary. "It's on Level Four, near the ordinary school for Earther kids. There's a well-guarded corridor leading there with all the hatches locked and four sturdy Ground Patrol at every air duct."

"And?"

"And what?"

"And you've scouted an alternative entry possibility?"

He smiled faintly without opening his eyes. "The créche can be entered from the outside by means of an old airlock that lets into, would you believe, the pantry?" He did open his eyes then, just long enough to watch my reaction. "I think the chamber was some kind of maintenance area when the rock was first hollowed." He grinned faintly and closed his eyes again. "There aren't any guards in the pantry."

"You have been doing your homework."

He shrugged. "I was feeling . . . You'd call it frantic. I don't know what I thought would come of it."

"We'll need space suits."

"And a rescue bag." He opened his eyes again. "I couldn't find a child-sized suit."

"But you got two full-sized?"

"That part was easy. It isn't as though we don't use them anymore."

"It is, however, as though the Earthers have them under a very close watch."

"That's why I couldn't get a kid-sized one. Rescue bags aren't as closely counted, but."

That "but" instead of "though" or "however" at the end of his sentence showed me how frayed his nerves were. I had seldom heard him speak Rock at all, and never by accident. "Jamin . . ."

"I'm okay," he said quickly. A little too quickly to be totally convincing, but never mind. "Now that we've talked about it, we'd better do something. I've never believed the Company listens to us over the PA or chamber phones, but it is possible, and we've said some careless things just now."

"Well, we've already discussed my lack of plans, but it sounds like you might have one."

"Not really."

"You must have thought of something when you stole two suits and a rescue bag."

"I just thought they might come in handy. Oh, hell. I guess I imagined we'd go clambering off across the outside of Home Base wearing the suits and trailing the bag till we came to the airlock and let ourselves in, grabbed Collis, stuffed him into the bag, and fled. Where or how we were going to flee I hadn't really considered. I told you I was feeling frantic."

"I guess."

"You could bring the *Defiance* around—"

"I don't have the *Defiance*."

He stared. "What happened?"

"Never mind. It's a long story. I've got an adequate substitute that the Company conveniently mistook for the *Defiance*. Probably because I had the *Defiance*'s registration numbers painted on her wings. Where did you want me to bring her around to?"

"I don't know. Near enough the airlock that Collis and I could float across."

"Won't work. The Patrol boats around this rock are thicker than the wild rocks in New England."

He closed his eyes again. "I don't know, then." He shifted irritably. If he'd been a Grounder or a Floater he would probably have gotten up and paced the floor. Being a Faller already weary of too much gravity, he stayed where he was and did a fairly convincing imitation of an armed bomb. "We have to do something."

"That's what I said when I got here." He didn't rise to that bait either, so I considered the problem. "Okay. We both go out, suited and trailing the bag as described. We get Collis. You bring him back in through the airlock in the ready room, while I create a diversion somewhere closer to Patrol headquarters."

"That's nice. Then what do we do? March on board your substitute *Defiance* right under the eyes of whatever Ground Patrol aren't taken in by your diversion, and wait patiently aboard till they let you out of whatever dungeon they're currently using for Insurrectionists, which will presumably be sometime at the end of the war?"

"May I take it you don't entirely approve of my plan?"

"It does leave something to be desired." He sounded more relaxed: that was a good sign.

"You got a better one?"

He thought about it. "Aren't there any of the old crew still around, or has everybody we know already left for Mars Station?"

"Most everybody we know who isn't an Earther."

"*Most* everybody?"

"Well, there are a few still here. I saw Jake when I landed."

"Jake?"

"You remember. She went along when I stole the Sunfinch from Station Newhome."

"Oh, Jake. You trust her?"

"I don't have any real reason not to."

"What's that? Yes, no, or maybe?"

"Maybe . . . I guess."

"Well, if she's on our side, what's she doing here?"

"That's why it's a maybe. I don't know."

"That's no good, then." He thought about it some more. "They won't believe I'd leave without Collis. Or Collis without me. If they know where one of us is, they think they know where the other is."

"So? They're right."

"But if I were with Company officials while you got Collis on board your shuttle—"

"All under the eyes of the Ground Patrol?"

"Yeah, well."

I sighed. "Maybe we could use the refugees somehow, but I can't think how. Really I don't think there's anything to do but grab him and blast our way off-station."

He scowled at me. "Brilliant. I wonder why I didn't think of that?"

"I don't like it either, but we have to do something."

CHAPTER TEN

It sounded simple enough. Just grab Collis and blast our way off-station. Right. With what weapons, for instance? I'd brought along the little laser I'd smuggled out of my quarters when I was here to get Rat, but that was all we had. It wasn't enough.

I took the space suits and the rescue bag when I left Jamin's quarters. Modern technology being what it is, they didn't make an impossibly large bundle, just an inconvenient one. To avoid Patrol curiosity we'd agreed to stick to pilot territory: there was an airlock off the Common Room that we could use to get outside. It wasn't even ridiculously optimistic to hope we'd find the Common Room deserted; it was mostly used as an overflow from the rec room and the ready room, neither of which had been anything like crowded when I'd made rockfall.

Unfortunately, not all the new Earthers at Home Base had formed the same habits the old pilots had when we lived there. The Common Room was not deserted. There was a card game I didn't recognize being played at one table, and a pair of lovesick teenagers having lunch at another. They all looked up when I came in with my bundle of space suits. Nobody said anything. And nobody did anything. They just all looked at me. Even the lovesick teenagers.

I went on across the room to the scarred rock wall in which the airlock hatch made a gleaming plasteel reminder of the vacuum outside. The Earthers watched while I put my bundle down against the wall and moved away from it to settle myself at the nearest gaming table. They couldn't tell what was in the bundle, though if they'd lived out here a little longer they could have made a damn good guess. Or maybe they couldn't. Earthers remained peculiar about space suits and the vacuum no matter how long they lived in the Belt. Witness the fact that they actually kept the suits under lock and key when they knew they would soon have a war on their hands. During a war, even more than in ordinary times, space suits would be needed: they could be the only thing between rock residents and the vacuum: and anybody with half a brain should have been able to figure out that it was absolutely essential that they be readily available as needed.

The Earther mind said the danger from saboteurs who had space suits was greater than the danger to residents who hadn't. Or maybe the danger of a few escaped freelancers or mutants was worse than the danger of a holed chamber. Either way, their solution was to risk all the residents' lives by making space suits a rare and oddly cherished commodity. Many persons were flatly denied them: refugees, of course, and the occasional mutant pilot like Jamin. Those who were permitted suits were made individually responsible for them. They were instructed to keep them safely locked away in their living quarters, and never mind how far those quarters might be from either the nearest airlock or from the first war-torn hole in a Home Base wall.

The racks in every chamber and corridor and near every airlock where we used to keep space suits were empty now. I hoped for the sake of all those innocent Earthers that nobody managed to hole Home Base, because not half of them would be able to get to their space suits and safely into them in time. Some people say if Earthers won't believe space is a hostile environment, they deserve what they get; but looking around at the ignorant kids who would, if anything went wrong, be the ones to suffer, I couldn't agree. The people in charge of locking up the space suits and failing to properly educate those kids deserved the worst that could happen to them. But the kids themselves deserved only decent education and training. If they'd had that, they wouldn't have sat so comfortably in front of empty suit racks with a war gearing up outside.

But they were sitting there, and I had to figure out how to handle it. Probably I wouldn't have resorted to stunning all the kids present, even if the Patrol hadn't confiscated my handgun; but whether I would have or not, I couldn't, so I had to think of something else. Jamin would be following me at a discreet interval—we had decided it might be best not to be seen trudging along the corridor together with the bundle of space suits in our arms, just in case—and when he got there we wouldn't really feel like sitting down to a nice game of Planets when we'd got all psyched up for the rescue of Collis.

But we couldn't just climb into our space suits in front of these kids and walk into the airlock as though it were an ordinary thing to do. However dumb they might be, one or more of them were bound to figure out we weren't acting on Company orders. Some of them were already eyeing me between moves in their card game, and they didn't look like they were pleased with what they saw. I doubt any of them recognized me, but they sure knew I wasn't an Earther.

It's not just a political boundary that separates Earthers from Colonials. We're all Terran humans, and within the wide racial variations that includes, we all look pretty much alike; but we don't all act alike. There's something about time spent in freefall that marks a person's movements as surely as time spent staring into the starred black of space marks his eyes. It takes a lot of time in freefall to make a noticeable difference, but the difference is real. None of these kids had spent that much time in freefall. I had.

Which was, of course, the answer to my dilemma, and I realized it just as Jamin stepped through the door. He would be in his element in freefall. I'd certainly be comfortable in it. But these kids wouldn't know which side was up. Moreover, the shock of losing gravity unexpectedly would probably scare them silly.

Since we were in pilot territory and I was as much a mechanic as most Belters, we could lose the gravity in the Common Room without much difficulty at all. I stood up to greet Jamin, using my words to cover his look of alarm when he saw the Common Room occupied by Earthers. They glanced at me when I spoke and it gave him time to adjust to their presence, realize it would be better if they didn't know how unwelcome they were, and arrange his facial expression accordingly.

"There you are, Tech Pulver," I said briskly. "What kept you? I think the problem is over here in the distribution panel, but I didn't want to open it up before you got here." I walked across the chamber to meet him, guiding his attention and incidentally that of the Earther kids to a maintenance panel set squarely into the rock wall at eye level near the big phone screen. If any of the kids happened to have a working knowledge of the life-support system of the average asteroid, we were in trouble. But apparently none of them had, because nobody challenged us. "I think we're getting cross-level interference from the master board here." I tried not to look at Jamin's face as I said that; it's difficult to spout nonsense to somebody who recognizes it for nonsense and hasn't the smallest idea why you're doing it. "I'll just get the cover off, and we'll take a look. . . ."

Jamin helped me with the panel cover without a hint of either confusion or amusement. "Do you think the trouble is limited just to the Common Room unit? he asked, straight-faced.

"Absolutely." I wasn't sure my expression was as competently deadpan as his, but I was working on it. "No need to involve any other areas, is there?"

"Probably not, if you're sure the problem is local." He threw a glance at the kids while I was putting the panel cover aside, and what he saw seemed to reassure him. "I think it probably is, at that."

I had my hands tangled in wires exposed by the removal of the panel cover, selecting the ones I wanted to pull free. "Why don't you go over there and get my tool bag ready?"

The kids had quit paying attention to us by then, or they surely would have figured out that suggestion was odd at best. The bundle I'd brought into the room was large for a tool bag; and if I had brought it for the purpose of working on this panel, why had I put it down beside the airlock hatch?

Jamin nodded sagely and crossed the chamber with his curiously careful, graceful stride to stand beside the bundle of space suits, making no move whatsoever to "get it ready" in any way, just staying in reach to keep it from floating away when I pulled the wires. He looked arrogant, indifferent, and dangerous. I had a sudden, ridiculous terror not of but *for* those Earther children, if they should happen to look at him now and recognize him for what he was. In gravity he was all but helpless, but we weren't going to have gravity in this chamber much longer, and any Earther who tried to interfere with him after that would be in real trouble.

But the kids never knew what hit them. I pulled the wires and more or less threw myself across the chamber, having very little desire to be anywhere near the Earthers when they started floating. They would, and did, become a tangled mass of arms and legs and girlish hysteria before we had the space suits unbundled.

We had no trouble getting the suits on and floating through the airlock hatch without attracting the Earthers' attention. One of them was sick, another was screaming, and I thought as I closed the hatch behind us that even if they survived their brief interval of freefall till automatic relays closed the gap I'd left and restored gravity to the chamber, they wouldn't have any idea where we'd gone. None of them were looking our way when we went into the airlock. They might be able to describe us well enough to make leaving Home Base a little more awkward than I'd hoped, but it was going to be awkward at best anyway, once we'd got Collis, and maybe the kids would be too sick and confused to make a coherent report till after we were safely off-station.

Jamin was staring at me through his face plate while we waited for the airlock to dump so we could go on out. "Don't they give them any freefall training?" The tiny transmitters in the suit Comm distorted his voice, but not so much that I couldn't hear the genuine shock at what we'd just witnessed.

"I doubt if they have time," I said. "They're recruiting like crazy, trying to supply enough Ground Patrol to handle all the refugees, and they can't all come from military training schools. These kids probably never expected to leave their oversized rock," by which I meant the planet Earth, "and down there they don't have a big need for freefall training."

"They aren't down there anymore. Space, how could they try to man a station with rookie Grounders who fall apart like that in freefall?"

"How not? What else have they got, that they can trust? Besides, I think they'd do better in freefall if they saw it coming. They just didn't know what happened."

"I hope they're all right. I mean, I hope we didn't hurt them. They're only kids."

"They're kids who'd as soon kill you as look at you, if they knew what you are. What I hope is that you know where we're going." The airlock had expressed willingness to let us out onto the surface of Home Base, and although I knew the general direction to take to find the level on which Collis was being held, that wouldn't be adequate to find him, let alone get him safely outside, drag him along to another airlock nearer the flight deck, and bring him back inside.

Jamin knew where we were going. He paused automatically to close the airlock behind us while I waited, anchored by one gloved hand to an ancient loop of metal cable placed for the purpose conveniently near the hatch. We were on the up-sun side of the rock, which meant we could at least see what we were doing without artificial lighting aids. At that distance the heat of the sun was no problem at all—I wasn't sure it even reached us—and the light was helpful, but it certainly wasn't that blinding glare that, if you're an Earther, you'll have automatically imagined when I mention the sun.

With the hatch properly fastened shut behind us, Jamin led the way off across the face of the rock at a brisk scramble, moving easily and gracefully in spite of the constricting limitations set on one's freedom of movement by even lightweight maintenance suits, which these were. He was in his element at last: the mass of Home Base was too small to generate any appreciable gravity on the outside, and the artificial gravity generators didn't affect us out here.

I'd spent half my life in freefall, and I moved well in it, being even more comfortable with it than the average Floater; but I wasn't a Faller, and I couldn't keep up with one, at least not on the ragged exterior of Home Base. Pride, of course, made me try: but when I'd missed the second handhold in a row and avoided floating helplessly off-station only by muscle-wrenching contortions that resulted in snagging one toe in a loop of cable and banging my face plate against a ridge of rock (which nearly bounced me right back out of the toe-hold I'd so awkwardly obtained), I decided it was more important to survive than to prove that there weren't any situations I couldn't handle just as well as Jamin could.

"Slow down, can't you?" My voice sounded cross and half-strangled even over the inadequate relays in the suit Comm.

"Oh, sorry." He didn't sound sorry. He sounded impatient. But he did wait while I caught up with him, and after that moved forward at a sufficiently reduced pace that I could keep up with him without serious risk to life and limb. I didn't have time to admire the view or anything, but we weren't out there to admire the view.

There wasn't a lot of view to be admired, anyway. On the down-sun side there would have been the infinite black of space, dotted with near and distant points of light in all the colors of stars and sunlight reflected off asteroids; but on the up-sun side there was only the rock we were on, the black of space "above" us, and the bright of sun that blanked out most other heavenly bodies. I couldn't even see whether there were any Patrol boats in orbit nearby. I just hoped that, if there were, they couldn't see me any better than I could see them. Which wasn't an altogether unreasonable hope: with their shuttle scanners they could almost certainly see us if they looked, but they hadn't any particular reason to examine the surface of Home Base, with scanners or without. At least, I hoped they hadn't any reason. If those kids in the Common Room were as disorganized and confused as I hoped, they wouldn't have a reason. A lot depended on the ignorance of those kids. I hoped my confident belief in their bewilderment was well-placed.

It was an absent-minded hope. I didn't spend much time or energy on anything but getting from one handhold or toe-hold to the next. Jamin moved as if there were nothing easier in the world than wandering the outside of a rock in a space suit, but I found it uncomfortable at best. One thing I hadn't mentioned when we planned all this, and didn't intend to mention now but was getting less and less happy about, was that I tend to get claustrophobic in a space suit. It took all my concentration to breathe normally and move carefully and keep my mouth shut about it. I wanted to shout as frantically as those kids had back in the Common Room. I couldn't see properly, I couldn't move my arms and legs without considerable effort, I was too warm, and I was becoming convinced there was something wrong with the oxygen distributor in my suit.

We were moving onto the down-sun side, adding seriously obstructed vision to the list of my anxieties, when Jamin finally said, "That's the hatch we want, over by the knob of rock to your right."

I looked where he pointed, and couldn't see a hatch cover, but the knob of rock was comfortingly near. I could go that much farther without giving into terror. Silently, because I was afraid that if I said anything my voice would reveal the state of my nerves, I turned toward the knob of rock and worked my way resolutely from handhold to handhold, manfully resisting the impulse to let go and kick into orbit in my rush to get to a hatch where I could get back inside and get this damn enclosing suit off. Had I kicked free of the handholds the chances are good I'd have kicked eternally free of that rock and any hope of help. Jamin might have caught me. Or he might just have got lost, too; we hadn't any propellants with us. Without a sturdy grip on that rock or anything to tether us to it we had every chance of becoming minor asteroids ourselves if we weren't careful.

It isn't easy to be careful when you're panicking, but I did manage to keep my grip on Home Base long enough to get to the hatch, and after that everything was a lot easier because I knew that within minutes I'd be able to get at least the helmet off, if not the whole suit, and breathe the familiar recycled air of a rock instead of the too-fresh and chemically tainted air of a suit.

We hadn't discussed what we might find inside the hatch, or what kind of reception we might have to deal with; and I tried not to think about the trip back outside that we would probably have to take with the added burden of Collis in a rescue bag. Thinking about it now wouldn't make it any easier when the time came. I had the little laser in a readily accessible pocket of my suit. That was the only preparation I could make; and that would probably be useless. I could hardly brandish it freely in an area crowded with kids, and if Jamin had selected the right airlock, the area inside should be crowded with kids.

CHAPTER ELEVEN

As somebody a lot cleverer than I once said, life sure does seem to consist of a series of events. The rookies back in the Common Room must have had more sense than I'd given them credit for; they'd not only called out the Ground Patrol, but they'd recognized us and identified our space suits for what they were—either that or seen us leave by the airlock instead of the door—which gave Ground Patrol all the hints they needed. They were waiting for us.

I had the laser ready when the inner hatch opened. We had an advantage in that it opened onto a small pantry, rather than onto a large chamber. Ground Patrol had stationed two of their members inside the pantry, which strained its capacity even though both of them were small females. They couldn't get more Patrolmen inside, and the ones waiting in the chamber beyond couldn't do much without endangering the ones who were inside with us.

They obviously hadn't expected us to be armed. They probably thought they'd just look smug, show us their badges, and lead us off to a holding cell without any fuss. The two things they hadn't counted on were my laser and Jamin's determination to reach his son.

They didn't even have their weapons out when the lock opened, so I showed them mine and did all the looking

smug that seemed reasonable, in the circumstances. Jamin
and I had fought together often enough before—fighting
others as well as each other—that we each knew how the
other would react, and what each of us could expect of the
other.

There was a brief stillness while the Patrolmen decided
what to do about my laughable little laser. One of them
decided to take a chance on it: she reached for her own
laser. That wasn't a good idea, and I was quick to let her
know it. Fortunately she was the one nearest me, so while
I was expending my precious laser charge on her handgun,
Jamin was free to tackle the other one barehanded.

Well, bare-gloved; we did still have our suits on. Which
was a minor disadvantage for us in one way, because
visibility out of a suit helmet is necessarily somewhat
obstructed; but it was a much stronger advantage in another way, because a fistfight between a suited and hel-
meted *berserker*—which was what Jamin became when his
kid was threatened—and a merely uniformed Patrolman
was pretty one-sided, despite the fact that we were in
gravity and the *berserker* was a freefall mutant. Without
the suit he wouldn't have had a chance against her; with it,
he was so effectively armored that she couldn't even figure
out what to hit.

Mine dropped her handgun when I'd heated it a little
(and I might say it was just lucky for all of us that it didn't
explode: I wasn't thinking rationally enough at the time to
worry about minor details like that). Jamin's took an automatic swing at his nose that must have hurt her hand when
it connected with plastic instead of flesh, and crumpled
under a single return blow from his gloved hand.

Then he looked at me. I looked at the Patrolman whose
weapon I'd lasered. She looked at my laser, which was
aimed at her midsection. There was an interminable silence while we all considered the situation. It probably
lasted three seconds. Then Jamin, whose face through his
helmet visor still looked wild and dangerous and possibly
mad, said in a voice that was absolutely calm and untroubled,
"Give me the rescue bag. And the laser. I'll get Collis.

You go back outside to the flight deck and bring your shuttle around.''

It wasn't an unreasonable plan, really. It might even have worked. But I wasn't going to let him face an unknown number of Ground Patrol outside that pantry, with only his space suit and one small half-charged laser to protect him. And I wasn't going to stay in my own suit one second longer than required. I shook my head, which is a singularly ineffectual gesture inside a space helmet, and said, ''No.''

The Patrolman was watching us with the vigilant interest of a child whose mother is baking cookies. I could see her fellows darting nervously back and forth outside the pantry door, trying to see what was happening within; but it wasn't hard to keep her between us and them. ''What, then?'' asked Jamin.

''You're absolutely a hero, no question about it,'' I told him, mostly just to see the look on his face when he heard it. If the Patrolman hadn't been right there, so obviously waiting for the smallest drop in my defenses to tackle me, I think he'd have tried to kill me; he really was a little off his head. ''But you can't take on half of Home Base's Ground Patrol with one miniature laser no matter how brave you are. At least, you can't do it with any sane hope of success. And I'm not going to let you try.''

The Ground Patrolman was trying to read our lips; our voices, carried between us by the suit Comms, were inaudible to her. She was getting impatient; the threat of that little laser wasn't going to hold her much longer.

''You damn near panicked out there, didn't you?'' Jamin smiled that damned superior smile of his. ''And you're not over it yet, are you? Whatsamattah you? Claustrophobic?''

He was perceptive, I had to give him that. It wasn't one of the things I loved about him. ''That's beside the point,'' I said stiffly.

''Okay, I give up. What is the point?''

The Patrolman had decided we were involved enough in our discussion that we wouldn't notice if she reached for something on her belt. I couldn't wait to see what it was, and I couldn't do anything about it without either killing her or risking the loss of the laser if she was just trying to maneuver me into reach; so I told Jamin to kick her.

He didn't kick her. But he didn't hesitate, either. It was just that it was easier for him to hit than to kick. He did it, without question and without taking time to see for himself why I asked it. That *was* one of the things I loved about him. When she was down he asked mildly, "What'd you do that for? Her presence, alive and upright, was helping keep the others safely outside. Now they'll be in here like a shot."

They didn't actually come in; they just started shooting. We ducked to cover on opposite sides of the doorway and I told him why I'd had him put her out of action. Then I reached for the fastenings on my suit helmet. He told me to wait, and I glared at him. "I want *out* of this thing."

"Not till we have some kind of plan. They can't overhear us while we're using the suit Comms."

He had a point, little as I liked it. "You're always wanting a plan."

He smiled benignly. "They seem so useful."

I had been looking around the pantry to see if I could find anything useful hidden on its barren and dusty shelves or forgotten in a corner or something. Jamin, less rattled than I, bent to pick up useful items that were in plain sight in front of us; the two Patrolmen's lasers. Both carried nearly full charges, and the one I had lasered wasn't visibly damaged. He handed me one while I was absently reaching again for the release to my helmet.

"These may be useful," he said.

"Good. Now can't I get out of this beastly suit?" I fumbled awkwardly with the fittings, too frantic by now to undo them easily; my fingers kept slipping.

"We still don't have a plan."

"I have a plan. I have her laser, and what's left of mine. I'm going to go get Collis."

"Just like that? Now who's the hero?" The dim light reflected shadows on his faceplate, but I could see the sardonic amusement in his eyes.

"There's no need to feel superior just because you're perfectly capable of living in an enclosed space with no oxygen for the rest of your life if need be, and I can't."

He smiled. "The rest of my life wouldn't be long if I tried that, would it?"

"Don't quibble. D'you have a better plan, or may I go after your son?"

"I may have a better plan. Yours seems to get us killed so soon. There may be dozens of the Patrol out there, and handguns or no handguns, there are only the two of us against all of them."

"What plan, then, damn it?"

"I thought I might call Cousin Willem."

I stared. "You think he could help us now? Then why didn't he, before? Why haven't you called him already? Why did we make that absurd trip outside, if Willem could have—"

"Slow down. Willem couldn't have done anything then; we had nothing to bargain with. Now we have two fine young Patrolmen at our mercy."

"And he has Collis. You think he'll trade?"

"Willem doesn't have Collis," Jamin said stiffly. "The Company has Collis. Willem never approved of—"

"But do you think he'll trade?"

"It's worth a try. Better, at least, than barging out into that corridor to get killed." A renewed burst of laser fire from beyond the doorway emphasized his point.

"It takes more than a few lousy Ground Patrol to kill the Skyrider."

"Sure it does." He said it soothingly, as to a child. "Do can I take off the uuuuu ruhi?"

"Don't you want to listen to what Willem has to say?"

"You can repeat it to me if it's interesting. Meantime you'll want a guard duty mounted, to keep the Patrol off us while you're engrossed in your cousinly conversation."

He sighed. "All right. Take off the suit. Try not to get yourself killed."

"I always try that."

The Patrol hadn't been quietly waiting in the wings

while we carried on this inane conversation; they'd been doing their best to get into the pantry with us. Which was at best an odd goal, since there was hardly room for more than perhaps one additional person now that we had Jamin, me, and the two fallen Patrolmen all crowded into a small space originally intended to provide room for two workers if they were chummy. However, the Patrol did want in, or anyway they wanted control of the pantry and us out of it, which amounts to the same thing. They'd been firing blindly at first, which had caused a certain jerkiness to our conversation as we tried to dodge laser rays that were already past us by the time we ducked; then they'd begun a more scientific effort. They were laying down a careful pattern of fire that would eventually have got us if they'd been allowed to complete it.

I saw no reason to give them the time. As soon as I had the hated helmet off my suit I felt sufficiently relieved to join somewhat more actively in the firefight that had, so far, been altogether too one-sided. Like the Patrol, I used my first shots blindly, more or less to let them know I was there. I must have got in a lucky hit, because I hadn't fired more than twice before their whole pattern was disrupted and there was a lot of extraneous shouting and carrying on somewhere beyond the range of my vision but apparently not beyond the range of my laser.

Figuring that what worked once might work twice, I fired in the same direction a couple more times for effect. It worked, all right: somebody screamed. I don't like it when they scream. I suppose it's their own business, and a person who's taken a laser hit has a perfect right to scream to his heart's content; it is hell of painful. But all of a sudden I wasn't fighting a group of faceless Earthers anymore. All of a sudden the corridor beyond my vision was full of boys like the one down on the flight deck who kept confiscating my handgun.

Well, if he hadn't confiscated my handgun, I wouldn't have been left with only lethal weapons to defend myself. Of course, if I followed the Earthers' rules I wouldn't *have* to defend myself; but that was irrelevant. The Earthers'

rules were impossible to follow at the best of times. Right
now they included that I was to leave Collis in the care of
strangers; and Jamin, as a result, trapped in an environment hostile to him both physically and politically. How
could I follow rules like that?

I still wished the damn kid would stop screaming. Whoever the hell he was. I knew it wasn't really the kid from
the flight deck, but it sounded like one his age. Damn it, I
didn't ask for this. I really didn't.

"Going soft, Skyrider?"

I whirled; Jamin still had his helmet on, and the voice
I'd heard hadn't been his. Like an amateur, I'd forgot the
two Patrolmen inside with us. They were down and disarmed, and I guess I'd decided that was enough. The fact
that I was rattled by that damn kid screaming wasn't an
excuse. You don't get a lot of second chances in the Belt;
you're supposed to do things right the first time.

"For gods' sake don't kill me now!" It was the one
Jamin had tackled first, and she wasn't making any effort
to get up. She was holding her hands up, palm forward, in
the universal gesture of submission, and the right one was
badly swollen from hitting Jamin's face plate. I didn't trust
Earthers no matter how they held their hands, broken or
not. But I didn't kill her.

"Why not?" I made my tone as pleasant as I could
manage.

"Because you need me."

"Like hell I do."

She had plenty of courage. She studied my face a
moment, let her gaze fall to the laser I aimed at her vital
bodily parts, and shrugged almost hopelessly. "Okay,
then, kill me."

"Why would I?"

"Kill me? I don't know. You seemed to want to."

"I meant why would I need you?"

"Because I know where the kid is. *And* how to get him
out."

"Why would you?"

"Know? Or help?"

"I assume you know because you're Patrol, Earther. Obviously the question is why the hell an Earther would help a Faller and a Floater who are both Insurrectionists and enemies of the state."

"A state which considered it quite reasonable to kidnap a little boy in an effort to convince his father to do their bidding."

"Is that supposed to mean you don't approve of your government's tactics?"

"Not always. Certainly not in this case, I don't."

"Okay, Earther. What's in it for you? Where's the catch? What's the trick? I have to admit I don't quite see it; if all you wanted was a chance to live a little longer you could've just kept your mouth shut and I'd probably have forgot all about you."

She hesitated, still holding her hands up in a half defensive, half submissive posture. Then the left hand—the one that wasn't swollen from an encounter with Jamin's face plate—slowly bent some of its fingers till it was making a certain sign in a certain way that was supposed to mean something and probably once, a long time ago, did. The swollen hand tried to make the corresponding but slightly different sign that would complete the meaning.

I spoke before she could strain something, trying to work with fingers that obviously didn't respond the way she expected. "So what? So you know a hand signal. So must half the Company by now. That was old stuff by the end of the last war, and it wasn't reliable even when it was new."

Her mouth twisted in a wry little smile. "I know. It's the best I've got. I didn't suppose it would convince you. I just thought it would explain my motives more quickly than a bunch of words that you wouldn't necessarily believe, either."

"Why should I? If you're such a Colonial sympathizer, why did you break your hand on Jamin's face plate? A gesture of friendliness? Sheer gladness to see us, maybe?"

"Would *you* have stopped to try to explain anything to that madman?"

"It couldn't be that you just like to be on the winning side? If the two of you had managed to overcome us, you'd have turned us over to the Company; but since you failed, you'd like to join us instead? And maybe wait till you see a nice weakness you can use against us?"

"That's a very sensible attitude."

"The one I suggest?"

"The one you have. I can't prove my beliefs. Why don't I just tell you what I know, and you use it or not, as you see fit?"

"If it pleases you. I don't seem to have anything better to do right now." The guy outside was still screaming, and nobody else was firing. The screaming was really getting on my nerves.

"His kid is just a few doors away from here. He's been separated from the rest of the créche; they did that when they heard you were going to make a play for him. He's in a room of his own." She described its location and locking mechanism. "You can get to it without passing any Patrol by going along the back corridor; the only problem is to get out of this pantry, and I think I can help you with that."

Jamin lifted off his helmet in time to hear part of what she said, and he stared at her with an odd expression. "I'll bet you can," he said. "Then we just unlock the door, bring him back here, stuff him into our rescue bag, and we're on our way again, right?"

"There'd be the little problem of getting back on-station at the flight deck," I said.

"There'd be more of a problem than that," said Jamin. The Patrolman just looked at him

"There'd be the little problem of surviving a rather nasty explosion." Jamin never took his eyes off hers.

After a long moment she smiled again, just as wryly as before. "It seemed worth a try. You've been talking to your cousin, I suppose?" At his nod, she shrugged. "We were afraid he wouldn't let us go through with it."

"With what?" My laser had been wavering away from her vital bodily parts. I brought it back on target.

"Sometimes it really amazes me how Earthers think," Jamin said absently. "If you can't use the Faller, kill him, right? And his troublesome kid along with him. And the Skyrider as a special bonus if you can get her."

"This is war now, you know," said the Patrolman.

"This isn't quite how Colonials usually conduct their wars," said Jamin. "We don't object to the occasional spot of sabotage, but we do draw the line at noncombatants and children."

"One Colony-loyal kid in exchange for two of the Colonies' best warriors didn't seem a bad exchange," said the Patrolman.

"Thanks for the compliment," said Jamin. "No, Skyrider, don't kill her yet."

He spoke just in time. I twitched my finger back off the firing stud and waited for an explanation. It wasn't immediately forthcoming; he just stared at her for a while. The kid outside stopped screaming. I wondered if he was dead.

"Speaking of kids," said the Patrolman.

"He had a laser in his hand." I said it too quickly. "That does make a difference, you know." My nerves were shaken; I don't usually explain myself gratuitously like that.

"Sure. A kid isn't a kid with a laser in his hand." She must have seen I wasn't happy about it.

"Like you said, it's war now."

"What was that about drawing the line at children?"

There were a lot of things I could have said to that. The kid I'd shot had made his choice; Collis hadn't. If one based willingness to kill on the age of one's opponent, one wouldn't last long in a war with Earth, where both sides took any willing and able volunteers over the age of fourteen and turned them into warriors. There'd be too many kids dead before we were done, and I saw no way to prevent it. This time I had sense enough not to answer her.

"Collis is where she said he is," said Jamin. "Willem will take us to him. He said he'd have the Patrol disarm the bomb by the time we got there."

I didn't look at him. "Willem is a Company-loyal Earther."

"He's also my friend," said Jamin.

"You're sure of that?"

He smiled dangerously. "If he isn't, or if he hasn't the control over his troops that he thinks he has, he's dead. He'll open the booby-trapped door himself."

"I think I'll stand well back while he does it."

"We both will." Jamin's voice was grim. "If the bomb goes, it won't just get whoever opened the door. It will also get whoever's inside the chamber beyond the door. If Collis is in there, and gets killed, I want to be around afterward to do a little killing of my own."

"Kamikaze mutant runs amok."

He looked at me, his eyes cold and distant. "You damn betcha."

The Patrolman on the floor tried to look disappointed. "If Willem's opening the door, the bomb will be disarmed first."

I looked at her. "I'll bet you believe in Santa Claus and the Tooth Faerie, too."

She had the decency to blush.

CHAPTER TWELVE

Somewhat to my surprise, things stayed fairly quiet in the corridor outside our pantry. Willem had told Jamin he would come to the pantry to meet us while someone else was disarming the bomb on the doorway to Collis. I pointed out to Jamin the various possibilities for a double cross involved in that apparently simple plan, but he wasn't having any.

"Instead of Willem," I said, "it'll be a new contingent of the Patrol complete with laser cannon."

"That would mean sacrificing not only these two sterling officers, but half this level," said Jamin. "A cannon blast in here would breach the wall for sure."

"There are airlock hatches all along the corridor. They could seal off this section and suit up everybody while we're waiting."

"Don't be silly. Willem said he'd come, and he'll come."

"Maybe he *meant* to come. Maybe he *thought* he'd come. Instead, they'll send up a cannister of tear gas; or something more lethal."

"They know we have suits." He sounded impatient.

"That's why something lethal; we wouldn't notice it till we were dead."

"We wouldn't notice it after we were dead, would we?"

"I meant we wouldn't have time to put on our helmets, rockhead."

"Skyrider, Willem will be here."

"You have such simple faith. Damn it, the man's an *Earther*."

He grinned mirthlessly. "So's your mother."

I made a face at him. "You leave my mother out of this."

We might have carried on like that indefinitely if there'd been no outside interference to stop us; but there was. No shooting, this time. It had been quiet in the corridor since the boy I shot stopped screaming, and suddenly the silence became so intense it was almost tangible. Jamin had been about to say something, but he paused with his mouth half open, as alert to the silence as I was.

I thought, Here it comes. Laser cannon, an armored squadron, I don't know what I expected, but I sure thought we were dead. It was that kind of silence: the interval between the massing of the troops and the attack. The Company had decided to sacrifice the two Patrolmen with us; they would blast the pantry; or they would descend upon us in such overwhelming numbers that we couldn't repel them all. They were going to make an example of us. See what happens when a mutant tries to defy the law?

The moment stretched till I was ready to charge out the doorway firing blindly, just to end the waiting. Just in time, Jamin reached across the doorway to put a hand on my arm. Nobody shot it off. I looked at him, and he shook his head in a curt negative gesture so self-assured that I obeyed without thinking. It wasn't only that I trusted him with my life. He was grand officer material. The Colonial Fleet would benefit enormously from a few good authority-types like him, who could put all the force of a military command into one brief headshake.

Having obediently relinquished the best possibility for filling that waiting silence, I resorted to the second-best: speech. "If Cousin Willem can just placidly walk up here and personally escort us first to Collis and then safely to the *Stead*—I mean, to the *Defiance*, why in holy space didn't you call him sooner, and save us that variegated EVA? Do two Patrolmen he doesn't even know really make that much difference?''

I couldn't quite interpret the look he gave me. ''They give him a believable excuse. I didn't know you were claustrophobic about space suits.''

''Shut up.'' I said it without thinking, and with undue force. The Patrolmen who'd offered to mislead us looked at me speculatively. The other one was waking up, but I ignored her; she wasn't near becoming a threat yet.

''If you'd told me,'' said Jamin.

''I'm *not* claustrophobic about the damn things. Or about anything else. You think I'd have made that EVA if I were claustrophobic? Hell, who do you think you are? For that matter, who do you think I am? This is the Skyrider speaking, remember? And I don't recall having been offered any recompense adequate to justify an EVA to a mercenary claustrophobe.''

''For that matter, I don't recall offering you any recompense at all.''

I shrugged. ''That's different.''

He was still giving me that look. It wasn't so much an expression as it was a shadow across the ice-blue of his eyes. ''How so?''

''Well, hell.'' I looked away from him. ''You know damn well . . .'' I paused, glared at the two Patrolmen on the floor, and turned toward the door through which Willem would supposedly eventually arrive. ''I never said I wouldn't do favors for friends. I'm not all *that* mercenary, and you know it.'' Having recovered my accustomed poise, I turned to face him. ''But I'm not a damn fool, either, and I told you a long time ago I don't go on suicide missions. If I were claustrophobic, that EVA would've looked like a suicide mission to me, right? Don't give yourself airs. You're okay, and everything, but nobody's more important than my life.''

He grinned. ''Sure, right, I guess I forgot.''

I swear I would've hit him if Willem hadn't interrupted just then. There wasn't a PA in the pantry, nor even a phone unit, so he used a hand-held amplifier to warn us that he was coming in, so we wouldn't shoot him before we saw who he was.

I felt like shooting him anyway, or like shooting somebody. Anybody. Jamin's cool inference that I had braved the terrors of a claustrophobic EVA just out of loving friendship had shaken me . . . because it was true. I told myself I did it because one has to face one's fears; because it's not a good plan for a person who lives in the Belt to be afraid of space suits, and any chance I get to use them is a chance to get over my irrational fear of them; and because I was so angry with the Company for holding a little kid hostage to keep a Colonial in line that I'd have gone to greater lengths to defy them: but the plain fact was, I cared a hell of a lot for that kid and his father and I would not have automatically and unquestioningly made that EVA for anybody else in the Belt.

I called myself "risk-taker," sure, but the risks were always for financial gain or for the adolescent thrill of cheating death, and there hadn't been any thrill in creeping across the rock face of Home Base in a space suit. This wasn't like the wild, mad ride I'd made to try to get Rat safely home to his rock. There hadn't been any overt mention of financial gain there, either, but there was always the tacit understanding between Rat and me that when he struck it rich he owed me. I'd made so many runs for him on credit that by now I probably had a right to half the malite a rock the size of his could hold . . . if it held any.

Far more important, though, had been the open battle with the Patrol Inner in space. That fit my image of myself. That was the sort of thing I did. Ostensibly for gain, sure, but I'd hardly have got the reputation I had for being the best and craziest pilot in the Company's employ if I had always waited till I had the credits in hand before I made a run.

I did, almost always, make sure I had the *promise* of credits in hand before I took on something hazardous, and I hadn't thought about that when Jamin and I set out after

Collis. I hadn't even mentioned it to keep up appearances. Sometimes I became all too aware that I wasn't entirely the self-serving loner, the greedy mercenary, the isolated rock-bastard outlaw that I pretended to be; but I'd never come so close before to letting anyone else see that.

What happens to the loner, whose whole life and public image is built on a solid foundation of egocentricity and indifference to others' needs, when she cares enough about somebody else to drop the careful cover and head out on what does, in fact, look to her like a suicide mission, without first asking about the pay?

Maybe what happens is that she finally starts growing up, whether she likes it or not. Maybe what happens is that she has accidentally joined the Human race while she wasn't looking, and now she'll just have to learn to live with it.

All that could happen right then was that I shove the whole matter to the back of my mind for later consideration; Willem had said he was coming in, but that didn't mean he wasn't bringing an army. Jamin already had his handgun centered on the doorway. I met his gaze, saw the mocking shadows still darkening the ice of his eyes, and made a face at him. Then I took up my position on the opposite side of the door from him, handgun aimed, ready to catch an army in our crossfire. Most of my attention was on the doorway, but I kept track of the fallen Patrolmen in the pantry with us, too. Even if Willem came in alone as he said he would, those two could screw up the deal if they came down with an unexpected attack of heroism.

Neither of them did. And Willem didn't bring an army. He came alone, as he'd said he would, and stopped squarely in the doorway with his broad back providing a barrier between us and anyone outside who thought he *should* have brought an army.

He didn't seem to notice the weapons in our hands, though they were centered on his chest and neither of us was feeling quite secure enough to lower them just yet. True, he and I had years of friendly enmity behind us that had left a recognizable bond; and he was Jamin's cousin, which is perhaps an even stronger bond. But he was also a Company man: an Earther. The bonds might not be strong enough to overcome the fact that the enmity between Earthers and Colonials was getting a lot less friendly lately.

He paid even less attention to the two fallen Patrolmen who were our hostages and supposedly the reason Willem had come to treat with us. Earthers have a policy about hostages. They take them from others as they had taken Collis, because it works with others. It doesn't work with Earthers, as a rule. You take one Earther hostage, and the others kiss him off. It's as simple as that. It's not an invariable rule, and not all Earthers approve of it (presumably, for instance, those taken hostage might have an objection), but it's reliable enough that not many of Earth's enemies bother to try the hostage game. Which is why they adopted the policy; it works. But that doesn't mean it's always a good idea.

Apparently Willem had managed to convince somebody that it wasn't a good idea this time. Maybe he didn't like the general policy any more than I did. Maybe he didn't like it that this time the hostage the Earthers were holding, for whom we wanted to trade the Earthers we were holding, was his cousin's adoptive son. Maybe he knew as well as I did that a Faller held by coercion in the Company's employ wasn't going to be much of an asset, particularly if he were forced to live on and work out of a gravity station.

And maybe he just had a trick up his sleeve that I hadn't yet seen. In any event, he was there, and he was looking at Jamin with an expression of sheepish uncertainty on his handsome black face that went a long way toward breaking down some of my defenses. One didn't often see Willem looking either sheepish or uncertain.

"Well?" Jamin schooled his voice to a flat, patient tone very close to indifference.

"They say they've disarmed the bomb." Willem's expression disclosed—perhaps involuntarily—both distress and concern. "Jamin, I never would have—"

"Save it." Jamin's voice was harsh and as cold as his eyes. I watched Willem's craggy features, wondering if he realized, as I did, how much of that harshness was due to the physical pain with which Jamin lived whenever he was in full Earth gravity, as we were now. His defenses against revealing that were down when he was forced to cope as well with the emotional strain of separation from and danger to his Buddha-faced blue-eyed boy. "How big an army d'you have waiting for us out there?" He gestured curtly toward the corridor beyond Willem.

Willem looked genuinely hurt. "I *told* you—"

"Tell me again," said Jamin.

Willem almost smiled. "I'm a politician, boy. You think you can read the truth in my face?"

"I think I can." Jamin's voice was dangerously soft. "More to the point, I *know* the Skyrider can."

For the first time, Willem looked directly at me. His gaze took in the handgun I still held aimed unerringly at his heart—if Earther politicians have hearts—but he paid it no more attention than he would have if I had been holding a plate lunch or a cup of caffeine. To his credit, he didn't make any effort to look innocent. His gaze was frankly appraising, and his shallow black eyes told me nothing about what was behind them. After a long moment his lips twitched in what might almost have been a smile. "I imagine you're right." His voice was as dangerously soft as Jamin's had been.

I had my doubts, but this didn't seem like an appropriate time to voice them.

"Good," said Jamin. "So tell me again. You've had the bomb disarmed, you've cleared the corridors, right?"

Willem nodded heavily. "I've cleared the corridors from here to the room your son is in. I would have waited for the bomb squad to finish, and brought him to you myself, but the boy wouldn't come out. He's alone in the room, and he's locked himself in. Says he won't come out until he knows you're outside waiting." Willem looked genuinely sad as he said it. "He didn't trust even me."

"Why should he?" I asked. "You're a Company man,

and he knows it's the Company that's taken him from his father.''

Willem didn't waste time with denials or arguments. "I can take you to him. You can get him out of the room. After that, I'm afraid things get more complicated.''

"In the Belt we call them chambers.'' I don't know why I said that.

Willem looked at me. "What? Rooms?'' He looked suddenly old and very tired. "I know, I know. There is so much . . .'' He closed his eyes, opened them, and straightened his back. "Be that as it may. This is not the time . . . This just isn't the time. I can get that boy out of that room, or rather get you to where you can get him out, and I've given orders to clear the way for us to the flight deck, but I'm not sure, Jamin. I'm not sure anymore. My people don't like this. I'm using my authority too arbitrarily here, and I'm not sure it will be enough. What I've asked is directly against Company policy, as you know. They wanted to keep you. I'm not sure they'll let go so easily, just because I tell them to. We are at war. I am a Board Member, but I'm not the only Board Member on Home Base right now; and even if I were, I'm not sure a Board Member outranks a Patrol Admiral anymore.''

"Oh, come on,'' I said.

He looked at me. "I'm serious,'' he said. "Of course officially I outrank an admiral. But I'm talking about reality. And the more time we waste here, the greater the chance is that somebody out there is going to decide to challenge my decision. If we're going, we have to go now.''

"What will happen to you after we're gone?'' Jamin asked.

Willem barely glanced at him. "I don't know. To tell you the truth, right now I don't care. If this is the way the Company is going to fight its wars—kidnaping children, tricking homesteaders off their rocks, packing internment rocks with everybody who doesn't have a firm Earther history and forty-two relatives to speak for him . . .'' He shook his head. "I don't know. I don't like it. If we're going out of here, damn it, let's go."

Jamin looked at me.

I looked at Willem. There wasn't really any way to know. All we could do was take a chance on his way, or find a way of our own, and I couldn't see any better plan than hoping he was being straight with us. "If this is a trap, you're dead," I told him.

He almost smiled again. "I know that, Melacha. I know you, remember? If this is a double cross, it's got to be a suicide mission. That's the only way we could play it against you. And to tell you the truth, much as I disagree with the Company's present policies, I'd really like to stick around and try to cope with them in a legal way. I'm not so disaffected that I'm ready to kill myself over it. And I'm certainly not feeling patriotic enough just now to kill myself for the Cause; not with Collis being held hostage behind a bomb. Not like that." And suddenly I really could see what was behind those flat black eyes. He knew I could, and he kept silent, waiting for my decision.

"It's a go, Jamin," I said.

"You believe him?"

"I believe him. Let's get out of here."

"What about these Patrolmen?"

I looked at the women in question. Both were awake now, and both looked cheerfully ready to kill any and all of us if they saw an opportunity. This in spite of the fact that one of us—Willem—was supposedly so much superior to them in the military scheme of things that they should be honored if he gave them permission to breathe. "We'll lock them in the pantry. If the corridors outside are cleared, that should give us time to get to Collis and away. And if they aren't clear, we'll have a hell of a lot more to worry about than these two wimps."

The nearest one considered charging me barehanded when I said that, but she thought better of it. I smiled at her. She didn't smile back.

When I looked up again, it was in time to see an expression of relief cross Willem's face. "What, did you think I'd kill them?'' I asked, and then paused, staring. ''Or are they a crucial part in the double cross?''

Willem just looked at me.

''Do you trust him, or don't you?'' demanded Jamin.

''I don't; I thought that was understood. He's an Earther, and he works with Earthers. I do believe him—up to a point—but I don't trust him. I just think we should go along with his plan and see where it gets us. If only because things can't get much worse for us than they are.''

CHAPTER THIRTEEN

After all that, there was really nothing to it. True, the corridors were still lined with Patrolmen despite Willem's orders, and my nerves were so much on edge that I'd probably have shot one if he sneezed, but none of them did. None of them did anything. They just watched us.

Willem walked with the calm, unhurried complacency of a politician about his rightful business: not unreasonable, since that was what he was. He didn't seem aware of the Patrolmen watching us.

Jamin walked beside him with the curious brittle grace he always had in gravity; not so much as if he were walking on something fragile, but as if he were himself fragile; which, in gravity, he was. Yet through the painful caution one could see the natural grace he would display in freefall: and the dangerous quality of his full awareness that the Patrol was there around us.

I don't know how I looked, but I felt stiff and awkward; as clumsy as the rawest recruit; and yet if anything had gone wrong I know I'd have taken a few dozen of those damn Patrolmen with me before I died. In fact, that was the trouble. I don't always know how to act when nothing *is* going wrong. If there's action to take, I can take it. If there's a battle to be fought I can fight it; a shuttle to fly, I can fly it; something to *do*, I can do it. Walking down that corridor with my weapon tucked demurely in my pocket and all those hostile eyes watching but nobody making a move against us . . . well, it was too much like waiting.

We made it to the doorway behind which Collis was being held. The bomb squad was still there; they assured us the bomb was disarmed, showed us its parts, and moved off. I thought of calling them back and making them stand there with us while we told Collis to open the door, but what the hell? We'd avoided open hostilities so far. If the bomb *was* disarmed, we needed more time with our guns in our pockets and nobody angry enough to try to stop us; if it wasn't, we wouldn't need much of anything anymore, and it wouldn't really do Collis any good to have a bomb squad die with him.

The bomb was disarmed. Jamin let Collis know he was there, Collis unlocked the door, and Willem opened it with no problem. He and I stepped back just in time to avoid being bowled over by a six-year-old whirlwind hurtling into his father's arms. Jamin was braced for that, and I'm sure Collis never saw the fleeting look of agony that crossed his face at impact. By the time they'd calmed enough to separate so Collis could look into Jamin's eyes, the only expression there was one of sheer joy.

I looked away from both of them and caught one of the Patrolmen in the corridor staring at us. I scowled at him with such ferocity he looked startled and glanced away. Willem touched my arm and I scowled at him, too. Good old Skyrider. Tough guy. Yeah.

"If we're going to get them down to the flight deck we've got to go *now*," said Willem.

"I know," I admitted, searching the dark of his eyes for something, I don't quite know what. "T'anks, eh?"

He just looked at me. "They're my cousins."

"Sure. No sentiment involved; just cousinly duty, right?"

"Right."

"Right. And I'm the Queen of the Cosmos. Let's go." I turned to Jamin and Collis, who were still doing their glad reunion number. "Come on, guys. We can't hang out here forever. Flight deck's this way." I gestured.

Collis took his face out of Jamin's collar long enough to
turn his summer-blue eyes toward me with fondly scornful
impatience. "Gosh, Skyrider, we *know* where the *flight
deck* is!"

"Prove it." My voice was harsher than I meant it to be.
"Get going. We don't have forever. And get down off
your father; he can't carry you in gravity."

"Can too," said Jamin.

"Don't be a rockhead. Maybe you *can*, but you damn
well *won't*. Put him down and let's get the hell out of
here."

"Why are you wearing space suits?" asked Collis.

"It's a long story." I took his free hand—the one that
wasn't clinging to Jamin—and looked at Willem. "Shall
we?"

Patrolmen stepped unhappily out of our way as Willem
led us toward the flight deck. They kept stepping out of
our way, all the way down the corridor. It wasn't until we
were back in more public territory, where workers and
refugees and tourists and a few loose Company officials
were going about their daily business without any knowledge of ours, that we began to lose our honor guard. There
were still Patrolmen in plenty, but they weren't concentrating on us anymore. The muscles in the back of my neck
began to relax, and I didn't have quite so much trouble
keeping my hand off my weapon after that, but I don't
mean to say the rest of the trip was easy.

We were still carrying illegal arms. Every Patrolmen
who happened to notice us—and most of them did—
controlled the urge to shoot first and think later only
because Willem was with us. I noticed we all had a
tendency to collect nearer and nearer him as we approached
the flight deck. Fortunately his face was well known on
Home Base, and he was a high enough muckymuck that he
could get away with quite a lot without being questioned
by a lowly Patrolman. I wasn't sure his diplomatic immu-
nity extended to escorting freefall mutants safely off-station,
but he certainly behaved as though he thought it did. He
strode serenely down the corridor like royalty out survey-

ing his domain. The refugees and tourists might as well
not have been there, for all the attention he paid them.
Most of the Patrolmen were beneath his notice, too, though
he nodded now and then to an officer; and once he smiled
at a fellow Company muckymuck.

I wasn't smiling at anybody. That was the longest walk
I had ever taken in my life. I'd far rather have fought my
way from the créche level to the flight deck. Just walking
like that, with everybody watching, and who knew how
many Patrolmen lining up their weapons behind us; knowing I didn't dare draw my own weapon till I actually saw
somebody else draw one against me, and knowing I wouldn't
see it, I'd just die. . . . Well, it wasn't quite as bad as the
suited EVA that got us to the créche in the first place, but
it was bad enough.

The best thing that can be said for that journey is that
we survived it. From the look on his face as we tucked
Jamin and Collis safely aboard the *Steadfast*, I'd guess
that even Willem hadn't been as sure of success as he'd
seemed. He tried to put me on board after Jamin and
Collis, but I wasn't ready yet. "Somebody here has my
handgun."

"Skyrider," said Willem, in a quelling tone.

I looked at him. "I want my handgun." I reached for
the lethal one in my pocket, saw three Patrolmen reach
instantly for theirs in response, and curtailed the gesture
before it could get me killed. "I was going to give you
back the one I took from the Patrol, but on second thought,
maybe I'll need it sometime."

"Melacha." Willem very seldom used my name, and
when he did, it meant something. I ignored him.

"But I'll still need my own weapon, and I want it." I
had the receipt for it in a zippered thigh pocket that I
could open without getting myself shot, and I did so.
"Here. Read it. It says here they'll give me my weapon
when I lift off-station. I'm lifting. I want my weapon."

He studied me a moment. "Okay, hotshot. You'll have
your weapon." He held the receipt in the air, and the
young Patrolman who had confiscated my weapon promptly

appeared, as if by magic, carrying my tagged and holstered stungun.

I don't know why I was so intent on having the damn thing before I lifted. Maybe it was just a gesture; maybe, as Willem implied, I was just pulling the hotshot Skyrider routine one more time. Maybe I was trying to prove to myself that even if I was willing to take on a suicide mission for love instead of money, I still hadn't lost the essential selfishness that would make me risk the whole mission for the sake of a personal toy. Or maybe I was trying to prove to Jamin that there were, after all, limits to what I would do for him. Whatever the reason, I got the handgun. The Patrolman who gave it to me retreated again into the background and Willem pushed me toward the *Steadfast*'s hatch. "I'm going, I'm going. I just wanted my damn handgun," I told him.

"If it were made of malite it wouldn't be worth the risk you just took."

"It is to me." That wasn't true, but I wouldn't have said the truth even if I'd known how.

"Okay." He shook his head, watching while I turned to close the hatch behind me, and once again I caught a glimpse of something real and personal and human in the flat black of his eyes. I think it was affection. "Be careful, damn it," he said.

"Sure." I held the hatch open a moment, looking at him. "Sure. I'm always careful. You know that."

"I've done what I can on-station," he said, "but I can't do anything about the Patrol outside. They'll be waiting for you."

"I know that."

"Melacha—"

I grinned at him. "We'll be okay. Thanks, Willem." I closed the hatch before he could answer that. There wasn't a whole hell of a lot he could have said. The man had just risked at least his life and maybe his career, his social standing, possibly even his freedom, and *he* hadn't asked first what the pay would be. I knew he didn't really give a damn about the Patrolmen we'd held hostage. He certainly

128   *Melisa C. Michaels*

didn't care as much about them as I cared about Jamin and Collis. It came down to that, no matter how I looked at it: we'd both risked a hell of a lot without asking what the pay would be because we *knew* what the pay would be: freedom for Jamin and Collis. That's fine for a Company muckymuck; it wouldn't hurt his reputation if people knew he was capable of an altruistic gesture from time to time. If the Earthers didn't break him for doing it for a Faller, he might even benefit in the long run. But what the hell had I done? I wasn't a muckymuck. The last thing I wanted was for anybody to think I was capable of an altruistic gesture.

A very small, self-conscious voice in the back of my mind said, "Yeah, but Jamin and Collis are alive and free."

I locked the hatch and turned to face them. *So far, they're alive and free.* We did still have a gauntlet of Patrol boats to run outside the station, and it would be a lot more useful if I concentrated on that right now instead of worrying about a reputation that wouldn't be worth rockdust anyway if I didn't get us off-station alive.

Having brought Jamin and Collis on board so openly, we had no need after all of the *Steadfast*'s smuggling capacity, but we would certainly need her powerful new conversion drive engines, and I felt a little guilty to realize how glad I was that it wasn't the real *Defiance* I was flying. I'd have tried it in the *Defiance*, and, hell, maybe we'd have made it. But the *Steadfast*'s extra power made it a much more realistic endeavor.

Jamin was already strapped into the auxilliary control seat with Collis in his lap. I considered pointing out that the boy would be safer strapped into a bed in the living quarters, then decided to hell with it; either we'd make it, or we wouldn't. If we didn't, we'd all be dead no matter where or whether we were strapped down; the Patrol would see to that. For ordinary bumps and jars of battle, Jamin could hang onto Collis well enough.

The Comm Link was already sputtering at me when I strapped into the pilot's seat. "Shuttle *Defiance*, you are not, repeat, *not* cleared for liftoff, I repeat, *Defiance*, you are not cleared for liftoff, please maintain position on the landing panel, do you read?''

"You better clear space, because we're lifting," I said, and flipped off the Comm switch; no reason to be distracted, during what might prove to be a difficult liftoff, by Comm Link orders I wasn't going to obey.

They made it about as difficult as they could. I'd hoped they might just leave it to the Patrol boats outside to stop us, but Ground Control deliberately risked a pair of short-runners, guiding them directly into my path. Their pilots were almost as good as I, which is why they survived. Ground Patrol tried to jam my computer, too, but you don't need the major computers for liftoff if you know your shuttle, and I'd made sure I knew this one very well indeed before I brought her in to Home Base. I took her out on manual, and threw her into an erratic dive the instant I felt the tug of the invisible barrier between the flight deck and open space.

It was as well I did, because the Patrol boats were lined up and ready, and half a dozen of them fired at once, their lasers flaring as they collided exactly where I would have been if I'd come out straight and level.

There were at least two squadrons waiting for us, mostly all Starbirds, and armed to their wingtips. Starbirds had been the logical choice; that was the best the Company had against a Falcon, which is what they thought I was flying. Even if they'd known that what I had was essentially a Sunfinch, they probably hadn't anything better than Starbirds available to chase her. The Company wasn't much richer in Sunfinches than the Colonials were.

Starbirds, properly piloted, can be quite a challenge, even to a Sunfinch. These were properly piloted. That was one strong advantage the Earthers had over the Colonials: trained manpower. Their teenagers were required to complete a standard course in military piloting sometime during their school years, and they had the money and equipment to see to it that the mandatory training was thorough. In addition to that, they offered optional advanced training not just free of charge, but actually paid for—that is, they paid the trainees, as if what they were doing were a regular productive job.

Beyond that, there was the military itself. Even in peacetime, Earthers had always kept an army ready in case of war. Warriors, weapons, and a military social structure with hundreds of years' history to draw upon . . . as far as I knew, the Earthers had always had that, even in the long ago days before space colonization. A peacetime army may not be as formidable as an army christened under fire, but it was a hell of a lot more formidable than the fleet the Colonies were assembling. Add the peacetime army to the Patrol, many of whose members *had* survived their christening fire in battles with crazy smugglers like me, and the total outclassed the Colonies by a frightening margin.

The only thing the Earthers didn't have that the Colonies had in plenty were those selfsame smugglers who had unwillingly helped train the Earthers' Patrol. We made up in madness for what we lacked in equipment, and there *were* no better pilots than we. Most of us had been flying since childhood, in adverse conditions more often than not, and in battle with (or evasion from) the Patrol on nearly every working flight. Where a Patrol boat might run into a smuggler once every few months to a year, an individual smuggler could expect to run into the Patrol on any given mission. The numbers alone suggested that.

We probably wouldn't make good Fleet members; as Michael had said, we weren't much good at following orders. But we'd make grand scouts and guerrilla invaders, pulling off swift and secret attacks and snatches like the one I was pulling now. I would suggest that to Michael; that the idea be formalized and missions planned to take advantage of our special qualifications, instead of trying to use us in the Fleet and bemoaning our rebellious temperaments.

I'd suggest it, *if* I survived the current mission. One of the Earthers was quicker than I expected, or luckier. I had continued the dive I'd taken off the Home Base flight deck, weaving a little to present an unstable target but generally letting the dive take me right on around Home

Base to get that mass of rock between me and the Patrol, so I would have room to get a really good run on them when I hit the thrusters and let the *Steadfast*'s Sunfinch engines power us out of there. One of the Starbirds saw what I was after and did some of the most expert maneuvering I've ever seen an Earther pilot achieve. He dropped out of his squadron, slipped into a neat one-eighty turn that lined up his lasers perfectly *and* put him on our tail, and we caught two of his shots dead on the aft shield, which promptly burned out. The starboard shield glared with a near miss. The whole ship shuddered and tried to go into a clumsy rolling yaw that would smash us against Home Base if I couldn't control it.

CHAPTER FOURTEEN

The Starbird's pilot was overconfident. The whole thing happened faster than I can tell it: the shots; the *Steadfast*'s uncontrolled, suicidal response; the Starbird's triumphant dive right on past us with a victory roll already started when I finally pulled the *Steadfast* out of her yaw, letting her roll, and caught the Starbird on my laser screens.

It hurt to pull the stud on a pilot that good. But he'd been smug. One thing you just can't afford in battle is smug. He died of it. My lasers both hit his aft shield at once and burned right on through like it wasn't there. The little Starbird exploded in fiery silence. I told myself the pilot never knew what hit him. But a pilot that good, however smug he was in the moment before I fired, was still alert enough to see me pull up. I thought I saw the hint of a nose-down pitch in the Starbird's attitude at the instant I fired, as if at the last moment the pilot saw his mistake and tried to dive out from under my lasers.

Whether he knew it or not, he had accomplished a part of his purpose. I had wanted to use the *Steadfast*'s phenomenal power to thrust out of Home Base's space without engaging the waiting Patrol boats at all, and if it hadn't been for that one quick thinker I probably would have made it. But the others, although they were slower than he, were by no means rookies. By the time I'd dealt with.

132

him, I'd lost all the advantage of surprise I'd originally gained with my dive off the flight deck, and I'd lost the chance of even a fractional breathing space in which to hit my thrusters and run. The remaining Patrol boats were swarming in around me like wild ore rocks around a collection ship before the last fragments of the blasted Starbird had faded from my sensors.

With no aft shield at all, and the starboard one damaged, I was crippled for most of the obvious maneuvers. I had to keep my tail to Home Base or they'd shoot it off for me. To defend the starboad side with its visibly weakened shield, I had to rely on the jockey thrusters for sideways jumps and awkward in-place maneuvers: pitch, roll, or yaw without any forward impetus. It would keep us alive till I could think of something better . . . *if* I thought hell of fast. We were a beginner's mark; a sucker's target; cornered and snarling our inadequate laser defiance without any real hope at all. I couldn't possibly keep track of eleven Starbirds. And as soon as my other shields took a few direct hits, they would be as vulnerable as the starboard one was already. Within a matter of minutes, we'd be dead.

Trickery is often helpful on such occasions, and I reached for the Comm Link almost automatically. But I hadn't anything to sell a batch of Patrol boats, and what else could trick anybody as effectively as an appeal to greed? I could hardly appeal to their finer instincts: Earthers hadn't any.

I almost missed the break when it came. One of the encircling Starbirds got overeager and I blasted him. Another danced neatly into the same space, trying to decoy me from one that nearly had my starboard shield in his laser screen. I blasted the one in front of me and dodged the one after my starboard shield, but I couldn't dodge all the ones around me, and we were taking hits faster than I could assess the damage from them. My computer was spitting out damage reports that were obsolete by the time the printout came off the board. Jamin was reading them,

134   *Melisa C. Michaels*

monitoring for anything I would have to know to keep
flying.

"Forward shield weakening," he said. "Port failing.
Possible damage to aft jockey thrusters K2 and K12."

"In other words, we've got to get out of here," I said.

"I hesitated to state the obvious."

That was when the break came: no Starbirds in my
direct forward path. None. They were concentrating on my
weakened shields, and nobody came up to take the place
of the two shuttles forward that I'd blasted. There wasn't
time to think about it. If there had been, I might not have
gone for it; with the aft shield gone, I was risking a hell of
a lot, relying on speed alone. But the *Steadfast* had it, and
it was about all she had left. I used it.

We plunged forward, out of the cluster of Starbirds and
away from Home Base with all the power the *Steadfast*
had. The thrust forced Jamin back against his seat with a
muted gasp of pain as the gravity forces built under acceleration. Somebody got in a wild shot that burned out the
last of the starboard shield and knocked us off the course
I'd set. It was a nearly random course anyway; anything to
get us out of there. Time enough later to plot a course that
would take us back to Mars Station. I let the *Steadfast*
dance sideways under the impact and held my grip on the
thrusters, watching the Starbirds recede in my screens.

If they'd known I wasn't flying a Falcon, we'd never
have got that opening. In a Falcon we'd have had very
little more power than the Starbirds; they could have caught
us easily, and harried us till all our shields burned out. But
the *Steadfast* wasn't a Falcon. We had more power than
the Patrol could possibly have guessed, and that brief
opening was all we needed. Despite the wild shot that
knocked us off course, we were essentially home free the
moment we burst out of the cluster of Starbirds. They tried
hard to catch us, but they hadn't a hope.

Jamin wasn't reaching for the damage report printouts
anymore. He couldn't. It was all he could do to hold onto
his son and wait for me to stop accelerating. After one
glance at his face I tried not to look his way again; I didn't

dare slow down till we had a lot greater lead on those Starbirds, and the gravity forces of acceleration, though not very strong for Collis or me, were just about the last straw for Jamin.

Collis, though Jamin tried to keep him ignorant of the severity of the danger of gravity to a Faller, knew or guessed what this situation was doing to his father. I've never seen a six-year-old sit so still. He seemed hardly to breathe. Any motion he had made would have added to his father's discomfort, but nobody had told him that. He'd worked it out for himself, and was acting on the knowledge in the only way he could. In that one glance at Jamin I saw Collis's face, too: as white as his father's, and just as stiff with pain he couldn't feel or share but could only imagine and endure. His blue eyes stared at me with patient terror while we all waited for the Patrol to fall safely behind.

The shot that had knocked out the starboard shield and sent us off course had been, in a way, a blessing; the course it left us on was erratic, and I did nothing to correct it. Once the Patrol lost us in their scanner screens I would choose a course that would confuse them further while it took us nearer home; meantime, we were running wild enough that they'd have a difficult time projecting our path far enough in advance to call in reinforcements to intercept us somewhere ahead.

I didn't know whether they would try that. How much expenditure of effort and expense was one freefall mutant worth to them? How badly did they want rid of the infamous Skyrider? I had a high opinion of both my own and Jamin's worth to the Colonies, but how much of that would the Earthers share? Maybe they'd be glad just to see us out of their sights, and would leave us alone.

Nice thought, but I couldn't count on it. I watched my own screens, guessing at the difference in power between them and those of the Patrol, and the moment I thought a course change would go unnoticed I made one. I had time for two more, selected more or less at random, before I felt confident we were far enough off their screens to cut our thrust and choose our path in a more leisurely manner.

I killed the engines completely and let her ride inertia for a while. Jamin desperately needed the relief from excess gravity, and I needed time to survey the damage reports while I watched the scanners to see whether the Patrol had really been fooled by my wild maneuvers.

The damage reports were not encouraging. "Jake's gonna kill me for this." I said it under my breath, half grinning at the thought of her probable fury if she should see her ship before I'd conned or bribed the Colonials into repairing the damage.

"She may not have to." Jamin was reading damage reports, too. He still looked pale and shaky, but at least he wasn't going into gravity shock. I had neither the equipment nor the training to handle that if it happened, and there had been a real possibility of it after that acceleration.

"Whatsamattah you? Think I can't drag this wreck home?" I didn't look at him. I was afraid of what he might read in my eyes.

"How could I doubt the hotshot's abilities?" Something in his tone almost made me look at him. I resisted the impulse.

" 'Ey. I got us this far."

"You sure did. Have you stopped to look at how far 'this far' is?"

Startled, I looked at the navigation screen. It revealed nothing but the multicolored snow of static. "Navigator out? Damn." I produced my most reckless devil-may-care grin. "Well, hell. If two of the Colonies' best pilots can't bring us a little to Quufiegh, we might as well concede the war right now."

"Fortunately," he said drily, "we haven't that authority."

"Come on, we know where we are. Roughly. And we're both well enough trained in navless flight. At least, I am. This is by no means the first time I've lost a navigator."

"The way you fly, I'd be surprised if it were."

"What's that supposed to mean?"

"Are you guys mad at each other?" asked Collis.

"Naturally," I said, at the same time as Jamin said, "Of course not."

Collis looked from one to the other of us, his eyes dark and wide. "Are we lost?"

He got the same response in different voices: this time Jamin said "Naturally," and I said "Of course not."

"You guys," Collis said with justifiable impatience.

"We've just lost our navigating computer," I said.

"Just," said Jamin.

"It's no big deal," I told Collis, "and your father knows it, or he wouldn't be fussing about it in front of you."

Collis grinned in relief. "That's true."

I looked at Jamin, then; the fear and affection for him that he might earlier have seen in my eyes was outweighed now by amusement and triumph. He met my gaze ruefully. "You guys," he said, in excellent imitation of his son.

"What do we do now?" asked Collis.

"Did we lose the Patrol?" asked Jamin.

"For now we've lost them," I said. "And what we do now is you get out the manual navigation instruments while I look over the rest of the damage and see what we've got left to work with. Collis, you keep an eye on the scanners while we're working. First sign of anybody out there—anybody at all—you yell, okay?"

"Okay." He looked important, hopping off his father's lap to stand before the scanner screens, watching more alertly than Jamin or I would have done, even if we hadn't any other tasks to tend to. With Collis on duty we'd hear about it if so much as a large rock floated into scanner range. Nor would his attention wander the way an Earther six-year-old's might have done; Belter kids took life-and-death duties like that seriously. They had to. They were taught from earliest childhood how vulnerable we frail humans were to the pitiless environment in which Belters lived. When they were given a job to do, they knew it could mean their lives if they neglected it.

In the early days of space colonization, parents had tried to shield their children from knowledge of the hostile environment outside their dwellings' bulkheads; they thought that knowledge would result in constant, unbearable fear, needlessly damaging tender psyches. What they hadn't realized was that their own fear could not be concealed; that the children, in the absence of reliable information, would imagine far worse perils than actually faced them; and that secrecy created a barrier to trust that was difficult if not impossible to overcome when the children grew old enough to be taught the truth.

They hadn't realized they were raising the first generations of people to whom the terrors of space were less than the terrors of Earth. The parents, raised on Earth, had expected their spaceborn children to feel as they did about things like gravity and the vacuum. But even children protected from specific knowledge of their environment became comfortable with the familiar, and frightened of the unfamiliar. To them, life in space was familiar as it could never be to their parents. To children raised out there, Earth was the frightening environment. I'd noticed that myself, when Collis and I went Earthside in search of a medical solution to the inner-ear problem that made him dangerously ill in freefall. Both Collis and I, who took wild rocks and the possibility of breached chambers for granted, were nervous about Earth's open space, indigenous life forms, and weather.

He didn't look nervous about being responsible for watching the scanner screens. He just looked capable and responsible and small. I left him to it and requested damage reports on my computer screen. When you have time to look at it that way, it's quicker and clearer than printout. The computer gave me the major categories first and let me have detail as fine as I wanted on specific areas. None of it was encouraging. The navigator was gone for good; it was physically burned out or broken in several places. Until I saw the report, I'd half hoped the problem was all in its mind, which I could have reprogrammed to some extent, thus saving time on the manual navigating we'd have to do. No such luck.

The shields were irreparable, too, from inside the shuttle

in flight, though I didn't think they'd be much of a problem to somebody who could get at them from outside and replace a few parts. Life support was completely undamaged, which was a relief. If anything major had been wrong with it we'd have heard the warning klaxons by now, and/or been aware of the effects; but there could have been something minor that would, without outside aid, develop into something major before we could get to Mars Station. It was the best protected of all the shuttle's systems, however, and it showed no damage at all.

The weapons were okay, with the exception of the starboard laser. That had taken some damage along with the starboard shield, and that worried me; the weapons were linked very closely with the engines. However, the computer said the engines were healthy; and when I ordered up a schematic scan I could find nothing wrong with them. Not that I could necessarily expect to, unless it were the grossest sort of damage; I knew almost nothing about the new malite conversion drive that fed them. Until I fired them up again—and unless something went wrong when I did—I had to rely on the computer's assessment of the situation.

Everything else checked out okay. We'd lost the navigator, the aft and starboard shields, some efficiency in the port and forward ones, and the aft jockey thrusters K2 and K12. The hull hadn't been breached, though there was obviously some exterior damage in the aft area. All in all we'd been damned lucky.

"Something coming," said Collis. "I think it's only a rock, but you look, Skyrider."

I looked. He was right: it was only a rock. "Keep an eye on it," I told him, and turned back to the main computer to see if by any lucky chance Jake had programmed a backup navigation check into it. Most smugglers did, but I wasn't so sure about Jake. The *Steadfast* was outfitted for smuggling, but Jake couldn't have made many runs since she left her undercover work with Earth's CID agency, where equipment was plentiful and pilots seldom went on any run alone. A pilot accustomed to company might expect to rely on a wingmate's navigation system if hers went wrong; and people who know that damaged equipment can be replaced at the next flight deck, docking, or planetfall might make no provision for doing without for any length of time.

Jake, however, was a sensibly cautious woman. The main computer was programmed to back up manual navigation. I showed Jamin the program and he, already immersed in the complexities of his tools, promptly instituted a deeply mathematical conversation with the computer.

"I think maybe you ought to dodge that rock now," said Collis.

I glanced at the scanners. "You're right. Thank you." I made the dodge as minimal as I could, using only jockey thrusters, both because I wanted to do as little damage as possible to Jamin's computations, which were based on our inertial ride before we encountered the rock, and because I was reluctant to fire up the main engines before I had to. If anything did go wrong when I fired them, I wanted what thrust I could get out of them to aim us more toward home.

Jamin glanced up when I fired the jockeys, frowned abstractedly, took new readings, and fed them into the computer. I punched up a readout on my screen in time to see the computer selecting from reference data regarding the orbits of Mars and Mars Station. It displayed the appropriate chart below the coordinates resulting from Jamin's calculations, then added a suggested flight path in the form of a discreet, dotted line.

"That's the best I can do for now." Jamin leaned wearily back in his seat and looked blankly out the viewport toward the distant stars from which he had selected his reference points. "I could do better with a reliable benchmark here in the Belt."

"Hell, if we had a benchmark in sight, or even a familiar local reference point, I could make the run blind."

Jamin sighed. "I'm sure you could, hotshot. I hope that doesn't mean you won't tackle the job all handicapped with my calculations the way you are."

Collis was standing between us. He shot me an agonized glance and said, "Papa!" with the sort of shocked impatience seldom achieved by anyone but children toward their parents.

"That's okay, Toad." Rather to my surprise, it really was okay with me. "He only acts that way because he knows I won't kill him in gravity."

"Considering your usual act-first, think-later policy, I don't see how anyone could be sure of that," said Jamin.

"Whatsamattah you? You wan' start one fight, or what?"

There wasn't time for him to answer that; Collis had not abandoned his duties, and he called my attention suddenly to the scanner screens. "Are those rocks?" he asked uncertainly.

They weren't rocks. Even at extreme distance they didn't look much like rocks. Magnified at maximum, they looked exactly like what they were: Patrol boats. "They're off our planned trajectory, and I don't think they have us on scan yet." I looked at Collis. "You'd better go strap down in a cabin; we're going to have to accelerate again."

"He can sit on my lap," said Jamin.

"The hell he can."

"I think I ought to go to a cabin." Collis looked uncertainly from one to the other of us.

"Make up your mind, hero," I told Jamin. "We've got to get the hell out of here before they get us on scan or they may have time to cause us some serious difficulty."

"I'll go to a cabin." Collis turned and went before Jamin could argue with him.

I waited, watching the Patrol boats on the scanner screens, till Collis used the intercom to say he was strapped down. "Okay, hang on," I said. "If they do spot us, this won't be a fun ride." It wouldn't be much fun, either, if the engines didn't function correctly on request, and in spite of the damage report I was worried because of that starboard laser. But I didn't see the need to mention it unless it happened.

Jamin was watching me intently. I could see nothing but mockery in the cold blue of his eyes. I ignored him.

The computer gave me the trajectory, feeding me numbers from the Backup Manual Navigation program, which I fed back into the same computer's Flight Control program. Computers seem very intelligent till you run into one of those quirks of categorization like that, which require an operator to tell one program what another program already knows. I checked the data to make sure I'd fed in all the numbers correctly, then invoked the program and put my hands on the thruster controls. "You ready?" Both Collis and Jamin assured me, with controlled impatience, that they were ready. I hit the thrusters and held my breath.

CHAPTER FIFTEEN

I don't suppose holding my breath made much difference to the efficiency of the *Steadfast*'s engines. I might try to make a case for the idea that it would have helped the *Defiance*, but the *Steadfast* hadn't that kind of soul. She was a sweet ship, and a fleet one, faultlessly obedient within the limits of her powers, and she had already got us out of at least one situation that the *Defiance* would have been too slow to escape. But she was only a ship. The *Defiance* was something more than a ship, at least for me.

However, it was the *Steadfast* that got us free from Home Base, and it was the *Steadfast*'s powerful conversion drive that whipped us neatly on our trajectory away from those Patrol boats and on toward Mars Station. If there was any strain on the starboard engine, I couldn't tell. She pulled us around in a neat parabola past the Patrol boats and gaining speed with every second, so that even if they had seen us they couldn't possibly have followed us, maybe not even if they'd been Sunfinches, which none of them were.

The duration of that acceleration was up to the computer; the information Jamin had obtained, that I had fed in from one program to another, was all the Flight Control program needed. From there the computer could select far more accurately than I could a trajectory that would eventually bring us to the place in space where Mars and the Station that orbited Mars would be by the time we got there.

I tried not to look at Jamin. The hyperbolic course curve of our acceleration created gravity forces the life-support systems couldn't negate, and Jamin had already undergone more gravity stresses than were healthy for him. I couldn't alleviate his physical discomfort, but I could do him the kindness of pretending not to see it.

In return, he would later do me the kindness of pretending not to have seen my concern for him. I wondered why we're all so intent on maintaining our unrealistic self-images in the face of such clear evidence that it's all just a game we play, often without fooling anyone at all . . . not even ourselves.

The moment the thrusters cut out I checked our position and compared it with the computer's projected course. We were right on target, with our nose aimed toward a rendezvous with Mars Station.

"Skyrider, can I come forward now?"

"Yes, Collis, come ahead."

"Course okay?" asked Jamin. His voice sounded almost normal.

"Perfect, as far as I can tell." I wasn't sure my voice was doing as well. "You okay?"

"Sure, why not?"

"Right." I decided to check our position again. "Probably what happened is that for a minute there I just forgot you were a hero."

"An understandable oversight. How many times d'you think you ought to take that same reading? Then if you really need to check our course, surely it would be wiser to use more than one reference point?"

"Damn you." I put the instrument down.

He ignored that. "Why don't you get some rest? Collis and I can take care of this shuttle, whoever and whatever she is, for a while."

"She's the *Steadfast*, and her engines are the new malite

conversion drive type from Earth's Sunfinches. What makes you think I need rest?"

"Intuition." He was laughing at me, though I couldn't see why. "I won't ask where you stole this thing—"

"I have her on loan."

"—or what you've done to the *Defiance*. I won't even ask how you knew my shuttle wasn't on-station at Home Base."

I stared at him. "My gods, Jamin, I didn't think! Why didn't you *say* something? We could've taken them both out."

"I just said, *Challenger* wasn't on-station. She was out on a run; we'll get her later. Now would you go get some rest?"

"Don't need any damn rest."

"I think you need a nap." That was Collis's voice.

I blinked, and there was Collis, standing in front of me, grinning one of his father's cat-grins at me. "Where'd you come from?" I asked.

"From aft. I asked permission." The grin faltered.

"I know you did. It's just that I didn't see you come into the cockpit just now."

"That's because you were asleep."

"Nonsense. We were talking."

"Then where did I come from?"

"Space, I don't know. Ask your father."

But they weren't to be put off with feeble jokes. "When was the last time you had any sleep?" asked Jamin.

"I don't know. I wish you wouldn't nag."

"Then get some sleep," said Collis.

I glared at both of them, but it didn't change anything, and I was tired. Now that I thought of it, I really couldn't clearly recall when I'd last slept, but it had been a long time ago. "Yes, all right. Just don't let the damn Patrol catch up with us, okay?"

"We won't," said Collis.

"I don't think you're indispensible," said Jamin, "but if it turns out I'm wrong, we'll call you."

They didn't call me. I might have known he'd find a

way to prove I wasn't indispensible. I slept all the way to
Mars Station, and went on sleeping while Jamin landed
Jake's *Steadfast* safely on-station. The only reason I woke
then was that he sent Collis after me. "Where are we?"
I asked stupidly, in the time-honored tradition.

"Mars Station," said Collis.

I stared. "We're *home* already?"

"You slept a long time." He looked uncertain and
maybe a little scared. "Won't the Patrol find us here?"

"They can't. This is the center of the Colonial war
effort. Headquarters, you know. Didn't you see all the
shuttles on deck?"

"Sure, but . . ."

"Sherbet what?"

"Well, we were at the Company's headquarters. Then
we just flew a while, and now we're at the Colonial
headquarters. How can that be?"

"How not?" I sat up and looked around for my dis-
carded flight boots. They were under the bunk. Collis
handed them to me, still looking bothered. "Come on,
Toad, give." I smiled encouragingly at him while I pulled
on my boots. "Whatsamattah you?"

"I don't know. Aren't we at war with Earth?"

I looked at him. "I guess we talk a lot about war, but
you never knew what it looked like, right?"

"I thought . . ." He hesitated, blushed, and looked
away from me. "I guess I'm just a dumb kid."

I felt like hugging him, but managed to overcome the
impulse by adjusting my boot straps instead. "Sure you
are. What else is new?"

"Kind of I thought if there was war you couldn't just go
from one headquarters to the other. I mean we're enemies,
right?"

"Right. And that's why the Patrol did their best to kill
us on the way here."

"But there wasn't . . . I mean, except for those Patrol
boats, there wasn't . . . anything to, you know, to stop us.
There's nothing in between. Except space."

"And a lot of bad feelings. What did you think there'd be between?"

"I don't know. Just something." He solved the hug problem by hugging me. Hell, nobody was watching. I patted his back awkwardly.

"Toad, there's nothing magical or mysterious about war. It's just like when you see two Belters fighting, only with war it's hundreds . . . thousands . . . on each side. It's still just a fight, no matter how many people get into it."

"I never thought of it like that. But when you guys fight, you don't want to kill each other." He leaned back to look at me and I stopped patting.

"Not usually, I guess. You're right, that is a difference between war and Belter fights." I didn't know what to do with my hands, so I put them on the bunk beside me. "When we fight, we're usually just letting off steam and there's no bad feelings, no matter who wins or loses. But have you ever seen a Belter in a fistfight with an Earther?"

He nodded slowly, looking thoughtful, leaning against my knees.

"Did you notice something different about that fight?"

He blinked and nodded again. "The Earther wanted to kill Papa."

"He should've stood in line."

"What?" He looked up at me again, his eyes wide and innocent, the hint of a smile pulling at his lips as he tried to determine whether I'd made a joke.

"Nothing, Toad. A joke only, and possibly not funny. What about your papa, when the Earther wanted to kill him? How did he feel?"

"Well . . . I guess he was pretty mad, too."

"He wanted to kill the Earther, right?"

"Maybe, sort of," he said reluctantly.

"You don't 'sort of' kill somebody." At his look, I grinned. "Never mind. D'you see what I mean, about war? It's just that fight, only there are a lot of other Colonists on your papa's side, and a lot of other Earthers on that Earther's side. And mostly we'll use guns instead of fists. It's still just another fight.''

"People die, though?"

I nodded gravely. "People die. You knew that. They've tried to kill us often enough. And we've killed a few of them. What about the Patrol boats I've shot out of our way from time to time? Those pilots died. Same like we'll die if they ever get good enough at killing. It'll take better than they've got right now to kill me, but they'll get a lot of practice, at war.''

He hugged me again. "I don't want you to die.''

I looked at the bright blond boy-hair under my nose and put one hand on his shoulder. "We'll be all right, Toad. You and me and your papa. We're hell of tough, you know. It takes a lot of killing to get us down.''

"I'm not so tough.'' His voice was small and frightened.

"Wanta know a secret?"

"What?'' He leaned his head back enough to look into my face.

"We're none of us very damn tough, inside.''

He looked uncertain. "D'you ever get, well, scared?''

It was a fair question and it deserved a fair answer. None of the casual lies or half-truths I used for grownups, and none of the concealed emotions, either. I met his gaze and said with absolute honesty, "Most of the time, kid.'' He looked startled, but I went on before he could speak. "We're all human, same like you. Even me. And humans get scared. 'Specially when they're in danger of dying. Which we are in every firefight, in a shuttle or out of it. Oh, we act tough, and we talk tough, and sometimes we ┍╍┅╌╌┄┉┅╌┅┅┄┄┅ tough. But believe me, anybody who isn't scared of dying is one damn fool . . . or dead already.

He grinned tentatively at that.

"Come to that," I said, "we're not just scared of dying. We're scared of a hundred other things. Some of them silly, and some of them not. Some of us are scared of big chambers, scared of wild rocks, I even know some-body who's scared of space suits. We're scared of each other, scared of ourselves, scared of the dark or scared of too much light. . . . We're just plain scared. Point out anybody on that flight deck and I can tell you three things he's scared of. And there'll be half a dozen things he's scared of that I don't know about.''

He frowned, uncertain whether I was making this up. ''But nobody *looks* scared, hardly ever. Except little kids.''

''Little kids are just the only ones who haven't learned to lie about it. Of course we don't look scared. Think I could win a fight with your father if he thought I was scared of him?''

''Are you?''

''Sometimes, my small. Same like sometimes prob'ly he's scared of me. Scared is just part of the human condition. It's not a nasty secret that belongs only to you. We're all scared.''

He frowned again. ''I thought war would be exciting.''

I grinned at him. ''I know. Once you asked your papa if you would 'get to' go to war with him.''

''I remember.''

''Well, here you are.''

''It's not exciting.''

''Sure it is. Being scared is exciting. It's not fun, but it's sure as space exciting.''

''Oh. I didn't think of that.''

''Well, think of it. And when you get scared in future, just remember that you're not alone.''

''If everybody else gets scared too, how do you not look scared?''

''Years of practice and self-denial.''

''No, I mean really.''

''Hell, Toad, I don't know. I'm not the person to ask about that.''

''Why not?''

''Because I'm an outlaw. A rebel.'' *Risk taker, law breaker,* said the familiar litany in my mind.

''What's that to do with it?'' he asked sensibly.

''Everything.'' When he frowned at me, I tried my best to tell him the truth. ''All that, being an outlaw and a rebel and the craziest Company pilot and a razzle-dazzle smuggler . . . All that just proves that I'm probably the scaredest person you know."

"It does?" He drew away from me to stare intently into my eyes.

"Sure it does. I'm the scaredest, and I'm the craziest. What I do, when something scares me, I go for it. Don't ask me why, because I don't know why. I used to think it was that excitement we talked about before. How being scared is exciting. But it isn't fun. Sometimes I think I'm always trying to prove something to somebody, but I don't know what it would be, or to whom. But the thing of it is, is, that I do all those brave and reckless things exactly because they *do* scare me."

"Then how do you not look scared?" he asked dubiously.

"I guess I just do it because I have to. If I looked as scared as I feel, I'd get thrown in a rubber room right quickly. And rubber rooms are even less fun than being scared."

He shook his head, frowned, and looked at me intently again. "Are you telling me the truth?"

"Absolute swear-to-gods Truth, my small, and if you ever tell a soul what I've just told you here, I'll kill you."

That did it. He nodded slowly and said with grownup seriousness, "I won't tell anyone, Skyrider."

"Thank you, Collis."

"What in space are you two doing in here?" asked Jamin.

We both looked up at him, wide-eyed in our innocence. "Just talking," said Collis. "Did you find out if they have someplace here where I can live, or what?"

"They do have gravity quarters here, don't they?" I never had got around to checking on that for sure, and the sudden thought that they might not have anyplace for Collis startled me.

"They have gravity quarters." Jamin's smile was mocking.

"Is it . . . is it far from the flight deck?" asked Collis.

"Guess what?" Jamin grinned at him, not at all mockingly. "You're not the only Grounder who's allergic to freefall. They've rigged up a little emergency vehicle, complete with gravity, to get people from here to the gravity quarters. It's waiting outside for you."

Collis's relief was evident, though he tried to conceal it. "Oh. That's awfully nice of them."

"Did you think they'd be mean to you because you're not a Faller and can't pretend to be?" asked Jamin.

"Well, yes, actually."

I had to resist the impulse to hug him again. "Why didn't you say so? I could've told you they aren't all Fallers. Lots of colonists live on Mars or on gravity stations. How could there be any Floaters like me if there weren't both Fallers like your father and Grounders like you? It's only when a Grounder and a Faller have a baby together that you can be sure of getting a Floater child."

"Sure, but they might've quit doing that, or something. You get Floaters when two Floaters have a baby."

"You also get both Grounders and Fallers, rockhead."

"Oh. I guess they wouldn't just throw away the Grounder babies, would they?" He looked pleased and, for the first time, excited. "Were any of those you mentioned, Papa, the ones that are Grounders allergic to freefall, were any of them kids? My size?"

"They were all kids," said Jamin. "I'm not sure whether any were just your size, but we can find out."

"I want to meet them, anyway," Collis said.

"What a good idea," I said.

"Are you sure?" said Jamin.

"Unless they're babies," said Collis.

"Well, let's get started," I said.

The emergency vehicle was a box just large enough for a small person, and it was entirely enclosed. No windows. When the tech who offered it to us held open its hatch, Collis hesitated inside the *Steadfast*'s hatch, safely within her gravity field, and frowned at the little plasteel enclosure. "Why doesn't it have windows?" he asked dubiously.

The tech looked sympathetic. "There's a personal Comm inside," she said, "so somebody outside can tell you what you miss seeing."

"But why can't I see out?"

"The med-techs tell me that even with gravity in there, you'd get sick if you looked out and saw us all floating around different sides up."

Collis looked around the flight deck, paled, and looked crossly at the tech again. "Why?"

"I don't know. I'm not a med-tech. They say that even if we could arrange for everybody to be the same side up, which would be quite a job, I'm telling you, it wouldn't do any good because the corridors aren't all the same side up and you'd get sick if you could see when you were being turned over or sideways or whatever, to go along a new corridor."

Collis looked at his father and me. Jamin looked oddly at a loss. I looked at the tech. "We'll need two Comm units outside, so we can both talk to him."

"Sure, I've got two with me."

"Okay, Collis?"

He studied my face, hesitated, then nodded. "Okay."

"Okay, close your eyes, and let your parents put you in the vehicle," said the tech.

"I can float that far," Collis said scornfully. He didn't correct her assumption that Jamin and I were a matched set of parents.

"Are you sure?" asked Jamin.

"I'm not a baby," said Collis.

"Of course not," said the tech. "Come on, then."

He drew his breath and held it, as if he were leaping into water. His face was white and determined. He looked at nothing but the hatch of that black box. It wasn't a long distance from the shuttle hatch to the box. He made it in one awkward little dive, and didn't even bang up against it too hard when he got there.

When he was safely inside, the tech made as if to close the hatch, but he stopped her. "Wait . . . please," he said with anxious courtesy.

She waited while he put on the Comm unit and saw Jamin and me put on our matching units from the tech's pocket. Then, with a brief, frayed smile at us, he nodded at her and she closed the hatch, shutting him inside. "He'll be all right," she told us.

"Papa? Skyrider? Can you hear me?" His voice was not quite steady, but he was working on it.

"Loud and clear," I said, at the same time as Jamin said, "We hear you."

He laughed at us. "I bet that's why they only wanted one person to talk to me," he said. "Two people talking at once is hard to understand when you can't see them."

"Sorry," said Jamin and I, simultaneously.

"We'll work out a system," I said, laughing.

The tech told us where to find the gravity quarters, and we set out with the black box floating between us. Jamin and I took turns describing the sights along the way, till we came to the gravity section. It was Jamin's turn, but he looked so startled—almost frightened—at the big warning signs on the closed hatch to that section that I took over.

"We're at the hatch to the gravity section. And wouldn't you know it, we've come along upside down. At least, the signs on the hatch cover are upside down. Whew! And what a lot of signs! WARNING: GRAVITY, THIS SIDE UP, that sort of thing. There's even a big fluorescent red arrow to point out which side up. They sure don't want anybody to wander in there by accident."

"Of course not," said Collis, who by this time had begun to sound as if he were enjoying his strange little enclosed adventure. "What if you floated in there by accident? You'd fall right down."

Jamin cleared his throat. "I'll open the hatch."

"Papa?" said Collis. "You've been in gravity a long time. The Skyrider could take me home, if you want to stay in freefall a while. I wouldn't mind, really."

Jamin's gaze met mine across the box. He wanted to accept the offer, and we both knew it. But he shook his head with such fierce determination that I didn't say anything. "I'll help you get settled," he said. "There'll be plenty of time for me to be in freefall later."

A new voice interrupted before Collis could respond.

"Melacha? Sorry to come in on your private frequency. This is an emergency. Do you read?"

"I read. Who's this? Michael?"

"Right the first time. Report to the flight deck on the double."

"I'm not one of your damn cadets!" The objection was so automatic that it surprised me at least as much as it surprised Michael.

He hesitated. "Okay. Granted. *Will* you report to the flight deck on the double, *please*?"

I looked at Jamin. He returned my gaze without expression. "That settles that," he said. "The Skyrider can't take you home, Collis. You'll have to let me do it."

"Okay." Collis sounded more pleased than not. "Skyrider, you be careful, okay?"

"I'm always careful. Besides, what makes you think I'm in any danger?"

"You're always either in danger or in trouble," said Jamin.

"Maybe both, this time," said Michael.

"You butt out of this," I told him. "I'll be there straightaway." There was a tiny click to indicate he'd gone off our frequency. "You two sure you'll be okay without me?" I asked Collis.

Jamin said, "We survived a number of years without you, before we met you."

Collis said, "She was talking to me, Papa. We'll be all right, Skyrider, thank you."

"I knew I didn't want to know where you got that shuttle," said Jamin.

"It isn't that," I said. "At least, I don't think it is; I did sort of have permission."

"Sort of isn't always good enough," grinned Jamin.

CHAPTER SIXTEEN

It was Jake who'd had Michael call me, but she didn't have any complaints about the condition of the *Steadfast*. I think she was so relieved to see her all in one piece, safely back at Mars Station, that she hadn't even considered the damage yet.

Besides, she had other things on her mind. "Where the hell have you been?" She came diving toward me the moment I appeared on the flight deck, and I barely had time to notice she'd been floating beside Jamin's Falcon *Challenger* before she caught me by the arm and we both banged up against a retaining pillar, tangled in each other's arms and legs.

"I was taking Collis to his quarters. Anything wrong with that? And how the hell did *you* get here?"

"In *Challenger*," she said impatiently. "Didn't you see her?"

"I see her, but I don't believe it. She can't outrun your *Steadfast*, can she?"

"Of course not." We were untangled now, floating warily on opposite sides of the pillar, and Jake glared impatiently around it at me. "I left Home Base before you did, or I probably wouldn't have got away at all. At least not in *Challenger*. And I certainly wouldn't have got here so soon after you."

"Was that important? To get here soon after me?"

"Unfortunately, yes."

"Why?"

"Somebody had to tell you what you'd done. And see what the hell you plan to do about it."

"What I've done? What d'you mean? I brought Jamin and Collis back, is that a crime?"

"Brought half the EFs in the Belt, too."

"I what!"

"Oh, we're not under attack, or anything. Not yet. They didn't even try to stop me coming in. They're just gathering out there. Waiting."

"What exactly are you trying to suggest, Jake? That the Earthers couldn't have found Mars Station without my help? Or that they wouldn't have got angry with us if I hadn't liberated their pet Faller?"

"Neither of the above." It wasn't Jake who answered me; she was too busy controlling the urge to kill me. It was Michael, appearing unexpectedly from the Flight Control booth beyond Jamin's *Challenger*, who answered for Jake. Unfortunately, he didn't stop at a simple answer. "Jake, I expect this sort of behavior from Melacha; she's got her idiotic reputation to maintain, and as far as I can tell she doesn't even want to grow up. But you! Space, Jake, I thought after all the years you spent living undercover with Earthers you'd have learned how to carry on a normal conversation without having to knock somebody down just to punctuate your sentences!"

"Wasn't a matter of punctuation," said Jake.

"I'll punctuate somebody," I said, "if you don't tell me what the hell's going on here pretty damn quick."

"Nothing's going on . . . exactly." My cousin could still look as suspiciously innocent as a boy if he thought it would serve a purpose, but the last war had left its mark on him. Since then, it had taken very little to strip the look of civilization from his hooded eyes, or to change the boy's disingenuous smile to the wolf-grin of a warrior ready for battle. "But you did bring the EFs back with you, you know."

"Rockdust. They knew where Mars Station was. If they wanted to come here, they didn't need me to show them the way."

"They didn't want to come here," said Jake. "They wanted to follow you."

"Why would they?"

"Maybe just to keep an eye on you," said Michael.

"Or a scanner, more like," said Jake.

Michael glanced at her, not quite impatiently. "In fact, I think we know why they're here. Before you went to get Jamin, did you talk to Rat about carrying a message to Earth?"

"Rat Johnson?"

"Do you know any other Rats?" said Jake.

"Probably any number of rats," said Michael, "but that's beside the point. Yes, Rat Johnson. You watched the newsfax, and then you discussed whether Earth knew what was really going on out here, right?"

"Oh, yeah, I guess." The conversation had taken place in the dim recesses of history, it seemed to me now, and I wouldn't have recalled it at all if I hadn't been reminded. "The newsfax was almost pure fiction. I don't think Earth must know the truth. I know the President. She's one tough lady, and she wouldn't hesitate to pull a scam to convince the public to back an action she liked, but this isn't her sort of action. Rounding up Fallers and using the Redistribution to trick freelancers . . . it's just not her style. Board Advisor Brown's, either, for that matter. Since they're both still in office, and this is happening, and the newsfax is telling lies, I think the whole Earth government is being told lies by its Company branch. I guess Rat and I talked about telling them the truth, but we'd have to bring proof. It was just an idea."

"Somebody took it quite seriously," said Michael.

"And you've blown the cover off an operation we've been working on for days," said Jake. "We've assembled the proof; what the hell did you think I was doing on Home Base, anyway? I've got holos, recordings, signed-and-sealed statements, the works. And you've got the Patrol alert to the whole maneuver."

"Well, hell, I didn't know anybody was really going to do it."

"Maybe they're not," said Michael. "Maybe nobody can, now. And don't tell me 'The Skyrider can,' or I'll slug you."

"I thought you disapproved of slugging as a conversational gambit."

"This wouldn't be a conversational gambit."

"Then I won't say anything. Hell, I didn't want to make the damn run, anyway. It's too dangerous, for one thing. For another, there's no profit in it. That combination of factors makes it look to me like somebody else's job."

"Only you've ruined it for somebody else," said Jake. "The EFs are just waiting out there."

"Let them wait. They're waiting for me, according to you. They didn't try to stop you coming in. They probably won't try to stop you going out. If they got a spy report about a proposed mission, it was my mission. They'll wait for the *Defiance*."

"Not after you convinced them, temporarily, that the *Steadfast* was the *Defiance*. They know that now, of course, and they'll stop anything big enough to hold you."

"You said they didn't try to stop you coming on-station. Have they tried to stop anybody leaving?"

"Nobody's tried it yet."

"Well, what are you waiting for?"

Michael blinked. Jake thought about killing me. Michael grinned suddenly, and stopped her before I had to do anything about it. "She has a point," he told her.

I looked at her. "Did all those years among Earthers teach you anything?"

"Yeah. Never trust a space-damned outlaw Belter pilot."

If she expected me to react with anger, she was disappointed. In a way, what she'd said was actually a compliment. I nodded agreement and managed not to grin. "Wise policy. I hope you keep it continually in mind."

Michael laughed out loud. "Thank the gods there's only one of you, Melacha. I don't think the Belt could handle more than one."

"Well, it doesn't have to. So now what?"

"That's what we're trying to determine." He looked at me seriously. "Did that little speech you made, about risk and recompense, mean you don't want to make the run, or did it just mean you want to run up the price before you start?"

"What price? What run? What are you talking about?"

"Told you, Michael," said Jake. "Listen, just let me make the run, okay?"

"You don't have the experience, or the acquaintances required," said Michael. "You're not exactly on a first-name basis with the President of the World, are you?"

"Neither am I," I said quickly. "Is that what you're talking about? Running to Earth with evidence of the Company's recent behavior?"

"What else?" asked Jake. "And I tell you, Michael, I can do it."

"You and what army?" The words were rude, certainly, but I kept my expression neutral. It looked like she really wanted to make that run. If so, I didn't seriously want to discourage her. Though I didn't see any harm in trying to get her to think about it first. She wasn't always well behaved, but I had no reason to wish her dead.

"Maybe *you'd* need an army." She looked superior and fierce, but controlled. "I can do it alone."

"Good for you." I allowed a grin to show, and turned to Michael, who was floating lazily above us, watching us with shadowed eyes. "You've got your pilot. What did you call me for?"

He looked steadily at Jake for a moment, then turned— reluctantly, I thought—to me again. "Melacha."

"That's my name." No matter how polite my tone or expression, I was being disagreeable. Intentionally. And Michael knew it.

He hesitated, but only briefly. "You have a price in mind?"

"Price?"

"Don't be so damned coy."

"Losing your cool, cousin?"

"Why do you even try to work with her, Michael?"
Jake sounded almost plaintive, like a small child denied an
expected treat.

"Because she's the best there is, and we need her."

"Well, that's putting it pretty bluntly," I said. "But I
don't guess I'll argue. Sure, I'll make the run . . . *if* you
outfit the *Defiance* with the new malite conversion drive,
same like Sunfinches and Jake's *Steadfast*." I hadn't meant
to ask for more than that, but something in Michael's
expression warned me. He looked too smug. "*And* you
guarantee me repairs at no charge for the lifetime of the
Defiance and her engines, no matter what condition she's
in when I bring her on-station. If I can land her, you put
her back together."

He swallowed. "I've seen what you can land."

I laughed at him. "I know it. Do we have a deal?"

"It's a hazard to the Station, but I guess I'm not encouraging you; you'd land her wrecked anyway, to avoid
salvage." He didn't like it, but he was going to agree to it.
"Okay, damn it. *If* you can land her. No free salvage
operations, though."

"Agreed."

"You want it in printout, or what?"

"I'll take your word for the repair agreement. And I
don't suppose you'll try to change your mind about the
engines once they're installed."

"Not if you make the run, I won't." Those wolf eyes
watched me with predatory attention. "How soon can you
leave?"

"How soon can you have the new engines installed?"

"They're in, already."

I stared. "You had it done yourself . . ."

"I'm afraid I did," he said, looking neither afraid nor
sorry. "It seemed a high enough price, even for you." He
permitted himself a tight little smile. "I hadn't thought of
the repair contract, though I should have. You drove the
same bargain with the Company, didn't you, when you
asked for the *Defiance* in return for rescuing the *Marabou*."

"A similar bargain," I said. "I'm learning. You have
your evidence already loaded on board?"

"We fed what we could into your computer. The hard copy is in the cockpit glove box. Your weapons have been checked out and fully charged, and I think you'll find ample supplies in the dispenser or the store-hold. Everything I could think of that you might need. D'you think you can get in to see the President?"

"She said I could." I had prevented her assassination, and she had been grateful. Whether she would still feel so, months later and with the world situation changing daily, I didn't know. "If I have any trouble getting to her, Board Advisor Brown should be able to help me. I *know* I can get in to see Board Advisor Brown . . . and I know she won't like the news I'm bringing."

Jake made a sound that might have been meant for laughter. If so, it wasn't very convincing. "Sure she won't."

"You don't know Board Advisor Brown."

"I know she's an Earther."

Michael and I looked at each other. He started to say something, but changed his mind and shook his head instead. There really isn't much you can say to someone who talks like that—and I speak as one who *has* talked like that.

"You worked with Earthers for how long?" I asked Jake.

"Two years." She made it sound like an eternity.

"And you came away feeling that there were no redeeming human qualities among them?"

"Well . . ." I think she almost blushed. "I don't suppose I'd put it quite that strongly."

"You just rejected Board Advisor Brown out of hand," said Michael, "solely because she's an Earther."

"An Earther politician," said Jake. "That's different."

"None of *them* have any redeeming qualities?"

She shook her head, sure she was on firm ground now. "None."

"I rather liked the President," I said.

"I'm fond of my mother," said Michael. "But then, she's only a mayor. Maybe that doesn't count."

Jake looked from one to the other of us, her eyes suspicious. "Is this some kind of joke, or what?"

"It's no joke," said Michael. "Surely it hadn't escaped your attention, after working with them for two years, that Earthers are people, too."

"Well, yeah, but . . ."

"But what?" I asked.

"But they aren't, they don't, they're . . ."

"They're all different. Same like colonists," said Michael. "Some of them are decent and some of them aren't. I don't know what the official Earther position will be on this war: I know some Earthers will think it's all a political matter, and some will treat it like a religious war. Some want to control the universe, and some just want to destroy everything in it that's different from them. And some don't want to think about it at all; they just do what the government tells them to, and hope everything works out for the best. Same like colonists." Jake was losing interest, but he didn't stop. "What I do know is what the official Colonial position will be on this war. From our point of view it's not a religious war. We're not out to rid the world of Earthers or anybody else. We just want room to live and the right to live in it."

"Sure, great," said Jake, "but the Earthers—"

"Forget it," I said.

"I won't forget it," said Jake. "D'you know what the Earthers did to my family in the last war?"

"No, but I know what they did to mine," said Michael.

I looked at him. "And the other side of our family, Michael? The Earther side? What did Colonials do to them?"

"That's just the point," he said, looking at Jake with curiously bleak intensity. "There are two sides to any war."

She was staring at me. "Which one are you on?"

I looked at her. "I can tell you which side I'll fight for. I can't tell you which side I'm on." Something in her eyes had given her away. "Are all your relatives Colonials?"

She didn't want to answer that. After a long moment she shook her head reluctantly and offered me a brief, frayed smile. "Right the first time, Skyrider. No, they aren't all Colonials. Now could we just forget it?"

"I thought you didn't want to forget it."

"Changed my mind."

"Right." I looked at Michael. "Do you really want to try logic on that?"

"Oh, hell." He relaxed suddenly, and managed a crooked grin of his own. "I guess we can finish fighting the last war later; right now we ought to be thinking of this one."

"I guess there's not much to think about," I said. "If the *Defiance* is ready, and you've got your evidence on board, I might as well be on my way. If you don't mind, I'd like to say goodbye to Jamin and Collis before I go."

"We need a little time anyway," said Michael. "I think we'd better assemble some kind of firepower to see you safely off-station and on your way."

"What, are you going to break out your new fleet already?"

"Such as it is," he said.

"I don't really need them. Why risk them?"

"What do you think we're training them for, if not for battle?"

"Well, yeah, but everybody likes to miss a battle when possible."

"Not everybody," said Jake. "Certain outlaws of questionable courage, maybe."

"Are you serious?" asked Michael.

That frayed smile again. "Not entirely," she said. "I've heard a lot about the Skyrider, including what a coward she is because she didn't fight in the last war. Whoever made up that one wasn't looking; cowards don't fly like she does. Remember, I was with her when she stole the Sunfinch off Station Newhome."

"Don't let's drag my history into this," I said. "The point is, why risk your precious new fleet so soon when you don't have to?"

"Who says we don't have to?" asked Michael.

"I do. Is there a better authority on this mission?"

"Since you're the only one on it, I don't guess there is," said Michael.

"But that doesn't make you right," said Jake.

"There are limitations to what even the Skyrider can do," said Michael.

"I've been told that before," I said. "What the hell, it's your fleet. Risk it if you want to. I'm going back to the gravity quarters for half an hour or so, and then I'm leaving. Do what you want to."

"Melacha." He said it just in time to stop me from kicking free of the retaining pillar and floating away from them.

"That's my name."

"You don't have to make this run, you know."

I stared. "Are you serious? You think you can get that new conversion drive away from me that easily? Listen, you met my price. You're stuck with me."

"There are other pilots who could do it."

"And get my new drive? No, thanks. I want it."

"Hell, if it's only the conversion drive—"

"Don't say it." I glared at him; if he offered me that drive whether I made the run or not, I'd just have to bargain for something more. It wasn't my fault if he suddenly remembered the hazards of war, and wanted to send somebody who wasn't his cousin and hadn't been his childhood playmate. There might be other pilots who could evade the EFs and successfully make the run to Earth; but there weren't any other pilots personally acquainted with the President of the World, Incorporated. And I couldn't make the run for free. "Just don't say it, Michael. We have a bargain. Leave it alone."

He studied my face for a long moment before he nodded, reluctantly, and said softly, "Okay, damn you." There was no anger in his voice, only pain. That's what comes of dwelling too much on the last war when you should be fighting the next one.

CHAPTER SEVENTEEN

Jamin had Collis pretty well settled in by the time I got back to gravity territory. Their quarters were pleasantly furnished in metal and plastic, with minimal rock since the station wasn't a rock, but with everything else calculated to make a native Belter feel at home: burnished plasteel walls, naked furniture and floor, bright blue heat shields on the beds instead of the fur and fabric covers Earthers use, and even a hologram disguised as a viewport onto the littered darkness of the asteroid belt.

Jamin and Collis both looked surprised to see me, but only Collis looked pleased. He ran to the door to hug me. "I thought you might've gone on another run without saying goodbye, I'm really glad you came back, do you have to go on a run already? Can we go with you?" He followed me to a big plastic chair and leaned against it when I sat down.

"Yes I have to go, and no you can't go with me. You wouldn't want to, anyway; I'm going to Earth."

"To Earth!" Jamin stared. "What for?"

"To tell the President what's happening out there."

"You don't think she knows?"

Collis turned to frown impatiently at his father. "Of course she doesn't know, Papa. She's a nice person. She wouldn't let this stuff happen to us if she knew about it."

Collis had played Planets with her. He knew her better than I did.

"She may be a nice person," said Jamin, "but she's still the President. She can't just do what she wants to; she has to do what she thinks is best for the World, Incorporated."

"But she wouldn't think stealing rocks from Belters was the best thing for the World. And putting Fallers in prison. She wouldn't do that, not for no reason."

"Things are a little different in war," said Jamin.

"It's just a big fight," said Collis. "People don't change their whole, um, you know, how they are—"

"Their character?" I suggested.

He threw me a grateful impish smile. "Yeah, that, I think. They don't change that just because they're in a fight."

"War is a little different from a big fight," said Jamin.

"Not that different," I said.

"Different how?" asked Collis.

"Go ahead, answer that one," I said.

Jamin shook his head, smiling affectionately at his son. "It's too much for me. What you need is a thorough grounding in politics."

"Why politics?" asked Collis.

"Because that's the difference between war and an ordinary fight."

"Oh. Well, if I really need it, they'll give it to me in school." He looked dubious. "At least, I don't *think* we've had it yet."

"Will they have school here in gravity that you can attend?" I asked.

"Oh, yeah, we already checked," said Collis. "And did you know my friend Jerry is here? His father's— oh. I guess you knew, huh? His father's your cousin, or something?"

"Michael. Yeah. I knew he was here, but I didn't know whether his family was here or down on Mars."

"Jerry and his mother are here. His other mothers and fathers and most of his brothers and sisters are down on Mars. Jerry's mother is a pilot, that's why they're here."

"That may be why she's here, but why did she bring Jerry?"

"For company, I guess," Collis said with a child's perfect logic. "Anyway, we'll be going to school together, and Papa doesn't have to look for a babysitter because Jerry's mom will stay with me and Jerry when she's not on a run, and she's got a babysitter for us when she is. Course, when Papa isn't on a run, I'll stay here with him."

"Of course." I looked at Jamin. "Sounds like you've got everything pretty well organized."

He looked mildly embarrassed. "Collis did the organizing. As soon as he found out Jerry was on-station he called up and worked all this out."

"When are you going to Earth?" asked Collis.

"I'll be leaving in a few minutes, why?"

He looked at his father. "Because prob'ly Papa'll want to go part way with you, just to make sure you get started okay, and I guess I better call Jerry and see if I can come over when you leave."

I looked at Jamin. "You're too tired, for gods' sake. There's no need. Michael is sending half the Fleet out with me."

He looked dubious. "There's a fleet?"

"Sort of."

"Right. I'll just come along for the ride, if they can give me a shuttle to fly."

"*Challenger*'s on the flight deck," I said.

He stared.

"But there's no reason for you to come along," I said.

"*Challenger* is on the flight deck here? How did she get here? Who brought her? Is she all right?"

"She flew, Jake, yes."

"I'm coming with," he said. "That is what you got me a shuttle for: to fly as your wingmate when you go into battle."

"Will there be a battle?" Collis asked alertly.

"I don't know." I looked at his father. "I'm afraid so. But that's no reason—"

"Shut up," said Jamin.

"Right." I looked at Collis and sighed. "Right. You'd better call Jerry, Collis."

"Okay." He went to the Comm unit, and Jamin and I eyed each other with mild hostility.

"You're sure *Challenger* is all right?" asked Jamin.

"Hell, I don't know. Jake said she was. But I haven't flown her."

He looked at me speculatively. "What did they offer you?"

"What?"

"To make this run. What did you bargain for?"

"Oh. Why, d'you think I should do it for free?"

"I know you wouldn't. What did you get?"

"The new malite conversion drive for the *Defiance*. Like a Sunfinch."

"You don't come cheap, do you?"

"I keep telling people that, but they don't always believe me."

"They will when they hear about this."

"Not necessarily. Some people are hard to convince. And for some reason people think the humanitarian gestures are the ones that should be done for free. The riskier, the freer, maybe. Nobody complains if I want to be paid to make a legal run for the Company, but if I want a profit on a smuggling run they get suspicious; and if I want to be paid to risk my life to save somebody else's, the few people who are forced to believe what I'm doing are often positively shocked." Jamin had been shocked when I asked for a Falcon in exchange for the *Marabou* run. He'd known me longer now, and he still didn't like it, but he wasn't shocked that I had bargained for—and got—new engines for that same Falcon before I would agree to make a run to Earth that might avert a system-wide war.

He almost smiled. "What would happen if you did make a run like that for free sometime?"

"Why speculate? It won't happen."

"But if it did?"

"Space, Jamin." I frowned at him, hoping it wouldn't

occur to him that it already had happened, when I went to get him and Collis. "What is this, a little home psych-tending? Don't be stupid. Nothing would happen if I made a run for free. Which is why I'm not going to do it. I don't have any reason to risk my life for free."

"What about helping others?"

"What about helping myself?"

He grinned. "I won't argue." He said it in the way people do who hope their smug superiority will provoke some inadvertently telling response.

"That's good; then I won't have to."

"I can go over to Jerry's whenever I want to." Collis returned from his close conversation with the Comm unit, clambered comfortably into his father's lap, and grinned at me. "Jerry says you got new engines for the *Defiance*."

"And a new maintenance contract," I said. "Don't forget the maintenance contract. If I can land it, they have to fix it."

"That's great. I guess Jerry didn't know about that."

"His father didn't realize what a hard bargain I'd drive."

Jamin looked at me. "They offered the conversion drive, so you felt you had to bargain for something more, right?"

"If they'd offered that much unasked, I thought they'd pay a little more if it was put to them nicely."

He looked at me speculatively. "You know, there's a lot of talk here about profits in return for ventures. How 'bout if I demand some recompense before I'll help you leave Mars' orbit?"

"Then you'll just have to stay here, won't you?" I laughed at his look of confusion. "See, it only works if you mean it."

Collis giggled, looking fondly up at his father. "You can't do what the Skyrider does if you aren't the Skyrider."

"Nicely put," I said.

Jamin grinned ruefully. "I knew there had to be a catch to it. I guess I'll never be a very good mercenary."

"I'm mercenary enough for both of us. So it's settled; you'll stay here?"

"No." He rested his cheek against his son's golden hair

in a gesture so unconsciously affectionate I could have
kicked them both. "There's a little something more than
finances at stake here."

"Yeah," I said. "Lives. I'm getting paid to risk mine.
You're not, so why risk yours?"

"Lucky the rest of the Colonial Fleet doesn't think like
you," said Collis, "or there wouldn't be one."

"One what?"

"Colonial Fleet."

"What, are you going all patriotic on me?"

"That's not a dirty word," Collis said sturdily.

Jamin grinned suddenly. "It isn't strictly applicable here,
either."

"Look, why don't you both just go chew rocks or
something." I got up and headed for the door.

"Skyrider," said Jamin.

I paused, not looking at either of them. "What?"

"Are you leaving without saying goodbye?" asked Collis.

"I was," I said.

"Are you still?" He sounded uncertain.

I sighed. "No."

When I didn't turn around, he got off his father's lap
and came to me. "Skyrider, are you mad at us?"

Those blue eyes would break a lot of female hearts
someday. "No, Collis, I'm not mad at anyone."

He hesitated, watching me. "There's nobody here but
us," he said.

I looked beyond him, toward the door through which I
should already have gone. "So you figured that one out?"

"What? That you don't like for anybody to know you
like us? Sure." He said it as though it were common
knowledge and not particularly remarkable.

"Damn." I hadn't really meant to say that. It was
barely audible, a sound more than a word, but Collis heard
it. I saw him hear it, I saw the pain in his eyes, and I felt
trapped. "Damn both of you." I turned away from him,
but I didn't leave.

"Melacha," said Jamin.

"Shut up." To my horror, my voice broke. I cleared

my throat and spoke more calmly. "Is it that *easy* for you?
Do you just . . . just say what you feel, without fear or
second thoughts? It isn't that easy for everybody, you
know. It just isn't all that simple. You don't just *love*
people, you don't just love them and you don't just *say*
you love them, not in the real world, not people like me,
not just . . . *damn* it!" I drew a deep breath, cleared my
throat again, blinked a couple of times, and turned around
to face them. "Okay. Okay, just don't speak. Don't say it,
okay? I know what you're thinking, both of you, and I
don't want to hear it."

Jamin looked genuinely bewildered. "What do you—"

"I said shut up!" I glared at him and paced the floor,
trying to avoid seeing Collis's startled blue eyes or Jamin's
lifting eyebrows. "Okay. Okay, I like both of you. I
pretend I don't, but we all know I do, so what the hell? So
I should be able to just talk about it when there's nobody
else around, right? Well, wrong. I can't." I looked at
Collis then, right into those stunning blue eyes, and said
helplessly, "That's just not who I am. I don't think like
that. I don't behave like that—" I looked at Jamin, seeking some reassurance in the cold blue of his eyes that
wasn't there at all. "It's not an act, you know. How I am.
I don't behave this way just to keep some public image
going. Oh, partly that, sure, but damn it, the public image
happened because that's *how I am!*"

"We know that," said Collis.

I looked at him. "What?"

"I'm sorry, Skyrider," he said. "I didn't mean to be
pushy."

"You must really be nervous about this run," said
Jamin.

I whirled to face him, but his expression wasn't mocking, and my anger faded under the remote composure of
his gaze. If he had been as sympathetic and concerned as
Collis was, I would have lost it. Maybe he knew that. And
if he'd been as sardonically amused by my antics as he
sometimes was, I would probably have forgotten his limitations and started swinging. Maybe he knew that, too.

Maybe that's why he took the middle course, neither concerned nor amused, not even intensely interested, just mildly curious and moderately friendly.

"Is that what?" asked Collis. He moved around me to his father's side and leaned comfortably against the arm of Jamin's chair. "Are you nervous about the run?"

"Hell, I don't know." I stopped next to a chair and sat down suddenly, more suddenly than I intended. "Why would I be nervous?" I looked at my hands. They were shaking. "I guess I am."

Jamin shrugged negligently. "Why not? It's a hazardous run. And you've been in action almost constantly since—"

"It's not that." I shook my head, still looking at my hands. "It's the Gypsies." I wouldn't have said that to most people; not everyone can hear the ghosts of the asteroid belt. Not everyone believes they're there to be heard. Jamin couldn't hear them, but he did believe I could. Maybe he didn't quite believe in ghosts, but my ability to hear them had saved our lives more than once in the past. He couldn't afford to *dis*believe.

"Singing?" His voice was steady, but it wasn't just mildly interested anymore, and without looking at him I could feel the intensity of his gaze. "They're singing?"

I shrugged impatiently. "What else would they do? That's what they ever do. When I, when something . . ."

"When you need a warning."

"Yeah."

Collis had looked from one to the other of us, his body growing tense and his eyes wide, while we spoke. Now he pushed himself away from his father's chair and ran to put his arms around me. "Skyrider, don't go!"

I patted him awkwardly. "There isn't really room in this chair for both of us."

He tilted his head back to grin at me. "That's not what to say when somebody's hugging you."

"I just said the first thing that came to mind."

"Will you stay?"

I shook my head. "I can't."

"Couldn't somebody else make the run?"

"Maybe. But not as well as I can. We don't have a lot of pilots personally acquainted with the President of the World."

Jamin cleared his throat. "But if the Gypsies are warning you . . ."

Collis put his arms around me again. "What good will it do to know the President if you're dead?"

I hugged him back, briefly, aware that the gesture was both awkward and oddly guilty. It didn't matter; it was the best I could do. "I don't think I'm going to die."

"But the Gypsies," he said.

I looked past him at Jamin. "I don't quite understand it, but I don't think it's a warning that I'm going to die."

"What then?"

There were a lot of possibilities. They had sung a lot of songs for me over the years, and while the meaning was usually clear straightaway, as it had been the time they warned me of a bomb on board the *Defiance* or the time they woke me from sleep to alert me to the impending arrival of Earth Fighters on my flight path, sometimes it wasn't clear at all until the moment of hazard arrived and there was action I could take. Occasionally they sang just for fun, but this wasn't that kind of song. A few times they had sung for reasons that I never had understood, but this was a different song from any I had heard before. It was similar in its emotional impact to those I had heard as warnings of impending death, but it was different, too. It frightened me more than any previous warning had frightened me. I didn't know why.

"They warn you of danger, right?" said Jamin.

I managed an uncertain laugh. "Well, not every danger. Unusual danger, okay? If they warned me of every danger that came along, they'd be singing all the time."

He tried to smile, but it didn't quite come off. "Okay. Unusual danger. So if it isn't the run to Earth, what would it be?"

"I don't know. Hell. Sorry I mentioned it. It doesn't make any sense, and there's nothing to do about it. Why *did* I mention it?"

"Because Papa said you must be nervous," said Collis.

"Oh, right. Well, chalk it up to the usual pre-battle premonitions, and leave it alone."

"Is that what it is?" asked Jamin.

It would have been simple to say "no." I don't suppose it would have changed what happened later, but it would have been simple, and it would have been the truth, and I didn't say it. Instead, I said, "Sure, I guess so. What else?" I achieved what I hoped was a convincing smile and changed the subject.

Jamin didn't like it, but he went along with it. There wasn't much else he could do. From then until we said goodbye to Collis and went off together toward the flight deck, I to begin my journey and he to help ward off the Patrol at the start of it, we talked primarily about the Colonial pilot school on Mars Station.

He tried to talk about the Gypsies again on our way to the flight deck. But, anxious as I felt about their song, I refused to discuss it because I could not figure out what it meant; because I thought it must be about the run to Earth, which I was intent on making no matter what; and because I believed it was a warning meant for me.

CHAPTER EIGHTEEN

The *Defiance* had been put back together better than ever. From outside one couldn't see any evidence of change; but inside, the alterations to her engines became obvious at once. The control board had been meddled with to a considerable extent. There were new dials and gauges, new scanner screens, new panels to monitor the new engines and other new panels to control them.

I looked over the changes carefully, then went into the galley to see whether anything had been changed there. Nothing had been, beyond the addition of needed supplies. The hidden controls for the concealed hold were untouched. I signaled the secret hatch to open and went on back into the regular hold to see whether it had.

It had. I went through into the concealed hold, found everything in order, and stepped back out. The hatch cover could be closed manually from there if one knew how to do it. I knew, and closed it; not even Jamin knew where my smuggling hold was or how to get into it, and even though I had no immediate plans for it I wasn't going to start getting careless now.

Satisfied that my secrets had survived the mechanics' intrusion, I returned to the cockpit and took my place in the pilot's seat. There were other modifications I had made to the *Defiance* when I first got her, but as they were to do with her weaponry they would certainly have been affected by the installation of the new conversion drive, which would power the lasers as well as the rest of the ship.

The photars were a separate system, and the mechanics had left them alone. They were outmoded weapons, really, which I had installed as a backup system that I seldom had occasion to use. Still, one never knew. I checked their controls and power supply carefully before I went on to the standard preflight checklist for the main weapons systems and the engines; the life-support system; the various on-board computers and their contacts, if any, with outside computers; and, finally, the payload.

Physical evidence was in the glove box. The research and entertainment computer verified storage of reports, statements, and studies for later transfer to Earthbased computers for readout. Everything checked out okay. And the Gypsies kept singing.

Ground Control had verified my Comm Link and was waiting for me to start liftoff procedure. If anyone other than Michael had been in charge, I probably would have been allowed as much time as I wanted before departure; my legend held most people sufficiently in awe of me that they hesitated to get bossy. Michael knew my legend as well as anyone and better than most, but he knew me, too. He had known me long before there was any legend; we were children together on Earth a long time ago, and when you've had spitting contests and bicycle wrecks and skimmer board races with somebody, it takes more than a legend to put you in awe of her.

"Well, Melacha?" he said, "Are you going to float on my flight deck forever, or did you plan to leave sometime soon? The Fleet is as ready as it ever will be. The longer you wait, the more Patrol boats you'll have to deal with when you get off-station."

"Always a kindly word." I hadn't put the Comm Link on visual, but I made a face at it anyway. "I'm going, already." I fastened my shock webbing and fired up the engines.

"You are cleared for liftoff, *Defiance*." He went through the whole formal routine before he allowed the smallest hint of personal interest to show in his voice. Even then, all he said was, "Good luck."

Liftoff was unspectacular, which is just how a liftoff should be. I went off-station ahead of the rest and synched with Ground Control once I was out, so the others would have a relatively stationary target with which to rendezvous. It was odd to have them all take up their battle formation around me; I was trained in formation flying, of course, but it had been a long time since I'd practiced it. Outlaw queens fly alone.

Jamin took the wingmate position off my port wingtip. I dipped my wing to him and he mirrored the gesture for me, which is exactly what I should have expected, but it seemed incredibly sentimental when he did it and I wished I hadn't provoked it. My nerves were on edge. The Gypsies were singing. I touched my head, absently seeking a thin, three-cornered scar that was the only outward evidence the surgeons had left of the metal plate they'd put inside to hold my head together. It was a habitual gesture, prompted by the Gypsies' song. *There are ghosts among the asteroids.*

The space around Mars Station was filled with shuttles, all ready to fight the Patrol to see me on my way to Earth. Old friends and strangers, experienced pilots and students from the makeshift school on-station, trainers and trainees in every description of spacecraft available to the Colonials, they formed their fighting wings around the one Jamin and I led, and waited to follow us to war.

And the Gypsies kept singing. It occurred to me they might be singing the death of peace. We had been gearing up for war for a very long time, but we had never wanted it. It was Earth that wanted war; the Colonials wanted only freedom from oppression. We would rather have got it by peaceful means, and we had on many past occasions shown willingness to live with temporary oppression if Earth would work with us toward eventual freedom for all peoples, ours and theirs.

But there was always that tacit dividing line. *Ours* and *theirs*. We were wholly alienated from each other. It wasn't just politics anymore, if it ever had been: it was racial estrangement. We could no longer understand each other, much less trust enough to live in even an uneasy peace. We had quite literally grown too far apart, in the generations since the pioneers had ventured so courageously out from Earth into space, and our efforts at understanding each other had begun far too late.

The pioneers probably never saw the danger. Why would they? They didn't live on Earth anymore, but they were Terrans, as we still were today despite genetic changes that adapted us to our new environments. From the perspective of Terrans colonizing space for Terrans, the possibility of eventual alienation extreme enough to cause a war must have seemed remote if anyone thought of it at all. Yet in the olden days of Earth, Terrans fought whole wars over colors of skin: if our ancestors would do that, how much more readily might we not fight over something so much more divisive as a difference in ability to survive a force so natural to Earthers, and so alien to Belters, as gravity? We were all Terran, but we could not all survive the rigors of Terra. Add to that the simple reality of physical distance, and the complexities of interplanetary commerce, and suddenly war seemed almost inevitable; though the process that brought us to it was slow and subtle.

Now it was the possibility of peace that seemed remote. If the Gypsies were singing for the loss of that, their song was overdue. We hadn't lost hope of peace suddenly today, with the conclusion of this battle with the Patrol: any realistic hope of peace was lost a long time ago, before the last war, and probably even before most of the warriors who would fight in this one were born.

"Ready when you are, wingmate," said Jamin.

I looked through the viewport and across the intervening space at his shuttle, bright with reflected sunlight against the dark background of the down-sun side of Mars. He hadn't said "wingleader," but neither had he made clear claim on the title for himself. He wasn't just being polite; I could hardly lead a wing I intended to desert at the earliest opportunity, but the wing would follow Jamin more willingly if I publicly named him leader. We hadn't any official rank, and my legend was much more impressive than his. As if legends meant anything in the real world! I smiled sourly at the viewport and said, "Ready on your command, wingleader."

He led us in a clean sweep Earthward from Mars Station, head-on toward the waiting Patrol whose ships hung invisible in the black of space somewhere beyond scanner range. Wing after wing of volunteer warriors swept outward from Mars Station behind us. Michael must have called out almost the whole Colonial Fleet to see me off. The Patrol surely couldn't have assembled in greater numbers than we had, in the time available. But those they did send against us would be more experienced in battle than most members of our fleet. It would not be an easy victory for either side. But then, we didn't need a victory; we just needed my escape. Then the remaining Colonials would be free to disengage from battle and return to Mars Station.

That sounded relatively simple in the abstract; but of course the Patrol might not let them disengage so easily. And if I had ever entertained hope of slipping past or through the Patrol ranks unnoticed, leaving the Colonials free to return without having fired a shot, I gave it up when we came in scanner range of the Patrol. There were more of them than I expected, and they were ranged over a wide area in double wings I would be hard put to evade even *with* Colonial support.

The Gypsies' song seemed, briefly, to intensify; then, as often happened when they sang me to battle, it faded to the merest background melody, so I was free to concentrate on the complexities of fight and flight. The Patrol knew what we were there for, and they had my escape effectively blocked. Instead of engaging us directly, they waited for us to make the first move. They weren't going to make it easy for us. They were outnumbered, but they knew they weren't outclassed. And they had all the time in the world; they hadn't any appointments to keep, or flights to Earth to make.

We were almost in firing range when Jamin broke Comm silence again. "Blue wing maintain formation: execute Alpha formation."

The wingleaders must have been busy on another frequency; I saw the wings on either side of us peel away seconds before we jockeyed neatly, as a unit, "upward" with relation to the waiting Patrol, who were arrayed on a plane facing Mars Station. When the maneuver was completed, the Patrol was still on their defensive plane, with their noses all pointed toward the Colonial Fleet. But though we still had our noses—and our weapons—directed toward them, we were no longer on the same plane with them as we had been when we made our first approach. We had altered our positions so that the plane of our formation was at a ninety degree angle to theirs.

It was a standard face-off maneuver, which the Patrol answered with expert readiness, rearranging themselves with relation to us with no apparent effort or confusion. But they revealed something about themselves by taking up exactly the same positions again, simply having changed their plane to match ours. I wondered if our wingleaders had performed the maneuver to learn exactly that: that the Patrol still habitually thought in flat planes, like Earthers.

We were still outside firing range. The other wings were arrayed behind us as neatly as when we left Mars Station. Jamin said softly, "Blue wing execute Freedom formation," and we did.

From the point of view of the Patrol it must have looked like sudden anarchy in our ranks; all our wings seemingly broke formation at once, although little was actually altered beyond our individual shuttles' attitudes, so that we held our positions in space and maintained our distance from each other, but when the maneuver was completed we were all facing slightly different directions, seemingly at random. We weren't even all the same side up. Of course there was nothing random about it; it was a formation the Colonials had devised after careful study and experimentation, that looked like chaos to anyone accustomed to thinking flat, but that was in fact a very effective attack and defense stance for an army that was truly comfortable in freefall.

We held there briefly, waiting to see how the Patrol would respond. They angled their plane, but that was all. They had all been on the same plane, and they stayed that way. There was triumph in Jamin's voice when he ordered our wing forward. The other wingleaders' orders came through on the same frequency this time as each wing was ordered forward, and every ship in the Colonial Fleet moved on its own individual plane. The result was far from chaos. Our ranks seemed to increase, because the space we occupied was increasing without any loss of efficiency. In fact, fighting efficiency in the Freedom formation actually improved, at least up to a point, with the increase in space occupied.

The Patrol nervously angled its plane again, then altered it completely, resuming the position in which they had originally awaited us. They could not match us ship-for-ship. They expanded their formation in an effort to cover us all; then contracted it at once when they saw how vulnerable the expansion made them. They were a neat boxed unit confronted with an apparently unpredictable tumble of wild shuttles, and they didn't know what to do. Both military neatness and the flat planes of gravity contributed to their bafflement. I was reminded of something I'd read in an ancient history text about British warriors who habitually fought in a neat boxed formation that was utterly useless when they confronted the unpredictable Native Americans in battle. They hadn't known what to do, either.

When we pressed the Patrol, they panicked and fired before we were properly in range. We kept coming till we were in range and could return their fire. My wing, though we had led the flight out, was now in one of the last positions to engage, so I saw the opening of the battle before I joined it. The Patrol's formations seemed almost to shrink as they tightened their ranks more and more in response to the alarming apparent disorder of ours.

They undertook brief sorties against our leading wings, but they came in on a plane that our shuttles wouldn't maintain. If a Patrol boat moved on a Colonial shuttle, another "above" or off to one side or "below" would have the Patrol on laser screen before he could back off. We lost a few ships, but they lost two for every one of ours; and the resultant holes in their ranks were much more damaging than those in ours.

Meantime, our wings were infiltrating and enveloping the Patrol wings. When they saw what was happening the whole Patrol backed off as quickly as inertia would allow and tried to re-form to face us down again, taking pot shots at stray Colonials as they went. They were disorganized and maybe demoralized, but they were expert fighter pilots. Most of us were not. We knew one superior wing maneuver, but that was all. It wouldn't be enough to hold the Patrol for long.

The solution to that was for me to break through their ranks and flee for Earth before the fighting continued long enough to do the fledgling Colonial Fleet severe damage. My wing advanced last, and I began to watch for weak spots in the Patrol formation where I might be able to slip through unnoticed or, failing that, punch a hole through and run like hell. The former would be preferable, but with my new engines the latter would work.

Unfortunately, the *Defiance* was clearly marked with her call letters, and the Patrol recognized her. They were here to stop me from running for Earth, and they were as intent on that as I was on breaking through their lines. As soon as my wing moved forward, half a dozen patrol boats that had been hanging back, keeping free of the battle, suddenly lost their diffidence and jumped forward to meet us. It wasn't a friendly welcome. They damn near knocked out a couple of their own ships in their eagerness to blast mine out of the way.

Jamin's *Challenger* dived across my path, coming between me and the Patrol boats, and his voice over the Comm Link said tensely, "Blue wing on Bodyguard!"

Suddenly all the shuttles in my wing were between me and the Patrol. Lasers flared all around me, and somebody's shields burned out. I caught a Patrol boat in my laser screen and fired at the same moment he did. He missed. I didn't. But I took out only his shielding, and didn't have time for a second shot to finish him: he was past me before I could press the button again.

Of the other five, one had been destroyed and four were dodging the other ships in my wing, so I flipped the *Defiance* and tried for an angle on the one I had damaged. She was a Starbird, and her pilot knew his ship. I couldn't catch her. She dodged and danced and ran and I was so intent on chasing her that I didn't notice until too late how neatly I was being maneuvered back into range of the rest of the Patrol.

Jamin noticed. For the second time in as many minutes his *Challenger* slid neatly between me and the Patrol. Lasers flared crimson. Jamin's shields sheeted green, then white for a brief instant before they burned out and the lasers cut into *Challenger*'s unprotected hull. At that moment I finally got the angle I wanted on the boat I'd been chasing, and the Patrol had one less shuttle between me and Earth. It left a hole at the edge of their ranks, and I went for it, pouring all the power I had into one clean dive through them and away, not really even aware of what I was doing because the song of the Gypsies dizzied me.

I could hear them even over the howl of my shuttle's engines and I knew at last, too late, what they were singing for: Jamin was dead. He had driven *Challenger* between me and a Patrol boat ready to fire, and had taken the laser hit meant for me. I had seen his shields burn out; and in the instant before I dived for freedom I had seen the deadly silent blossom of an explosion that must have been *Challenger* dying.

The realization of what I had seen was simultaneous with my dive for freedom. I froze at the controls, staring into the aft scanner screen in shock while the *Defiance*,

obedient to my last command, hurtled through the Patrol
lines and safely out the other side. They couldn't possibly
have turned quickly enough to follow me, and the few of
them that were alert enough to see me go couldn't get an
angle in time to fire effectively, which was as well; I was
in no condition to dodge or return their fire. I could think
of nothing but the view in that aft scanner screen, and the
implacable Gypsies' song.

There was nothing, really, to be seen in the scanner
screen. What I saw was more memory than reality. The
angry red ember of coming laser fire; the blinding yellow
and sickening green of screens sheeting under a load they
couldn't handle; and that final deadly rainbow blossom of
explosion. . . . My hand still numbly clutched the thruster
control, automatically teasing the engines to greater and
greater power and speed while I searched the scanner for
some last sign of *Challenger*, and didn't find it.

The new conversion drive engines were all that saved
me. The unfamiliar power and incredible speed were so
great that even though the moment I fully understood what
had happened I flipped the *Defiance* onto her back to ride
tail-first with the thrusters still burning, fighting to overcome inertia, we were out of range before we'd even
begun to slow down.

By then, of course, I knew we couldn't slow down. We
couldn't stop. We couldn't go back. Jamin was dead,
and it was not my job to avenge him, at least not yet; I
was out of this battle and I was meant to stay out of this
battle. My job was to run for Earth with the evidence the
Colonials had put aboard my shuttle.

It took more courage than I knew I had to flip the
Defiance again and turn her nose toward Earth, but I did
it. I had to. Jamin died to give me that chance. He died to
give us all a chance . . . a chance to live in peace. A
chance to live.

Even if I didn't want it, I had no right to reject that gift
on behalf of the rest of the Solar System, which is what I
would have done if I'd gone back to fight instead of
completing my mission. That would have committed us all

to war. On some level even then I understood that there were those who still had reason to hope for peace. I wanted only death; destruction; some end to the incomprehensible agony that twisted my heart: I wanted war. But I fled blindly toward Earth on a mission of peace.

CHAPTER NINETEEN

I have no idea how long that flight to Earth took. I used full power the whole way down and burned most of the fuel I had on board, not because I was in a hurry but because I was so filled with rage and despair that only the all-out howl of engines and the feel of my shuttle straining for ever greater speed gave me any comfort. I didn't sleep. I didn't eat. I sat at the controls and listened to the engines and watched the black of space that filled the viewport, lighted by distant stars that were slowly washed away by the increasing glare of the sun as we plunged in-system.

That much use of power necessitated constant course corrections and calculations, and would, when I neared Earth, result in the need for all my remaining power to fight inertia and catch Earth-orbit instead of whipping on past and down toward the sun. The course corrections and calculations were something, anyway, to occupy my mind, and my shuttle's energy expenditure wasn't as soothing as if it had been my own, but it was better than no energy spent at all. If I could have, I would have physically *run* all the way to Earth, or as much of the way as it took me to kill myself in the effort. It wasn't exactly that I wanted to die, so much as it was the sort of gut-level, heart-wrenching *need* to use myself up, any way I could: to go,

186

and to keep on going, until sheer exhaustion finally numbed my senses enough that I could rest.

It wasn't all—or even mostly—grief that drove me. It was guilt. Guilt, and a childish rebellion against the weight of terrible responsibility. The flight to Earth was easy, but Jamin didn't die for that. He died for me. He put his shuttle between mine and a laser blast that would have killed me, and it killed him instead.

Somewhere along the way the rebellion died. Time dulled the killing edge of loss and self-loathing. Reason didn't fully reassert itself, but something did that was close enough to live with: I was capable of cold, calculating logic: I was able to survive. When the Patrol challenged me at the perimeter of Earth space I even answered them with creditable calm instead of with lasers. Their shuttles looked very like those we'd fought at Mars Station. If not these Patrolmen, then their brothers had killed Jamin and, with him, some undefined but essential part of me. And I spoke to them on the Comm Link with cool reason, dispassionate logic, indifference. Killing a few Earther Patrolmen, and consequently getting killed myself, might have been infinitely satisfying, but it wasn't what I had come so far to do.

They recognized my shuttle, and I confirmed the identification and requested an audience with the President of the World, Incorporated. If I had been anyone else, that might have been sufficient cause for them to kill me or at least to seriously question my sanity; lowly colonists weren't frequently granted audience with Earth officials. And if those Patrol had known what was going on in the Belt just then, my mere presence might have been my death warrant. But they knew me, and they didn't know what was going on in the Belt. They let me pass.

I was given an honor guard of Earthers this time, and I let them guide me safely down toward Earth's capitol, on the up-sun side of the white-and-blue ball on which Humankind was spawned so long ago and had since grown to a semblance of adulthood. It was a fragile jewel in the bottomless black of space. The jewel grew till it filled my

forward scanners and the viewport; and grew again till it
seemed to fill the universe. Then we were on our way
down into Earth's atmosphere on our final approach, with
screaming winds buffeting our shuttles and the Comm
Link communications between Patrol and the ground blacked
out in the heat and turbulence. That didn't matter; I had
heard enough already to know the President had agreed to
see me, and that was all I needed.

All that I needed, short of death.

I thought of Collis, wondering who was with him and
how I would face him if I returned to Mars Station. It
wasn't the first or the last time I thought of him on that
long sunward journey, but by then at least I had gone
emotionally numb enough to endure the pain. It was a
form of death, I suppose, and it protected me as nothing
else could have done. It kept me from seeing, over and
over again in memory, the beautiful deadly colors of the
lasers exploding across *Challenger*'s shields; or from being
haunted by the remembered blue innocence and the imagined agony of Collis's eyes.

The wild ride down through the atmosphere took all my
attention fighting the winds and physics; then we were
safely down, caught fast in Earth's killing gravity, our
shuttles' heat shields still faintly steaming in the cool damp
air of a misty planet morning. There were clouds in the
lucent blue sky, and people in shirtsleeves visible from my
landing site. I think I would have popped the hatch and
exited the *Defiance* just as readily, this time, if they hadn't
been there. Last time I'd landed on Earth I'd had a vested
interest in survival. Now it was only a necessary corollary
to the completion of my mission. I would survive, certainly, if it was convenient, at least till I'd seen the President. I would even make a reasonable effort to survive if it
wasn't convenient; I was, after all, a reasonable creature.
But the instinct for survival was gone. After all the years
of closed environments I stepped without a thought out
into the sun and wind of Earth.

It seemed to burn me. The morning was mild, even
chilly, causing me to hug my flight jacket closer around

my shoulders on the brief walk from the *Defiance* to the
groundcar the President had provided for me. Sun and
wind were disconcerting to a Belter, however numbed by
circumstance or sorrow. The light was blinding, and the
heat of solar radiation was easily discernable on my shoulders and on the top of my head. Wind whipped tears to my
eyes and I blinked against them and against the light and
listened to the whisper of my flight boots against the
landing surface and tried not to think.

The waiting groundcar contained two Ground Patrolmen
who greeted me with the uncertain civility of military
types confronted with a person of unspecified but possibly
high rank. I ignored them and settled into the empty seat
without a word, surprised to find my body trembling with
reaction and exhaustion.

I saw the two Patrolmen glance at each other before
starting the car. One of them shrugged, and the other
looked at me and quickly away again. I rested my head
against the back of the seat and closed my eyes and
waited, breathing carefully, trying to slow the lurching
rhythm of my heart. The driver started the car and we
drove off the landing field in uneasy silence. At least, they
seemed uneasy. I was past that; to be uneasy, one has to
care.

The drive wasn't long; or, if it was, I slept through
much of it. My eyes were closed, but if I did sleep it
wasn't a restful sleep and I woke as numb and weary as
before. The car stopped before an ordinary door in an
unremarkable tunnel corridor. Both the Ground Patrolmen
disembarked before me and silently waited for me to follow them, which I managed to do without betraying the
effort it cost me. Even the simple exercise of standing
upright had become an awkward, chancy thing, requiring
an impractical expenditure of energy and concentration.
Walking was so difficult it made me feel sick.

The ordinary door opened into an equally ordinary chamber, unusual only in that it was somewhat overcrowded
with Ground Patrol and Special Service personnel. We had
a brief moment of awkwardness when the Special Service

folks wanted to relieve me of my handgun and I was disinclined to part with it. They gestured and explained, their faces tense and distrustful. I understood, but it was a matter of principle with me. I had parted with my weapon too often lately. I didn't even try to explain; I just refused to hand it over.

The President solved the impasse by telling the Special Service people to forget it. They argued. It gave me time to look around the chamber, admittedly without much interest, till I found the Comm Screen on which the President's image was projected. When I saw her she seemed to be looking directly at me, so I attempted what must have been a rather demented grin in her direction, which she answered with surprising warmth.

"It's good to see you, Skyrider," she said. "Gentlemen, show the Skyrider in to see me now, please."

The Special Service didn't like it; it was their sole and exclusive duty to protect her life. Not an easy task. This wasn't the first time I had seen them obliged to obey her instructions even when they were counter to the Special Service's advice. But she was their boss. If she asked them to bring her an armed Colonial, a known Insurrectionist whose business on Earth they hadn't even ascertained, they could suggest alternatives; but if she was adamant (and she was), they had to obey. She was, after all, the President.

They took me to her, and very reluctantly left me alone with her in a chamber that was not nearly as ordinary as the one through which we had come from the tunnel outside. That outer chamber had been bare of any furnishings but Patrol work tools: computer terminals, Comm Link screens, work tables, and a few hard chairs. The chamber in which the President received me contained many of those same tools for her own use, but it was also completely and rather elegantly furnished in the style of Earther homes; wood-and-fabric chairs and tables, oversized decorative holograms on the walls, bright fabrics draped from the ceiling down across the walls in wide swatches for no apparent reason, and a thick soft fabric like fur on the floor.

There was a small work area with an anachronistic writing table of rich brown wood with a matching chair, the seat and back of which were covered with a golden fabric matching that hung on the walls. A small lounge area nearby held soft-looking chairs entirely covered with fabric, and a low table made of wood and glass on which rested an enormous basket of fresh ripe fruits from Earth. It was to one of those soft chairs that the President directed me, dismissing the Special Service guards with a brisk nod and an impatient word when they hesitated. When they were gone she sat in a chair across the table from me and studied my face intently. "Do you want food or drink?" she asked.

I shook my head and frowned at the fruit on the table before me. "No, thank you, I'm fine." The colors of the fruit seemed to melt into each other, and I blinked at it.

"You don't look fine. You look exhausted." A frown pulled at her forehead. "You can't even see straight, can you? What is it, Melacha? What's happened? How can I help?"

That may not have been why she was President—kindness and perception weren't necessarily an asset in the business of climbing up the corporate ladder to the presidency, and I doubted that many people were granted that glimpse into her character—but I had seen it once before, and it was why I had brought the Belt's problems directly to her. She would give the Colonies a fair hearing. The measures that had brought us to this crisis might have originated on Earth, but if the President was aware of them, she never meant for them to be used in the way they had been used in the Belt. She didn't want war any more than we did. She would stop it, if she could.

I showed her the evidence I had brought, and connected her computer with mine on board the *Defiance* so she could examine all that the colonists had assembled for her information. She was stunned and horrified and increasingly angry. I watched while she conversed with my computer and asked for printouts. Her face became pale and stern and remote. I'd been right in thinking the Company had

acted without her knowledge or approval. Earth had believed the fiction the Company had sent to the news ser-
vices. They had no reason to doubt it.

I had brought them reason. And the President was paying
attention. Satisfied, I closed my eyes for a moment. When
I opened them again the President was leaning back in her
chair, looking at me, her eyes weary and her expression
grim. "I've been in touch with the Belt Branch," she said.
"And with the Colonies. We'll see. Meantime, I think you
need a lot more sleep—didn't you sleep at all on the way
in? But let me order a meal for you, first, and you can
tell me what you know about the situation while you eat.
The tapes and records you brought are fairly complete, but
they contain only facts. You know people. Tell me how this
happened. Tell me about the people. Both sides." She
smiled fleetingly. "That's one advantage to dealing with a
known renegade like you; you're conversant with both
sides." The words could have been offensive, but her tone
made them a compliment. Another believer in the great
Skyrider image? The thought wearied me.

"Are they still fighting at Mars Station?"

"Apparently not." She hesitated. "Want to tell me
what happened?"

I closed my eyes. After a moment she phoned someone
and ordered a meal—no mere dispenser food for the President of the World—and then waited. I could feel her
watching me. "When I was here before . . . during the
Station Newhome affair . . . you met a friend of mine. A
boy named Collis."

"I remember." There was genuine affection in her voice.

"His father . . ." I paused, and swallowed, and started
over again. "The Patrol tried to stop me coming here to
bring you all this information. The Company didn't want
you to know."

"Of course." Her tone was encouraging.

"The Colonial Fleet helped me break through." I'd
been staring absently at one of the holograms on the wall.
It was a summer meadow, dotted with flowers and crowned
with rich blue sky, deep as forever, bright with sun. I

closed my eyes. "He was a freefall mutant. Collis's father. He was my wingmate. He died."

She touched my shoulder in an impulsively sympathetic gesture. "I'm so sorry."

I shook my head quickly. Too quickly; it made me dizzy. "It doesn't . . ." I swallowed again, and forced myself to look at her. "He saved my life."

She nodded. There were a lot of things she could have said that would only have added to my pain and anger. She didn't say any of them. What she did say was perhaps the only thing she could have said that wouldn't hurt me: "You've done me another service for which I owe you, my friend. Will you name a price, this time?"

"Fuel and safe passage off Earth."

"You'd have those in any case." She smiled suddenly. "In fact, I'm not sure I'd have to take a hand in getting you that much; the Patrol might provide it just to be safely rid of you. I think you impressed them; you provided quite a vision of controlled savagery when you arrived." When I didn't return her smile, she sighed. "I owe you a lot, Melacha. Just about anything you could ask."

I shook my head, then smiled faintly as a servant came in with a tray heavily laden with the meal she'd promised me. "Well, maybe *food* and fuel and safe passage."

She watched as I reached unsteadily for a delicately trimmed sandwich. "Still not enough. Shall I surprise you, then?"

"I expect you would, anyway; Earthers usually do."

CHAPTER TWENTY

The President seemed to take no offense at my bitterness. Instead she studied the colonists' evidence a moment longer, then leaned forward in her seat, watching me with a fierce, almost frightening intensity. "How could the Company get away with this, Melacha? How could they *do* it? I don't understand how such a thing could happen. How could the colonists allow it?"

"That's easy." I put down my fruit juice and reached for another sandwich: they were made of cooked meat and the leaves of some vegetable, with genuine butter for a spread, and wonderfully thick nutty bread; a fit accompaniment for nectar of the gods, which is what real fruit juice tasted like to me. "We're gullible. Earth says come in; claim the rocks that are rightfully yours, that we took from you in the last war; claim your heritage; we're ready to admit you're human. And we, being all too human, arrive in droves. On the slaughter."

"But surely, if nobody was really granted a claim . . ."

"Oh, some were granted. Know whose? Relatives of Company muckymucks. Distant enough relatives, in several cases, that we didn't make the connection in time: and afterward, nobody was just straightforwardly denied a claim. I mean, the Company never said somebody just couldn't have his rock for no reason. It always turned out

194

somebody else already owned the rock. Somebody related
to the Company, of course. So people were stuck at Home
Base, forbidden to return to their rocks, sometimes with
their shuttles confiscated so they wouldn't try to return to
their rocks, and always with their weapons confiscated so
they wouldn't make trouble. What could they do? They
were on the enemy's home ground, with nothing to fight
with and no clear enemy to fight. Just officious little
bureaucrats who went all meek and stuffy and apologetic
when challenged, and probably really didn't know what
was going on any better than we did. They couldn't do
anything, and nobody could get an audience with anybody
high up in the Company who *could* do anything."

"Why did they keep coming in?"

"Who could tell them not to? The ones who'd already
come in? They were kept safely away from the Comm
Link. They couldn't even get back to their ships. The
Company wasn't going to warn anybody, or let anybody
be warned. And you have to remember this is the asteroid
belt, not Earth: the claimants were landing inside a big
rock to register their claims. From outside, you couldn't
see that anything was wrong, not like a landing field or a
parking lot on Earth that you could see and examine from
a distance, before you landed. And once they were down,
even if they noticed something wrong right away—which
wasn't there to notice until so many of them had come in
that the Company could no longer conceal all those excess
shuttles—they couldn't lift off again. I heard that a few of
them tried. They didn't make it. The only reason they
could even try was that there *was* still some legitimate
coming and going, and the Company couldn't be too
restrictive about it or somebody would have caught on too
soon. That's why I could land and lift off more than
once. . . . They really didn't have a reason to stop me. Of
course, if I'd been a freefall mutant like Jamin they probably would have anyway. They tried to stop us when I got
Jamin and Collis out. But when I was alone . . . Well, the
Company is cagey. Hell, granting free access to a few of

us even *helped* them; people who might otherwise have been suspicious were lulled by that."

"Because they thought if the Company were really using the Redistribution Act against you, they wouldn't have let anybody out to tell about it?"

"Exactly. Hell, that reassured *me!* For a while, anyway. We contributed to our own downfall in so many ways. Disbelief. Just plain innocent, ignorant disbelief. Much as we distrust Earthers, much as we've struggled against oppression all these years . . . since before the last war . . . we still couldn't believe this was really happening."

The President had leaned back in her seat, still watching me with that unnerving intensity. "You sound so bitter about that. Don't. Trust is not a bad thing, you know."

"Sure, praise the poor dolts for falling into the trap."

"You know better than that, don't you? From me?"

"I don't know, anymore. I'm sorry."

She sighed and shook her head. "It's nothing you should be sorry for. Any apologies should be to you, not from you." She watched while I lifted another sandwich, looked at it, and put it back down. My hands weren't quite so unsteady anymore. But I didn't feel well. "I meant," she said, "that it's a hopeful sign that the colonists are not so embittered that they would refuse to come in at all. I worried about that, you know, when we passed the Redistribution Act. From what I knew of affairs in the Colonies, I thought there was every chance the colonists would be so distrustful of promises from Earth that they would refuse to stake their claims, preferring to keep their rocks illegally and put up with the high cost of smuggling to supply their needs, rather than risking loss . . . risking exactly what did happen, in fact." She closed her eyes. "But maybe they will be that embittered, now."

She wanted an answer, and I didn't have one. I really didn't know. "I hope they are."

The President looked at me. "Don't hope for that. If it comes to that, there'll be no hope left. No chance to avoid another war."

"I'm not so sure there's a chance, now."

"I think there is. The Redistribution is real, you know. We can give those people back what we took from them. It's not too late for that."

"You can't give back life to people from whom you've taken that."

"Of course not." Her tone was sharp. "But don't forget, it's not just colonists who have died."

"Maybe I'll remember." I lifted my fruit juice. "But tell it to somebody else. I'm just a misfit renegade; it doesn't matter what I believe."

"It matters," said the President. "It matters to me."

I didn't ask why. "The point is, what matters to the colonists? And the answer is, freedom. Just that. We're perfectly willing to work with Earth, and to work for the Company. But we want to do it because we *choose* to, as people; not because we have to because Earth doesn't recognize our rights."

"What rights? Nobody has any God-given *rights*. You get what you can take, or what you're granted by the people in charge."

I almost laughed at her, but the sound that came out was broken and harsh and not much like laughter. "You can oversimplify anything," I said. "I don't really need to be reminded of that. The point is, we are human, and if we aren't granted human rights, we'll damn well take them."

"What rights do you consider to be 'human'?"

"Nobody loves a devil's advocate."

She grinned fleetingly. "I'm more serious than you know. I haven't been out there, Melacha. I know what laws we've passed, and what our intentions were. You know what has actually happened."

I hesitated. "What do you think of freefall mutants?"

She looked puzzled. "What about them?"

"Are you serious?"

"I don't think I understand." She seemed genuinely bewildered.

"They're second-class citizens. Monsters. Tolerated . . . grudgingly. They aren't human, you know."

She stared. "What are you saying? That's ridiculous
MAMA propaganda. No rational beings believe that. You
might as well say people with blond hair aren't human, or
people with high cheeckbones, or brown skin!"

"It's been said."

"Historically, sure, by primitives; I mean, nobody could
seriously believe that. People were frightened by superstitious terrors—"

"People are still frightened by superstitious terrors. And
while we're on the topic, I've read some history. Respected scientists once believed that skin color was indica-
tive of more than pigmentation. Learned papers were written
on comparative brain size, learning capacity, intelligence
quotients. . . ."

"I know, I know, but even science was primitive then."

"To our descendants, our science will look primitive."

"What are you trying to say?"

"Do you seriously claim you don't know?"

She frowned and shook her head briefly. "I know that
people are frightened of the unknown, the unfamiliar. I've
heard MAMA's spokesmen. But . . . I can't take their
propaganda seriously. You can't mean I should have taken
them seriously. Are you trying to tell me . . . Do you
mean to say that people honestly believe . . . You can't
mean that. A few people, sure; but most people are intelligent, educated. . . ."

"And frightened of the unfamiliar."

"I don't believe it."

"That people are frightened of the unfamiliar? You just
said it yourself."

She stared past me. "You could be right, of course. It
would explain MAMA's political success, and some of the
reports I've had from the Belt. But it's so absurd!" She
blinked and looked absently around the chamber. "I don't
have time to observe the popular press. My advisors say I
should *take* time, but I've always thought . . ." She pressed
a call button, and we waited while a Special Service
officer entered, ready for action, with his weapon drawn.
"Gerald," she said, "put your weapon away."

Gerald straightened almost imperceptibly, gave me a bewildered and only half-hostile look, and put away his weapon. "Yes, sir. What can I do for you, sir?"

"You can tell me what you think of freefall mutants."

He tried to conceal the automatic distaste he felt, but he was no actor. "Sir? I don't trust them, sir." His gaze slipped almost furtively toward me and away again. "I understand they're allowed to run free in the Colonies, just like regular people, but it's not a safe practice. Strictly speaking, sir, they aren't human."

"How do you know?" asked the President.

He looked startled. "Sir?"

"How would you recognize a freefall mutant? They look human, don't they?"

He said with kindly condescension, "You don't know them, sir, that's why you think that. They're not—" He glanced at me, blinked, and looked back at the President with grim apology. "Contrary to what some people might think, sir, they're obviously not human. You can tell, all right. I understand some of them try to pass, but you can tell."

"How?" insisted the President.

Gerald leaned toward her almost conspiratorially. "Their heads are too small." He said it triumphantly, with a quick furtive glance at me. When the President looked dubious, he added quickly, "It's a scientific fact, sir. Maybe you can't tell in freefall where they live, I mean just by looking, because from the outside the difference isn't so great— what I mean is, sir, their *heads* are almost human-sized, but their *brains* aren't, because they have a lot more skull bone than humans. That's a fact, sir. And what difference there is to see, they cover by growing extra hair. They're great hairy things, take my word, I've seen photographs. Where you or I have a little hair, they have a lot. You can tell in the holos. I was watching an article the other day on the newsfax—" He paused, perhaps remembering to whom he spoke, or perhaps seeing something quelling in her expression. After a second's hesitation he finished awkwardly, "They'd give themselves away right quickly, sir. They can't speak Company English like the rest of us; their brains aren't big enough to learn it properly. They speak some damnfool baby talk.''

"Pidgin?" asked the President.

Gerald hesitated. "Sir."

"Pidgin is the common language in the Belt, Gerald," said the President. "Nearly everyone speaks it."

Gerald could hardly contain himself. "Sir, I know, but they have to, don't you see, because they're dealing with all those muties who can't learn English. All humans can speak pidgin, but no mutie can speak English. I mean, no freefall mutant. Everybody knows that."

"Melacha?" The President looked at me expectantly. I wondered briefly whether she really expected me to deny or confirm his opinion.

"You heard him. And you know what you've seen—and what you've heard—elsewhere. Make up your own mind."

She frowned in irritation. "Don't be silly. I meant, is this the common belief? Is this what you expected to hear?"

I shrugged. "More or less. Does it really matter? There are variations in what 'everybody knows,' but the hatred is always the same."

The President looked back at Gerald. "And this *is* a common belief?" she asked. "I mean, would you say that most of the people you know would agree with what you've just said about freefall mutants?"

He produced a very unattractive smile. "There are always liberals."

"You mean there are people who would disagree?"

"If you watch the newsfax—"

She stopped him with an impatient gesture. "Thank you, Gerald. That will be all."

He didn't like to leave her, inadequately informed as she obviously was, but he couldn't disobey a direct order. "Yes, sir. Thank you, sir." He left less quickly than he had entered.

The President leaned back in her chair and looked at me. "Obviously you were right about that. And that may explain why the Company has been able to get away with some of the outrages in the Colonial evidence you brought me—internment camps for Fallers, for instance. But surely that doesn't explain how they could use the Redistribution Act against other colonists? Or does the discrimination extend to heterozygotes—Floaters, like you?" When I said that to some extent it certainly did, she looked bewildered. "But I can imagine ways of finding out whether a person is a Faller; it would become apparent in a gravity environment, if nothing else. How would you tell a Floater? How could you discriminate against somebody you can't tell from so-called normal people?"

"That's probably the basis for much of the fear, in our case," I said. "Think of it: somebody you think isn't quite human, but there's no simple way to *tell* him from the humans."

"I can't quite make sense of it." She shook her head. "It seems to me that would be enough to kill the whole idea. If you can't tell he isn't human, surely you'd admit he *is* human?"

"Nonsense. Then what would we do with that fine old concept of non-humans trying to 'pass'? In the olden days, if a person whose ancestry was dark-skinned, whose own skin was perfectly brown—or whatever was the accepted color—"

"Pale, I think," the President said with a smile.

"Well, whatever. If a person whose skin was the right color was considered to be 'trying to pass' if he didn't announce the skin color of his ancestors, isn't that just as silly as what your Special Service person said about Fallers trying to pass? Naturally Floaters would too—I didn't tell him I'm a Floater. In his opinion I'll bet that qualifies me as 'trying to pass.' I'm not a freefall mutant, but I am a mutant. Mutie. Never mind the fact that he is, too—that the whole human race has changed since pre-space days, so that I doubt there are very many humans left alive without the determinant genes. The thing is, everybody

who lives on Earth tends to be Grounders since they live
in gravity and don't intermarry with Fallers and Floaters.''

"That's an idea I hadn't considered.'' The President
looked almost cheerful again. "We don't know a whole lot
about the the mutation here on Earth. There have been a
few studies, but nothing much; the problem didn't seem
relevant, here. Do you really think we would find that?
That the genetic change is there, and it's only that we all
have two genes for gravity?''

"As far as our scientists have been able to determine,
from routine studies of the genotypes of residents and
immigrants to the Colonies, the environmental determinant gene is now the human norm.''

"Of course, it would be difficult to prove that wasn't
always the human norm. Which still leaves Fallers and
Floaters out since they don't have two genes for gravity.''

"Hell, you surely weren't putting your hopes on prov-
ing we're all mutants. We probably are all mutants. Always have been. Several respected theories of evolution
include that, as a matter of course. Successful mutations
adapted us to new environments as we moved, right up to
and including the move into space. But even the scientists
who propose—and believe in—the theories won't call themselves mutants. Mutant is a nasty word. Always has been,
as far as I can tell. It seems to call up images of all manner
of genetic freaks and failures. Never hope for a nice
scientific explanation to calm the masses. Think how people reacted to clones. They killed all the 'nasty inhuman
monsters,' confident that clones had no souls. But they
didn't and don't kill identical twins, or believe one member of the pair has no soul, and it isn't just because they
can't tell which twin is the clone.''

She nodded. "You're right, of course. It won't be that
simple. Nothing ever is.'' She sighed, and looked at me
again. "And it isn't your problem. You're exhausted; I
shouldn't be keeping you here. You've done your job.
Will you tell me what I can do for you in return?''

"Fuel and free passage.'' I really couldn't think of
anything else I wanted—at least, nothing she could grant.

She looked troubled. ''You're not going to go right back out into battle and get yourself killed, are you?''

I smiled and shook my head as if the idea had never crossed my mind.

CHAPTER TWENTY-ONE

My mission was accomplished. I'd done all I could do on Earth for the Colonies. It was time to go home. Not to battle, though I had given the idea serious consideration; but to Collis. There was little enough I could offer him, but I owed him what I had.

The last time I had flown from Earth, I'd had Igawa to keep me company: now I had only memories. They were not good company. The only real sound on board the *Defiance* between planets was the almost subliminal rumble of her engines, no longer straining for demonic speeds; and whatever small sounds I made myself in the business of living; and I heard the echo of Collis's delighted laughter in every chamber. I was the only living thing aboard, yet I saw shapes move in the corner of my vision and turned more than once with a word half-spoken, expecting Jamin or Collis, and seeing only my own reflection on some gleaming plasteel surface.

I tried to sleep, but the memories wouldn't let me. The way Jamin had looked the first time he came on board the *Defiance*, weakened by too much time spent in gravity . . . pale, aloof, arrogant . . . his long, lithe body stiff with pain and exhaustion that he tried, unsuccessfully, to conceal. . . . His pale eyes startled me. And the unexpected gentleness of his voice. . . . And the image of the

glaring rainbowed blossom, silent in the dark silence of
space, when the lasers collided with *Challenger* and stilled
that soft voice forever. . . .

I filled the hours back to Mars Station with all the
housekeeping and general maintenance tasks I could find.
There are a lot of those on any shuttle, and more on one
that's been pushed as hard as I'd been pushing the *Defiance*. I turned up the air filters, turned off the gravity, and
went around with a big dusting brush, stirring things up;
then I changed the air filter material, which by then was
gray with the impurities I'd swept into the air, and that
took care of the housekeeping—always the easy part. Then
I started on the maintenance.

Systems and computer checks came first: checking the
software and then letting it check what hardware it could.
That turned up a number of small tasks to be seen to, and
when they were done there was still all the hardware the
computers weren't programmed to oversee: structural in-
tegrity, the condition of bulkheads, the ongoing wear and
tear on all the mechanical bits and pieces that, when
assembled, constitute a space ship. There was a lot to do,
and it was good hard work that really kept me busy.

But it didn't keep my mind busy.

I suppose I went a little mad. I tried to keep my whole
attention on my work, but with the mindless tasks I was
performing, that would have been difficult at the best of
times. This was not the best of times. Inevitably, my
attention wandered. The madness developed in slow stages,
and I by no means remember every step, though I know it
started innocuously enough with the ordinary sort of day-
dreams, half memories and half imagination, that usually
accompany work that occupies the hands but not the mind.
I could control it, at first, and when the memories hurt I
could push them away.

I don't know how far into the trip we were, the first
time I caught myself speaking aloud and looked around in
surprise, almost as if I expected to hear someone answer
me. There was no one to answer. I shook my head with a
wry little smile at my own foolishness and went back to

my work. But it happened again, and after a while I don't think I even noticed it anymore.

Sometimes I was back in the time before Django died, and I shared the *Defiance* with him without the smallest uneasiness about the fact that I hadn't *got* the *Defiance* before he died. We laughed and played and told Gypsy jokes and watched the distant stars together. . . .

Sometimes it was Jamin and Collis who shared my shuttle, and we might have been on our way to rescue the *Marabou* all over again. That, too, had been a happy time; one much more pleasant to live in than the present I was trying to avoid.

I couldn't always wholly avoid it: sometimes I was alone again, on my way to Mars Station, to Collis. In a way, those were the maddest times. I knew Jamin was gone. On some level, I think I always knew that. But I created faerie tales to comfort me: the battle had taken place exactly as I had seen it, but instead of diving between me and the Patrol boat that killed him, Jamin had blasted it out of space. Or he'd dived to save me, but the Patrol boat's lasers had missed both of us. Or the Patrol boat hit *Challenger*, but only a glancing strike that didn't burn through the shields and didn't kill him. . . .

At some point I became so set on the idea that he had survived that I actually called ahead by Comm Link to ask whether the colonists had rescued him yet. When they said they hadn't, I demanded an all-out search, and threatened to attack Mars Station when I was told there would be no further search. I couldn't understand the colonists' indifference. Jamin was alive, maybe wounded, certainly helpless in a damaged shuttle, and they wouldn't find him and pull him in. I argued, I raged, I tried to reason with them, I may even have cried. All to no avail. They had made a sweep of the battle site, picked up what pilots they found and dragged home whatever debris seemed potentially useful, and neither Jamin nor any part of *Challenger* had been found. Yet they wouldn't go back and look for him. I couldn't understand it.

"Melacha, if he'd been there, we'd have found him."

Michael's voice cracked with more than Comm static. "Just get yourself home; we can talk about it later."

"He could be dying! Don't you understand? If he could, he would have called you by now; that means his shuttle is damaged, and he can't get home. What if his life support is damaged? What if—"

"Melacha, listen to me. We already searched."

"You didn't search well enough: you didn't find him."

"There were three independent reports—"

"I don't give a damn about independent reports, I want you to—"

"*Listen to me*. Three different pilots saw *Challenger*'s shields burn out. She must have been destroyed. If there'd been anything left, we would have found it."

I didn't want to hear that. "Damn you, I don't care what reports you had, he's out there."

He sighed audibly. "Just come home, Melacha. We'll talk about it."

"In the time it takes me to get to you, he could die."

"He's dead. Face it, Skyrider. He's dead. We can't do anything for him. *You* can't do anything for him. Collis needs you here. Just come home."

The argument went on, but it didn't lead to any new conclusions. Michael was adamant; the Colonials had searched already, and were not going to search again. Jamin was dead. Michael even produced two of the three pilots who'd seen *Challenger* take that last hit, and let them tell me their stories: but I found loopholes even then. They hadn't been looking any more directly than I. They hadn't actually *seen* him die; they'd only seen what I had seen. The Patrol boat firing, the lasers striking, the shields flaring. . . .

I was so persuasive in my arguments that I got one of the pilots to admit the possibility that Jamin hadn't died immediately under the Patrol's lasers. "But," she said, "we did search, you know. We picked up three pilots and five severely damaged shuttles, and brought them home. Jamin wasn't among them. All we left behind was debris nobody could use. Certainly nothing large enough to shelter a man. I'm sorry, Skyrider.''

"He's alive." I sounded cross and stubborn, like a small child denied an expected treat.

"Okay, maybe he is alive," she said. "Where is he?"

"I don't know. I don't know. You missed him."

"We didn't miss anybody. Hell, one of the pilots and two of the ships we picked up were Patrol."

"I don't care. You missed Jamin."

"I don't see how."

"I don't care what you see; I *know* he's alive." And by then I had convinced myself that I did know. I thought if he had died I would have felt it; that there was a little invisible light in the universe for every human, perceptible only to those who loved him, that would go out when he died; and Jamin's light hadn't gone out. I wasn't quite mad enough to imagine these were a real, physical manifestation like stars or planets or human bodies. It was more a feeling that we could be—and were—somehow aware of each other's life forces. And Jamin's hadn't died.

Oddly, that one impression is the strongest memory I have of that time . . . and the idea never quite left me, even after I went back to look for *Challenger* and didn't find her. I spent hours searching for some trace of her, even examining the bits of remaining debris I could find to see if any of it was identifiable as having come from *Challenger*, and none of it was. Maybe if I had found a piece of her I'd have believed she was destroyed, and her pilot with her, but I found no part of her at all. And I could not quite believe there wasn't anything to find.

Michael came out to the battlefield to find me and coax me home. Once before, seemingly a very long time ago, he had come to find me in a place of death, and had coaxed me carefully back to life. That time, I had been listening to ghosts. This time, they weren't singing. This time there was nothing but silence, and emptiness, and my own mad determination to find something that wasn't there.

"Come home," he said. "You need rest and food and

time. If you still want to, later, you can come back and search again.''

I flipped the *Defiance* to face him in an abrupt, practiced battle maneuver that caught him off guard. ''If you come any closer I'll knock you all the way back to Mars Station,'' I said.

He didn't make a move. He had the Comm Link on visual, and whether I liked it or not I could see his calm blue eyes staring with evident concern up out of the Comm screen. He said my name, softly, with terrible sympathy.

''Leave me alone, damn you.'' I looked away from the Comm screen, but I didn't turn it off.

''Have you looked everywhere?'' His voice was gentle and cautious, as if he were speaking to a demented child.

I passed a hand wearily across my face and looked at him again. ''Not everywhere; I haven't found him.''

''Where haven't you looked?'' His pale eyes seemed to penetrate my soul.

''Wherever he is.'' I sounded petulant.

''Melacha, this is crazy. You *know* you're not going to find him.''

''I know he's alive.''

''Okay, he's alive. But he's not here. Come home.''

''I have no home.''

''Then come to Mars Station. Collis needs you. Come to him.''

''Not without Jamin.''

''Jamin's dead.''

''He's not, damn you. He's not dead.'' I started to move away, feverishly searching my scanner screens anew.

''Melacha, you're worn out. You'll search better after you've had a rest. And Collis needs you *now*. Come back.''

I wasn't so crazy that I didn't know he was right. I just didn't want to believe it. But he kept talking, saying the same things over and over again, always in that gentle, encouraging voice, till finally he just plain wore down my resistance. I followed him home like a drunken puppy, too exhausted to fly a straight line.

210 *Melisa C. Michaels*

There was another argument when we got to Mars Station. He didn't think I was fit to land the *Defiance*. I disagreed. He threatened to order Flight Control to refuse to synch with me. I threatened to land manually if he did that. I meant it, and he knew it, and maybe I could even have done it; I've made more difficult landings in my time. But I didn't have to make that one manually; he gave in gracefully and probably held his breath till I was safely down on the panel with all my flight systems off.

Collis was waiting for me. Michael had been right; he needed me. Moreover, though I wouldn't have admitted it, I needed him. Michael floated with me to the Grounder quarters and helped me with the hatch cover between freefall and gravity when my exhaustion-numbed fingers refused to punch out the opening sequence.

We had positioned ourselves carefully upright with respect to the gravity field we were about to enter, but I nearly fell anyway when I stepped inside. Michael caught me, and steadied me without a word till I got my feet properly under me and was sure my knees would hold me. I'd been in freefall since I started housecleaning on the *Defiance*, and it took a moment to remember how to move against gravity. That's usually an automatic adjustment for Floaters, but in the condition I was in nothing came automatically except the internal processes like breathing and heartbeat and grief that go on regardless of one's environment if it isn't lethal.

"He's in my quarters," said Michael. "I didn't think he should be alone. My wife is with him."

"What did you tell him?"

He looked at me. "The truth."

"Whose truth?"

"Melacha . . ."

"Jamin is alive," I said, and shook my head, and sighed. "Never mind. It doesn't matter. Where are your quarters?"

I needn't have asked. Collis must have been watching for us. He came out of a door just down the corridor and ran to meet me, hurling himself into my arms with such fierce passion he nearly knocked me down. He didn't say anything. He just pressed his face against my neck and held me with all his strength, as if he were in danger of falling some terrible distance; or as if I were the last safe anchor in a world gone mad . . . which I suppose, in a way, I was.

I hugged him back. Maybe I was a little awkward about it, but if I was, I don't think he noticed. He knew the Skyrider had a heart of mush, at least where he was concerned.

The quarters we had shared with Jamin were nearer than Michael's, so I took him there. Michael followed us, and hovered uncertainly in the doorway till I invited him in. Collis and I sat in the most comfortable chair in the place, and Michael chose a chair pulled out from the table. "Dial us some caffeine, will you?" I asked him. "And some hot chocolate for Collis."

"I'm not thirsty." Collis's voice was harsh with pain.

"Try to drink it anyway," I told him. "It's good for you."

He pressed his face against my neck again and sniffled.

"Have you eaten lately?" I asked him.

"Not hungry." His voice was muffled by my tunic.

"Neither am I, but I think it would be a good idea to eat."

"I dialed a meal," said Michael. "You both need to eat."

"That's what she *said*," said Collis.

"He's only trying to help," I said.

Collis didn't say anything.

Michael looked at me. "Will you two be all right by yourselves?"

"We'll be fine." I hoped I sounded more assured than I felt.

"I really ought to get back to work, but I don't like to leave you."

"I'll take care of her," said Collis.

"Is there anything I should know about your reception on Earth?" asked Michael.

"Haven't you heard from the President?"

"Yeah, it looks good, if she can handle the Company. They won't give up easy."

"I'll report later," I said. "I don't know anything you need to know right away."

"Okay." He hesitated. "You're sure you'll be okay?"

"We'll be okay."

"Your food's on the table."

"Thank you."

He started to say something else, changed his mind, and left us.

We stayed where we were for a long while; but I could smell the caffeine, and I needed it. When I said so, Collis moved anxiously in my arms, but didn't release me. After a moment he said, "Okay," but didn't move. Then he said, in a very small voice, "Why were you gone so long?"

"I had to run all the way to Earth, to deliver data to the President. Didn't they tell you that?"

"Yes." His breath felt warm and soft against my neck. "They said when she started fixing things, too. Why didn't you come back then?"

I didn't answer right away. I wasn't sure what I was going to say. Finally I settled for a half-truth: "I don't know."

"What were you *do*ing?"

"I don't exactly know that, either."

He thought about that. "I needed you."

"I know."

Another silence. Then, "I wasn't sure . . . I, I thought . . . you know. You an' Papa were friends. I wasn't sure . . ."

"You thought I wouldn't come back?"

He nodded against my shoulder.

I touched his hair. "Your papa and I were friends. But I'm your friend too, Collis."

"I see that now." He was trying to sound reasonable and adult. "I just wasn't sure, *then*. Because you were gone so long."

"I'm sorry, Collis. I should have come back sooner. I was . . . I wasn't doing anything useful. I was just sort of . . . acting out, I guess. Doing crazy stuff. Things that didn't make sense. Because I was too upset to know what did make sense."

He nodded again. "I understand."

I pushed him away enough to see his face. "*Do* you, Collis?"

He blinked, looked away from me, and reluctantly looked back again. "When you didn't come . . . and they didn't find Papa . . . I was upset." He blinked again. "I threw things, and I yelled." His chin trembled. "I was mad at everybody. I told them I didn't care if you never came back. I said I didn't need you." He buried his face suddenly against my neck again. "I didn't mean it, Skyrider."

After a moment's hesitation I hugged him, hard. "I know, Toad. I know." He was crying. I wished I could.

CHAPTER TWENTY-TWO

The President of the World, Incorporated dispatched Earth Fighters to the Belt within twenty-four hours of my visit to Earth. But they weren't sent out against us this time; they were sent to our aid, to help restore order in the Colonies and to force the Company to give back what they had taken from us. Earth government even expressed willingness to listen to our case for self-government in the Colonies.

The President sent out a message by newsfax to all the World's citizens that said, in part, "Earth families don't have any greater desire to send their sons and daughters to war in the Colonies than the colonists have to be forced to defend their homes from Earth Fighters. We of Earth have been misinformed by our government in the Belt; and we have been misled by our own ignorant prejudices and greed. Once order is restored, we will listen to the colonists . . . and we will learn from them The time has come when we must give up our provincial outlook, our divisive beliefs, and our old hatreds: we must recognize that we are no longer the only inhabited planet in the Solar System. Mars, Luna, and the asteroid belt are inhabited not by Earthers and Colonials, but by Terrans. My people, it is time for us to quit our long, senseless struggle; time to lay down our arms, and to welcome our cousins, the colonists, into the human race. If we do not, we will not be fit members ourselves.''

All very stirring and grand, of course, but it wasn't quite that simple. The Company put up a fierce struggle in the Belt, and the Corporation on Earth had unrest of its own to contend with; racial bigotry, greed on the part of those who had a vested interest in what the Company had been taking from us, and a lot of hatred left over from the last war, to name a few of the major bones of contention. But Earth is a very large planet, with a great many resources; and the President, once alerted to the situation in the Belt, was determined to right it. She had enough Patrolmen to deal with both Earth and the Belt.

She had all her Patrol boats clearly marked to distinguish them from Belt Patrol. She used only Ground Patrol for the problems of Earth, and sent us every Patrol and Earth Fighter shuttle she commanded. More important, she sent them with instructions to obey Colonial Command for the duration. And she sent out ambassadors, researchers, med-techs and psych-tenders, mechanics, computer experts, retired generals, political aides . . . in short, every professional man or woman who might conceivably be of use to us either in war or in the aftermath of war.

The Earthers were reluctant at first, but most of those who came to us were able to overcome their prejudices and see past their expectations to the realities of life in the Colonies, and it wasn't long till they were helping us as willingly as the President did. I'd like to say they joined our cause *en masse*, but of course they didn't. Some joined; some even decided to emigrate, and sent back for their families. Some were willing to be convinced. Some weren't interested in anything beyond the immediate problem. Some maintained throughout that the Colonies should be governed from Earth no matter what. All helped us, one way or another.

Some Company personnel came over to our side when they saw the support we had from Earth. A number of persons whose names had been used in the claiming of Belter property under the Redistribution came forward voluntarily to relinquish their claims. Some Company officials even helped the Colonial Fleet and the Earth Fighters to overrun Home Base and to release the prisoners held on internment rocks in the Belt. The war didn't last forty-eight hours after the arrival of Earth forces in the Colonies; it was effectively over before it had begun. But it was a bloody little war while it lasted.

I slept through much of it. I'd fallen asleep right after that meal Michael dialed for Collis and me, and I stayed asleep for a long time. When I finally woke, I wasn't fit to go into battle at once, though I probably would have done anyway if Michael and Collis hadn't been there to stop me.

They insisted I eat another meal and change clothes and listen to the President's personal message tape to me. Probably they were just anxious to hear the tape themselves; it was encoded to my handprint and they couldn't find out what was in it till I did.

It was my payment for the last run to Earth. A fitting payment, I suppose. Certainly a surprise. She'd promised me a surprise.

I'm not God, she said on the tape. *I can't offer you anything but material goods or power; those are the things at my command. Since you don't need material goods, we'll have to settle for power.* There was laughter in her voice, and I wished she'd included a visual so I could see her expression.

Michael and Collis were looking at me speculatively. Michael, I thought, was trying not to grin. He knew me too well: what sort of power was I fit to command?

What sort of power indeed I grant you! asked the President. *You're not exactly Board Member material, as I think you'll agree. You don't have the required political frame of mind. And you'd hardly do well in the military, where there are so many rules and restrictions to tempt you to disobedience. The same goes, of course, for any active law enforcement agency, and I could hardly put the Belt's most infamous smuggler in charge of something that essentially legal, anyway.*

So I've created a department just for you. Well, actually it's for the Colonies; but you'll be in charge. In fact, at first you'll be the department.

I was reaching for the power switch on the tape player when she said, *Don't turn it off, Skyrider. Hear me out.* Everybody knew me too damn well, it seemed. *I really think you'll like it,* she said. *Do you know what an ombudsman is? It's a pretty archaic word, I'll grant you, but it covers what I want you to do: an ombudsman is a public official appointed to investigate citizens' complaints against local or national government agencies that may be infringing on the rights of individuals. So you see, I only want you to go on doing what you're already doing, only we'll make it official from now on.*

"That's just stellar," I said. "What the hell does it mean?"

As to exactly what that means, beyond the definition I've just read you . . . I don't quite know, said the President. *As I said, it's an archaic word, and an archaic political position. I guess you'll have to make it up as you go along . . . I know you're good at that. There are no rules, no regulations, no restrictions that I'll place on the job. Do the best you can. We'll talk about it later.*

"They always say we'll talk about it later when they mean don't ask questions," said Collis.

There was a computer code at the end of the tape. The President had really decided to trust me; I had the highest clearance rating there is, and a credit rating to match it.

"I guess you'll be pretty busy now," said Collis.

"I don't know. Why?"

"Well, I was talking to Sarah."

"My wife," Michael said before I could ask.

"And she's taking Jerry—"

"My son," said Michael.

"—and going back down to Mars," said Collis. "She invited me to come with. I didn't like to leave you, if you weren't doing anything, but if you're going to be flying all around like . . . like Papa always did, you know, a lot of runs and hardly ever home . . . Well, I thought I might like to live in a family.'' His blue eyes watched me, troubled and anxious. ''Just for a change,'' he said tentatively.

I hesitated. ''Would I be able to visit you there?''

''Of course,'' said Michael.

''Sure,'' said Collis, ''or I wouldn't want to go.''

''Then I think it's a good idea.''

His smile was never as joyous as it had been when Jamin was with us, but at least he looked genuinely pleased. ''You *will* visit me, won't you, Skyrider?''

''Of course I will. You're my best friend. You'd be hard put to keep me away.''

The smile, which had faltered briefly, brightened again.

''And now that I've slept, and eaten, and changed clothes, and listened to the President's tape like you guys wanted me to, will you *please* let me turn on the newsfax and see what's happening in the world?'' They let me turn on the newsfax. I'd asked just in time: the Patrol was making a stand out near Rat Johnson's rock, and he wanted volunteers to help fight them off.

''The Colonial Fleet and the Earth Fighters will go,'' said Michael. ''There's no reason for you to go, too.''

''Why not? Just because I'm not a Fleet member or an Earth Fighter?'' I was already reaching for my flight suit and Collis was pulling my flight boots out from under the bed where I'd left them.

''No, of course not,'' said Michael.

''That's good. I wouldn't want to think you were excluding independent pilots from your war.'' I grinned at him. ''That would probably be something an ombudsman should look into, you know. Whatever the hell an ombuds man is.''

''It's you,'' said Collis.

''Right. And that means it's a warrior.''

''Hotshot pilot is more like,'' said Michael.

''Which means that when there's a battle I should be in it.''

''I don't think that's quite what the President had in mind,'' said Michael.

"She said I could make up the rules as I went along. That's a rule; I just made it up."

"Your logic is astounding."

"Besides, I have to be sure Rat's okay."

"Because he's an old friend, right?" asked Collis.

"Because he owes me money."

"But you don't need money," said Michael.

"Shut up," I explained.

GORDON R. DICKSON

☐	53068-3	Hoka! (with Poul Anderson)	$2.95
	53069-1		Canada $3.50
☐	53556-1	Sleepwalkers' World	$2.95
	53557-X		Canada $3.50
☐	53564-2	The Outposter	$2.95
	53565-0		Canada $3.50
☐	48525-5	Planet Run with Keith Laumer	$2.75
☐	48556-5	The Pritcher Mass	$2.75
☐	48576-X	The Man From Earth	$2.95
☐	53562-6	The Last Master	$2.95
	53563-4		Canada $3.50
☐	53550-2	BEYOND THE DAR AL-HARB	$2.95
	53551-0		Canada $3.50
☐	53558-8	SPACE WINNERS	$2.95
	53559-6		Canada $3.50
☐	53552-9	STEEL BROTHER	$2.95
	53553-7		Canada $3.50

Buy them at your local bookstore or use this handy coupon:
Clip and mail this page with your order

TOR BOOKS—Reader Service Dept.
P.O. Box 690, Rockville Centre, N.Y. 11571

Please send me the book(s) I have checked above. I am enclosing
$_____ (please add $1.00 to cover postage and handling).
Send check or money order only—no cash or C.O.D.'s.

Mr./Mrs./Miss _____

Address _____

City _____ State/Zip _____

Please allow six weeks for delivery. Prices subject to change without
notice.